Discovering
MR. X

ELLE NICOLL

*To Han, the most incredible and
loyal friend I could ever have.
There is no-one I would rather stay up all
night talking to about sexy book boyfriends,
whilst in a cabin in the woods.
Thank you for being you.*

ONE

TANNER

EIGHTEEN MONTHS EARLIER

Drew: Don't fuck it up!

I BLOW OUT A BREATH AS I CLOSE THE TEXT AND SLIDE MY cell phone back into my suit pocket. What the hell does he think I am? An idiot?

I drum my fingers on the counter. Why does it take so long to make one regular coffee to-go? I have another glance at my watch. My flight will board in ten minutes.

"A peppermint tea and a double-shot caramel latte, please," a delicate voice calls out. I look at the two flight attendants ordering next to me, their figure-hugging red uniforms attracting the glances of every man behind them in the queue.

One, an attractive blond, drops her voice to talk to her friend.

"Are you sure about this, Rach?"

"Holly, it's fine. It's just pictures of my feet and

legs," the one with the delicate voice says, her back to me.

I cast my eyes down her petite frame to her red high heels. *Nice.* She turns in my direction, bending to zip her purse into her wheelie case. *Fuck, she's beautiful.* Dark hair and sweet red lips—a sexy Snow-White fantasy right there.

"So, do you just take photos and send them those?" her friend asks as the beauty I'm naming Snow turns back around, oblivious to me.

"Yeah, some guys will even buy stockings or underwear I've worn."

I lean forward, my coffee forgotten as I eavesdrop, not wanting to miss anything. Selling underwear? Maybe this Snow-White isn't so pure after all.

"Doesn't it make you feel a bit, I don't know, weirded out that some stranger is fantasizing about you?"

"Yeah, a bit, but this is the best chance I've got at saving a deposit, having something of my own for the first time in my life." Snow clears her throat. "You know how much that means to me," she continues, her voice heavy with emotion, "I will never make it on our salary alone."

Her blond friend sighs. "I know better than to argue with you when your mind is made up; you're the most stubborn person I know."

The barista slides my coffee across the counter, and I thank him as I stall over the sugars and stirrers, not wanting to leave before I hear the rest.

"Just be careful, please. There are so many weirdos nowadays," Snow's friend continues.

"I will," Snow says, straightening her back, "but I just need to remember that difficult roads lead to beautiful destinations."

What the Hell? I almost drop the scalding coffee all over myself, hearing her utter those words. Thankfully, they're too engrossed in their conversation to notice me.

"If anyone can say that it's you," her friend says, smiling at her.

"Yeah, fucked up, but still going. That's me."

Interesting. What's your story, Snow?

"So, how do you do it, Rach? Set up a website?"

"Yeah. *'Scent from Rachel'* has been live for a week now, and I've already had five inquiries about photos."

"That's crazy!" Her friend's eyes widen as her hand flies to her mouth.

Grabbing my coffee, I straighten my jacket and stride off towards the boarding gates. As much as I'd like to listen to the rest of their conversation, I can't miss this flight. My company's been working for months to land this contract. If all goes well at the meeting in New York, then a refurbishment project on one of the most iconic hotels in Manhattan will be ours. And I'll be living in New York myself for a year to head it up.

My flight's almost finished boarding as I get to the gate.

"May I see your passport and boarding pass,

please, sir?" the female staff member asks, one manicured hand extended.

I hand it to her, and she scans it through her computer.

Hang on a minute, where's my laptop bag? I swing my head around as though it may have magically reappeared by my feet.

Fuck!

I was so distracted listening to that hot flight attendant talk about her kinky side business that I've left my fucking laptop at the coffee bar. This can't be happening!

"I've left my laptop; I just have to run back for it," I say to the gate agent, grabbing my passport and boarding pass back from her.

Her brow furrows. "I'm afraid we're about to close the gate, sir. You may miss your flight if you don't board now."

"What?" I stare at her.

I can't afford to miss this flight. There isn't another one that will get me there on time for the meeting. I will have blown months of preparation.

Shit, think, think.

"Look, I'm just going to run back for it now. I'll be quick. I'll pay you one thousand pounds to keep the gate open for five more minutes for me!" I say as I slam my coffee down on her desk and spin around, starting back towards the departure lounge.

"Sir!" she calls after me.

"Two thousand!" I yell as I run.

I've fucked up. I can't miss this flight, and I can't afford to lose that computer. I pray it hasn't been stolen. The amount of sensitive information on that thing is a fucking lawsuit waiting to happen if someone decrypts it.

My stomach drops as I round the corner and see the coffee bar up ahead.

Closed.

I swallow down the sour taste in my mouth as I run over and realize it's not completely empty; there's a security guard speaking into a handheld radio. His eyes are cast down suspiciously on my laptop bag, which is exactly where I left it—on the floor, leaning up against the counter.

Shit! I'm causing a major security incident that's evacuated the coffee bar. My chest tingles as the realization that I've really fucked up seeps in. There's no way I'm making that flight.

"That's him!" a familiar voice calls out.

I'm so focused that I almost run straight past and miss her standing to the side with another security officer.

"That's your bag, sir?" the officer with her asks, tilting his head with a grimace to my offending bag as though it's a disgraced dog that's shit on an antique rug.

"Yes!" I pant, coming to an abrupt stop in front of them. My hands go to my hips as I try to catch my breath.

"It's definitely his," she says again, barely looking at

me. Her eyes glance at her watch and she frowns. "He was in front of me in the line. I recognize his suit."

The security officer standing with her looks me up and down, and I hold my breath, praying that he will not insist my bag is re-scanned or some shit.

"Go get your bag, sir." He nods at his colleague to indicate I can approach.

Thank you, God.

I stride over and swipe up my bag. The officer standing with it huffs out a sound of irritation. "Don't leave your luggage unattended again. More trouble than it's worth."

"I won't, I swear." I grip the bag's handle tightly in my fist. *I'm never letting go of this fucker again.*

The two officers walk away, and I turn back to thank the dark-haired beauty—fuck, I could kiss her right now on those sweet, red lips, I'm so happy to see my bag—but she's already rushing away in the direction of the departure gates.

"Thank you so much. You've no idea how much hassle you've just saved me," I say as I catch up with her. Okay, maybe my day isn't turning to shit as much as I feared.

"You're welcome," she replies.

"Let me thank you somehow, please." I match her stride. She's barely looking at me and keeps glancing back at her watch.

"It's nothing." She shrugs, speeding up.

"Not to me, it isn't. You've stopped a massive business deal from going down the pan," I say as I see the boarding gate for my flight coming back into view. Thank fuck, it still looks open.

"I'm sure you could have handled it without the laptop." She gives me a polite smile without looking up.

"That's debatable. Have you ever met Griffin Parker?" I joke.

"The guy who owns the Songbird hotel facing Central Park?" she says lightly, like we're talking about the weather and not the most prominent hotelier in all of Manhattan.

"You've heard of him?" I ask, impressed.

"Don't sound so surprised." She smirks, keeping her eyes straight ahead. "I meet a lot of people in my job." She leans her head towards me as she walks, and I catch a hint of her perfume—sexy and floral. "A piece of advice; get him talking about his boat, and you'll be fine."

I slow down as we near my gate, but she keeps going, her red heels clicking against the tile floor as the gate agent calls me.

"Sir, you need to board now if you want to make the flight."

"I'm coming." I head towards her, glancing back over my shoulder.

"How can I thank you?" I call to the dark-haired beauty.

"You just did," she calls back, never breaking her stride.

"I'll send you something. Tell me your name!"

She shakes her head. "There's no need. Besides, I can't accept anything. It's against company policy." She gives me a small wave before she turns the corner and disappears.

I take my seat on the plane. *Fucking hell, that was close.* She has no idea how much she just saved my ass. This deal is worth millions if my company gets it. No way could I miss the flight and my meeting.

I glance out the window as the plane backs from the stand and run my hand through my hair. There's something intriguing about this Rachel, as well as the fact she's sexy as fuck. I love how determined she is to get what she wants, setting up her own website business like that. It takes balls, and despite not knowing her, there's no way in hell I like the idea of other men buying photographs of her to add to their wank banks.

No fucking way.

Her words, "Get him talking about his boat," have me thinking. *Okay, Snow, let's play your card and see.* If it pays off, I'm going to owe her big time. I know her first name is Rachel. How hard can it be to send something to the airline for her as a token of my appreciation? But she said it was against company policy, and I don't want to cause her trouble. I'm going to need to be more discreet.

There must be a way I can thank her. I'm not sure how yet, but I'm going to make damn sure I do something.

TWO

ORDER ACKNOWLEDGMENT

From: Scent from Rachel
To: Mr. X
Subject: Welcome!

Dear Mr. X,

Thank you for your first order from '*Scent from Rachel.*' I take client satisfaction seriously. If there are any special requests you may have, please do contact me to discuss them.

In the meantime, I hope you enjoy your purchase.

Rachel x

THREE

RACHEL

PRESENT DAY

"You don't have to leave, you know?"

I glance back at Chris, propped up against the pillows with the bedsheets tangled around his tanned legs, his eyes showing that calmness that comes not long before sleep.

I raise an eyebrow at him. "I know. You should also know that I never stay; it's just not who I am." I finish pulling on my boot before stretching up the bed and giving him a brief kiss on the lips, moving back before he can pull me back into bed. "Thanks for the company... again." I smile as I grab my bag and head towards the door.

"Anytime, babe." He yawns, stretching his arms above his head, his blond hair messy. "Call me whenever you need a friend." He chuckles.

"You know I will," I call back from the hallway as I head out the front door, letting it swing shut behind me.

"Rach, is that you?" I hear my housemate, Megan, call as I come through the front door.

"Who else would it be?" I say as I shrug out of my jacket.

"You're home early." Megan appears from the kitchen wearing her flannel pajamas with unicorns all over them, a glass of wine in her hand.

"Yeah, have I interrupted something?" I glance back over her shoulder as I kick off my boots, hoping to see a half-naked man, but knowing unicorn pajamas probably wouldn't be in play if there was one here. It would take an incredibly special guy to appreciate those.

"I should be so lucky." She giggles. "Nope, it's just Nigel and me watching TV. It is early for you, though?" Her eyes land on my face suspiciously.

"I wasn't really in the mood once I got there but stayed for one shag, so it wasn't a complete waste of a cab fare."

Megan snorts. "Only you, Rach. How's Chris?" she calls behind me as I head into the kitchen and grab another glass and the rest of the bottle of red wine.

"He's fine," I say, heading into the living room behind her and sinking down into the soft cream sofa. Nigel, our house rabbit, hops over, so I lift his big grey fluffy body up into my lap, giving him a kiss on the nose as he settles on top of my ripped jeans. "You know Chris, he's never one to turn down a booty call, even though he has to operate the early Washington flight tomorrow."

Megan sits down next to me, her fingers absentmindedly twirling a loose curl of her long auburn hair around one finger as she sips her wine. "I think he's nice. Whenever I used to fly with him, he was always so friendly."

"Meg, this is Chris we're talking about. *Of course,* he was friendly. He makes a new 'friend' on every flight," I say as I stroke Nigel behind his ears where his fur is fluffiest, his little black eyes close halfway as he relaxes into my lap.

"Doesn't that bother you?"

"Why should it? I don't want to date him. Ugh," I groan, "I can't think of anything worse. Having to stay the whole night and make small talk in the morning. Them becoming all pathetic and needy. No, thank you! What he does is none of my business; I'm happy with our arrangement. At least I might get a dreamless sleep tonight with any luck." I take a sip of wine.

"You're so weird. I don't know anyone else who has sex dreams about politicians when they need to get laid." Megan shakes her head as she smiles into her wine glass.

"You call it weird; I call it unique." I smirk. "Maybe it's how wrong it is. They aren't meant to be sexy, but once I get hold of them in their suits, they turn into right kinky bastards."

"Ew!" Megan wrinkles up her nose. "I would stick with calling Chris, given a choice."

I laugh. "You're probably right."

Megan eyes me over her glass. "I'm not sure I could ever have a 'friend with benefits'. I quite like the idea of a hot man getting pathetic and needy over me." She giggles. "That's another thing I don't miss about flying, all the random hook-ups so many of the crew have. It was never my thing."

"You don't know what you're missing; it's much simpler." I watch Megan wrinkle her nose up again. "You know you're always welcome to come with me on any of my trips anytime you feel like it, don't you? Just because you don't fly anymore doesn't mean you should miss out."

"I know, thanks." Megan smiles. "If we can get someone to watch Nigel, then maybe I can come to LA with you and visit Holly and Jay before the baby arrives?"

"I would love that." I sigh as I lean my head back against the cushions as my phone beeps. "Speak of the devil," I say as I read Holly's text out loud to Megan.

Holly: Thinking of you and sending you good luck for the auction. Think positive thoughts; your new home is just around the corner! Miss you, H

"She's so lucky, meeting a Hollywood Heart-throb like Jay Anderson on a flight and getting swept off her feet." Megan sighs dreamily. "Doesn't it make you want it?"

"Want what?" I scratch at my wrist as I remember the day Holly moved out of this house to leave for LA permanently. I was so happy for her; I've never seen a couple as in love as her and Jay. I'm so glad Megan was looking for somewhere new to live at the time though, I hate the idea of living alone. We've become good friends over the past year, living together. Although we couldn't be more different in our views on love and dating.

"You know, the whole romance thing? I would have loved for that to happen to me while I was working a flight. Too late now."

I look over at her. She looks like a puppy that's just been kicked with her big, sad eyes. "Meg, you don't need that. You've got your own cool artist thing going on. You're so talented. You don't need a man to make you. Girl, you're already doing it!" I cry enthusiastically, causing Nigel to open one eye and give me a dirty look. I swear this rabbit is really a cranky old man in the wrong body.

"I know, you're right. It would just be nice to know I'm not headed towards being a single old cat lady."

As she says "cat," Nigel farts out loud. I swear he's like no rabbit I've ever heard of.

"Nigel!" we both groan as he slides down my legs and hops off to his bed in the corner of the living room.

"Remind me again why we rescued you?"

"Aww, Rach. Don't say that. Remember how sad he looked at the shelter? No one wanted him because he was so huge and old."

I remember. I look over at Nigel, who has sprawled out on his cat bed. Because of the size of him, it was the only thing he fit in at the store.

"We love you really, old boy," I call and blow him a kiss. "You're the only man I can ever live with."

Megan giggles as I turn back to her.

"Seriously though, Meg, how's work going?"

She crashes back against the sofa. "Ugh. Well, it could be better. You know how I told you that my boss is a bit of an idiot?"

"A jerk, yes."

"Well, he either totally mis-sold the job description to me, or I'm in some kind of initiation that includes getting his coffee and lunch and hardly doing any actual drawing." She looks down, picking at the fabric of her pajamas.

"God, Megan! He's such an asshole. It makes me so mad he thinks he can treat you like that!" My blood boils every time she talks about this guy. "You need to stand up to him. Take it higher if he won't listen. What's his boss like?"

"I can't do that. I'm lucky to have the job as it is. There are so many illustrators and artists who never get the opportunity to work for a company like that."

"It's not right, though. You're so talented, and you're supposed to be using your talent and growing. Not running errands for a jerk who's too lazy to get his own lunch," I grumble, knocking back my wine.

"I know, I know. Maybe it's just because I'm new. It's only been a couple of months. I can't expect to do all the exciting stuff straight away," she says dejectedly.

"Just know that I believe in you and when you're ready to tell him where to shove his coffee and lunch, I'll be right there to back you up."

"Thanks." Meg smiles. "Well, it's just as well you didn't stay out too late having no-strings sex with Chris. It's the big day tomorrow!" she squeals excitedly, changing the subject.

She's right; tomorrow is a big day. I've been saving for as long as I can remember to afford a deposit to buy my own place, have something of my own for the first time in my life, and I've finally got enough. It's not going to be a mansion, with the prices the outskirts of London attracts, but there's enough for a small two-bed house, like the one we rent, so that Megan can move with me.

"You're right." I can't help but smile back at Megan's infectious grin. "Tomorrow is a big day. We've got to be at the auction early. If we miss the lot number, then I'm screwed. It's the only one that's in the right area with a guide price that's within budget."

"Just think, all those months looking at houses, and now tomorrow, you might finally get your hands on the keys to your own house!" Megan's grin grows even wider.

"That's what I'm hoping for. If the house weren't up for auction, I don't think I would have any chance of affording it. It's a shame the old owner died. A family's life had to get turned upside down for me to have a chance at my dream." I sigh as I reach over to the coffee table and pick up the auction catalog. There, circled in red, is the house I'm bidding on tomorrow. My stomach knots at the sight of the pretty white terrace house, its shiny red front door glistening like a cherry on a cake.

This is it; this is going to be my house!

"It is sad, but you can breathe life into that house again. You can make it into a home. The house will be happy to be loved again." Megan smiles at me.

I love the childlike innocence she has. Maybe that's why she's such a talented illustrator; she captures a kind of magic in her work somehow.

"You know, we really should toast someone who made this all a lot more possible." Megan continues, raising her glass to mine.

"Oh." I smile knowingly at her. "You're right; there is someone who I am very thankful for. Without his valued business, there would be no house bidding at all happening yet. It would have taken so much longer. Who knew selling panties was such a lucrative business?"

"Who the heck knew?" Megan giggles. "To Mr. X, may he have a lifetime of *scent-sational* happiness."

Excitement bubbles in my stomach, replacing the knots that were there just moments ago. Selling panties I've worn on my flights was never something I imagined happening, but I'm glad it did. The past eighteen months of emails back and forth to the mysterious Mr. X, along with his regular deposits to my

PayPal account, brought me to this. The moment I've longed for my entire life, to finally have a home of my own. I can't ever regret his part in making that a possibility. Although I've been saving hard, I would not have been in this position for years had it not been for him. He insisted on being my only client and paid more than double for the assurance that I dealt only with him.

"To Mr. X, whoever he is." I smile as we clink glasses and drink.

FOUR

TANNER

"TELL ME AGAIN WHY YOU STILL DO THIS?" DREW ASKS me, taking a swig from his takeaway Starbucks cup as his eyes roam around the drafty auction house.

It's a good turn-out. People are sitting in every chair that's set up facing the Auctioneer's podium at the front of the room. And a whole load more are piled in at the back standing, like us.

"I like to do it; it helps the students. Nothing like getting your hands dirty and getting stuck in to learn," I say seriously, making some more notes on the auction catalog.

"Come on, man, don't give me that shit. What's really in it for you?"

"Drew." I eye him sharply. "I like to do this. It reminds me of where I started. Now I'm giving others the same chance. The really promising ones come and work for us."

"Ah, so that's it." He smiles smugly, nodding his

head. "I knew there would be some shrewd business decision behind it somewhere."

"It's always about business," I say gruffly, sliding my pen into the back pocket of my jeans.

"What's got into you today? I thought you'd be all happy having escaped Mandy the money-grabber now we're back from New York?"

I look at my best mate and Head of Staff, Drew, his eyes alight with mischief. "You know, maybe I should have left you over there for another year," I say, my face deadpan.

"Relax, Tan, I'm just yanking your chain." He bumps his shoulder against mine. "You make it far too easy, mate, far too easy." He chuckles to himself. "Anyway, I enjoyed working out of the New York office. American women, phew, they're feisty." He grins. "It is good to be home, though."

I clear my throat. "Looks like it's about to start." I nod towards the front, where the auctioneer has arrived. I'm pleasantly surprised to see it's an attractive blond woman. She's wearing a fitted wool dress with a low-cut neckline that shows off her ample cleavage. I run my hand back through my hair as I watch her climb up the stairs of the podium.

"Check out the cougar. Better than the old codger that used to be here last year. What do you reckon? Popped his clogs?" Drew says, inclining his head towards the podium where Blondie is standing.

I scowl. "No idea, but you need to stop talking. We've got four lots to bid on, and I want them all. If we miss one because you don't know when to shut up, you'll be looking for a new job in the morning."

"Alright, Boss." Drew holds his hands up, his empty cup between one thumb and forefinger. "Now I know you're pissed. I guess now that Mandy money-grabber isn't rinsing your wallet anymore, you're also not getting your balls milked."

His smirk leaves his face as I hiss, "Don't you even think about my balls."

I notice Blondie's eyes roaming up and down my body all the way from her place at the podium. She raises an eyebrow at me, and I respond with the faintest of smiles. At least this auction won't be boring.

Almost an hour later and we've won three out of four of the lots I came for. The houses themselves are all one or two-bed starter homes on the outskirts of London. Perfect projects for the local colleges' trade apprenticeship programs my company helps to fund. They get to learn hands-on like I did when I started out as a builder's apprentice all those years ago. It's a win-win for the company. It provides great publicity opportunities, and I hand pick the most talented tradespeople to come and work for my property development company. We're doing well. Offices London and New York, and talks over some major new Los Angeles and Las Vegas contracts are in motion.

"Tan, this is the last one, Lot sixty-nine," Drew says

to me, keeping his voice low. The last thing we want is for another bidder to overhear which lots we plan bidding on, or worse, how much I'm willing to pay for them.

I shift my feet as Blondie starts the lot. "Okay, ladies and gentlemen, onto plot sixty-nine." She looks me in the eye as she says the number. I try not to roll my eyes at her blatant flirting. I shouldn't discount the potential for a fuck later, but I'm already losing interest in all the obvious glances she keeps throwing my way. I look around the room as she drones on about the "charming curb appeal" and "perfect location, close to Heathrow Airport". There are a lot of heads bobbing and catalog papers being shuffled. This is obviously going to be a popular lot.

"Who will start the bidding at Two Hundred and Eighty thousand?" she calls out. There's a pause as she scans first the seated portion of the room and then the standing bidders at the back. "Make no mistake, this plot will sell," she says, glancing around again.

A hand with hot red painted nails rises out of the crowd. "Thank you!" Blondie calls.

"Any advance on Two Eighty?" She scans the room again. I tip the top of my rolled-up auction catalog towards her. "Thank you, sir." She smiles as she acknowledges my bid.

"Two Ninety?" she asks red nails. I can't see a hand, or even where the person whose hand it is sits, but whoever it is must have bid again because Blondie's eyes are back on me.

"Two Ninety-Five?" she asks sweetly, her eyes dropping to the crotch of my jeans and back up again. God, hurry up, woman. I nod, irritated that she seems to be dragging this out.

"Three Hundred and Ten Thousand!" I hear a voice call out. Blondie's eyes flash, annoyed at the interruption. She looks into the crowd, and I can see the same small, delicate, red-nailed hand extending up through the crowd.

Oh, she's stubborn.

I sigh. I really don't have time for this. Drew and I have some proposals to look over today before we head out tonight.

"Three Hundred and Thirty Thousand," I say, boredom creeping into my voice. Heads in the crowd are whipping back and forth, watching the bidding war.

"What happened to the Three-Two-Five budget?" Drew whispers from the side of his mouth.

"That's my plot, Drew. I just want to get out of here now. It's worth the extra five just to hurry this the hell up," I bark.

Drew rolls his eyes as he crosses his arms across his chest. "Your call, Tan."

Blondie smiles at me before casting her eyes back into the seated crowd near the front. "Three Hundred and Thirty-Five Thousand?" she asks. There's a murmur around the room as we wait.

After a long pause, Blondie looks back up at me. "It's your bid, sir, at Three Hundred and Thirty

Thousand pounds." Red nails must have maxed out. Good. I never usually go over budget.

"Going once." She scans the room for any last-minute bidders. "Going twice." Silence. "Gone! To the handsome gentleman at the back," Blondie calls out, her eyes on me as she licks her lips and brings down her gavel with a loud *thud*.

There's some excited chatter around the room as I hold up my bidding number so a member of staff can note it down near the podium.

"Congratulations, sir," Blondie says, but I'm past caring about her. A man has stood up and left one seat near the front, and I now have a direct line of sight to the person sitting in front of him—the woman who must have been bidding against me. She's turned around in her seat, a murderous expression on her face as though she's fantasizing about tearing me limb from limb with her red nails.

My breath catches, and my cock twitches as I stare back into the beautiful face belonging to Snow.

FIVE

RACHEL

"I can't believe it! Fucking wanker!" I spit as I pace up and down the living room. Nigel watches me with undisguised boredom as he chews his carrot.

"I know! And the way he smiled at you afterward," Megan says. "Smiling at you with his insanely perfect teeth. Do you think his hair always looks that good?" she trails off, staring into the distance.

"Megan!"

"Sorry. You're right, Rach. Total and utter asshole. Who does he think he is? He bought three other houses as well. Why so many?"

I freeze and spin to face her. "He did what?"

"I saw him. While you were busy focusing on the lot coming up, I was enjoying watching the room. The woman next to me even brought packed sandwiches with her," Megan says incredulously.

"So, Mr. Wanker had already bought three other houses? He didn't even need mine!" I shriek, my heart racing in my chest. "He's probably got a ton of money, and they're going to get swallowed up into his property empire or something." I seethe as I think of the smug asshole's face. I wish I had gone and given him a piece of my mind, but he'd disappeared by the time we made it out towards the exit.

He was lucky.

"There'll be other houses, Rach. This one was obviously not meant to be." Megan comes over and pulls me into a hug. "I know how much it meant to you, and you'll get there, you will."

My shoulders slump as I give in to her hug. "There won't be others like that, Meg. Not for ages. I can't afford anything on the open market, and the next local auction isn't for at least another six months."

"Something will turn up. If it's meant to be, it will be." Megan's eyes shine into mine.

"How can you be so optimistic?" I narrow my eyes back at her.

"I just have a good feeling. I think Mr. Wavy Hair did you a favor. That house probably has rats or something living under the floorboards."

I raise an eyebrow. "Mr. Wanker," I correct her, "better hope he doesn't cross paths with me again soon. I need a good anger release."

"That'll have to wait until your next kickboxing class. Right now, we are going out." Megan grins at me.

"Out?" I try to sound anything other than pissed-off, which has been my single setting since leaving the auction house.

"Yes. After today, you need a drink."

Actually, that sounds like a great idea.

Even Mr. Wanker can't spoil that.

The club is packed when we arrive, the atmosphere electric. It only opened this weekend and has a retro dance feel about it—neon lights and booths packed with people.

I went for my go-to 'don't fuck with me' outfit of a bright red body-con dress and black patent stilettos, which can probably pierce through bullet-proof glass. Megan smiles over at me, her auburn ringlets tumbling over her shoulders.

"Your hair looks so beautiful like that, Meg," I call over the loud music.

"Thanks." She smiles self-consciously, smoothing her hands down over her short, black dress. "Let's get a drink."

I look at the round bar as the barman fixes our drinks. It's lit up in blue and pink neon lights, one giant tube shelf of different liquors running up its center.

"Ladies," the barman says as he places our drinks down on the bar. We thank him as I tap my card against the payment reader.

I flash him a smile as I read his name tag. "Keep them coming, won't you, Greg?"

"Sure thing, gorgeous." He winks at me as he

throws a bar towel over his shoulder.

"Rach, not chatting up the barman, are you?" Megan giggles as he moves away to serve someone else.

"Just making friends. Look how busy it is here tonight. We will wait hours to order another drink otherwise."

"Smart thinking, I like it." She smiles.

"Thanks!" I raise my glass of whisky and clink it against Megan's cocktail.

She winces as I knock back the shot in one smooth movement before holding my empty glass up towards Greg.

"Make it a double this time, please," I say as he refills my glass.

We find an empty table near the bar and slide up onto the stools.

"You're on a mission tonight." Megan eyes my freshly filled glass.

"Hell yes. I want to forget all about houses, auctions, and smug wankers for tonight and just drink and dance with my friend," I say as I grin at her.

"I'll drink to that!" Megan says, raising her glass to her lips and taking a sip of her cocktail before eyeing my drink. "Seriously, Rach, I don't know how you drink that stuff."

"Practice and habit." I smirk. "When I was growing up in foster care, one of the older kids used to steal whisky and make us younger ones drink it as a dare or punishment if we stepped out of line."

"That's horrible; what a bully!" Megan looks over at me, listening intently. I rarely talk about where I grew up. I don't see the point. It's all in the past.

"Yeah, he thought he was big, but I had a growth spurt that summer and soon put him in his place. He never bothered the younger ones or me again."

"What did you do?" Megan's eyes go wide as she leans towards me.

"Gave him a corker of a black eye the next time he pushed one of the younger ones about. He gave me a wide berth after that."

"Oh my God." Megan clasps her hand over her mouth as she giggles. "You're a total badass."

"I hate bullies," I say as I down the rest of my drink. "Come on, finish that cocktail. We're going to dance!"

Megan throws her head back and downs the cocktail in one go, her eyes glassy as she looks at me. "I might regret that later; I've got a head rush already." She laughs as she takes my hand, and I lead her out onto the packed dance floor.

We get carried away with the music, dancing to song after song of sexy beats. The base is turned up so loud I can feel the vibrations of the music flowing up into my body through the floor.

I don't know how long we've been dancing before I become aware of eyes on me. I can feel their heat burning my skin. I spin as I dance next to Megan, searching for where they're coming from.

That's when I see him.

Dark eyes burning into my skin, his hand running through his dark, wavy hair.

Mr. Wanker from the auction.

Oh hell, you picked the wrong club tonight, asshole.

Megan's eyes follow mine to see what I'm looking at. When she does, they widen and come back to my face.

"Rachel... don't."

But I'm already striding off the dancefloor towards him. His smug face is still watching me, his eyes never leaving mine.

He's asking for it.

Game on, Wanker.

He stands up as I reach the booth he's in with his friends. A look of amusement plays across his face—an exceptionally smooth, masculine face complete with dark, chocolate-colored eyes. I watch him run a hand through his dark, wavy hair again. I scowl as I give him a quick glance over. Designer shoes and jeans, smart shirt rolled up at the sleeves, expensive watch. Yep, he's definitely some kind of smarmy property tycoon with more money than morals.

Now I'm right in front of him. He towers over me in height, despite my heels. I can feel my anger rising in my chest. This guy, this stupid, selfish moron, stole my house from me! I'm literally shaking with rage as I glare at him, and he's not even flustered.

"You!" I hiss through gritted teeth as I glare up at him. "You stole sixty-nine from me."

He eyes me coolly. "Excuse me?" he says in a smooth, deep voice.

"Rachel, come on, let's go get another drink." Megan pulls at my arm. I shake off her hand, my eyes never leaving his.

"No," Mr. Wanker and I both reply in unison.

I glare at him even harder. I swear, if looks could kill.

He turns toward Megan. "You're obviously a good friend to Rachel here," he says my name slowly, as though seeing how it feels on his tongue, "but it seems she has something she wants to get off her chest?" He looks back at me and raises an eyebrow, his dark chocolate eyes challenging me to continue.

"You bet I do!" I take a step closer to him. I expect him to move back, but he stays perfectly still and watches me intently. "That was my house. You do not know how long I've been waiting to find it," I say slowly, trying to keep my breathing even.

"Oh, I can imagine—" he says, but I cut him off.

"That was my house, and you and your fancy watch and shoes think you can just swoop in and steal it. You already bought three others. What could you possibly need them all for? Except to make more money to buy your stupid, worthless designer labels with." I snarl and give him a filthy look.

"Feisty one, isn't she?" One of his friends from the booth behind pipes up and laughs. Mr. Wanker glares at him, and his friend shakes his head and goes back to his conversation with the other two men there. They are dressed the same: designer labels and fancy accessories, a bottle of expensive top-shelf whisky on their table.

"You're very presumptuous about my needs, aren't you, Rachel?" He takes his time saying my name again as his dark eyes study my face.

"So, I'm wrong then, am I? You actually need all four houses to live in yourself? Or you've got four sweet old grandmas who all need a new house? No, wait..." I look him up and down, my finger tapping against my lips, "you've got four girlfriends who don't know about each other."

The briefest flash of anger passes over his face before he smirks at me. "Now you're just acting childish, Rachel," he says calmly, making my blood boil even more.

Who the hell does he think he is?

"Sixty-nine should have been mine." I point my finger at his face.

Before I even see it coming, he grabs my wrist in his large, muscular hand. He strokes it gently with the pad of his thumb as he leans down, closing the small distance between us until his lips are almost touching my ear. Goosebumps run up my arms as his warm breath flows over my skin. "I will happily give you a different sixty-nine, Rachel," he says smoothly.

"Ugh, please." I yank my wrist free of him and take a step back. "That's just the sort of thing I would expect you to say. Don't you have any imagination?"

I watch his lip curl up into a small smile at my

words as he pushes his hands into his trouser pockets. I can see what Megan means; he could be quite sexy if it weren't for the slight issue of his personality.

"Oh, I can imagine, Rachel. I can imagine lots of things." His eyes drop to my lips and back up again.

"You do that. I'm done wasting my breath on you," I fire back as I turn my back on him and grin at Megan. "Shall we get another drink, Meg?"

She breathes out in relief. "Thought you'd never ask."

We walk off back to the bar without looking back, and Greg greets us with a drink when we get there.

"To having a great night and not even glancing in that asshole's direction again," I say as I clink glasses with Megan.

"To avoiding the insanely hot man's eyes for the rest of the night." She nods.

"Megan! You really think he's hot?"

"Well, obviously, I'm just talking about his physical attributes." She smirks. "Did you see the size of his biceps?"

"No, just the size of his over-inflated ego."

"Well, they were huge." Her eyes widen. "You know he hasn't stopped looking over at you since we walked away?" She glances over my shoulder toward his booth.

"Let him look then," I say as I lean over the bar, so my cleavage is accentuated. I grin at Greg, who almost misses my glass with the whisky, as his eyes drop to my chest.

"He looks really pissed now," Megan whispers.

"Even better." I grin.

We spend the rest of the night drinking and dancing and having a great time. I feel the heat of his eyes burning into my body all night, but I don't even glance in his direction again.

If he thought he won, then he's mistaken.

Mr. Wanker is no match for me.

SIX

TANNER

SINCE THE NIGHT AT THE CLUB, I HAVEN'T BEEN ABLE TO get Snow—or Rachel—out of my head. I don't know what the hell's wrong with me. It's clear she doesn't even remember our brief meeting a year and a half ago, but then she was in such a rush that she barely looked at me.

Fuck.

I've never been so pathetic over a woman I never expected to see again, a woman I barely know anything about. Although, that's not strictly true. I know some things about her, like her innermost desire is to be independent and take care of herself. It's so fucking sexy. Yet, I was the one who unknowingly stole her dream from right in front of her. No wonder she was so mad.

The sight of her in that tight, red dress, the fire in her eyes when she laid into me, God, I would love to see that fire really in action. My cock stiffens at the thought. That woman has passion, all right. I just need to persuade her I'm the perfect man to unleash it with.

I stretch my arms back behind my head and blow out a breath as I stare out of the window of my office, London sprawled out below. I need to do something. This is insane. I'm not going to get any work done wondering about when I will see her again. Plus, there's this fucking guilt I feel over buying the house I know she's been saving years for.

I slide my fingers down my pen, turning it upside down and repeating the motion again and again as I wrack my brains for an idea. I smile as one hits me, and I sit forward, pressing the intercom to my PA.

"Yes, Mr. Grayson?"

"Penny, could you get me the auction house on the phone, please?"

"Of course, one moment," Penny replies.

Snow might have given me a frosty reception so far; she will be a challenge, and I never can resist one of those.

Time to heat things up.

"Hello?"

Even her voice is sexy. She sounds so different when she's not fighting with me.

"Hello Rachel," I say slowly, a smile spreading across my face as her pause tells me she's trying to place my voice.

"Matt? I'm not falling for one of your prank calls again." She huffs, and the line goes dead.

What the...?

She hung up on me. I dial back, and she answers on the first ring. I cut in before she speaks, "Don't you dare hang up on me again, and who the hell is Matt?"

There's silence for a moment before she speaks.

"Mr. Sixty-nine. How did you get this number?" Her tone is cold; she sounds pissed.

"You told me to use my imagination," I reply.

I don't fancy recounting the long dinner I had with Blondie from the auction house. I had to endure three hours of her laughing like a hyena and grabbing at my cock under the table. There would have been a time I would never have turned down an easy shag, but all I could think about was getting the hell out of there once I got what I went for—Snow's number.

She's turned me into a fucking soft cock. God help me.

"So... what? Am I meant to be impressed that you found my number? Probably sweet-talked someone at the auction house."

What?

I clench my teeth. I need to up my game.

"So, what do you want, anyway?" she asks, sounding irritated. "To gloat some more over your huge... portfolio?" I can hear the smirk in her voice. God, this woman is infuriating.

"Actually, I was phoning with a proposal for you."

"What could you possibly have that I would be

interested in?" she snaps back, but I sense she's intrigued, judging by the fact she hasn't hung up again.

"Well, a friend of mine has got a house coming up for sale, but he needs a quick sale and wants to avoid paying agent's fees."

"Why's he need a quick sale?" Her voice rises in suspicion.

"He needs the cash quickly to invest in another business deal he has going on. If he goes to market, it'll take too long. He's only just found out about this other deal, so he's missed the local area auction for another six months," I explain.

"So, what's your proposal?"

I lean back in my chair and cross my legs as a sense of satisfaction fills my chest. I've got her.

"I thought you and I could look?"

"You can just give me your friend's number, and I can arrange a viewing myself," she answers quickly. "No need to put yourself out," she says with mock sweetness, "I'm sure you're a terribly busy man playing big boy monopoly with all your houses."

I adjust myself as my cock twitches in response to her downright snarky attitude. Drew was right that night in the club. She is feisty.

"Well, if you're going to be like that—" I trail off.

"Hang on," she cuts in, and I feel my smile widen. "I suppose your input might be useful, given the number of houses you must have seen over the years."

"Over the years? Just how old do you think I am?" I

frown, checking out my reflection in the shiny glass of my desk.

"Old enough to know that I won't fall for any of your charming—run your hands through your hair shit—that might usually work for you."

"Just give me your address, Rachel." I sigh. "I'll pick you up in the morning at ten."

She reels off a street address to me, and I write it down.

"Hey, you never told me who Matt was?" I say. But all I hear is the beep of the phone. She's hung up on me.

Again.

Ten minutes to ten the following morning, I knock on the door to Rachel's house, and her friend, who I recognize from the club, answers.

"Hello Megan," I say, extending my hand out to her, "it's nice to see you again."

She takes it in hers and smiles at me—at least she has good manners. "You too, err?"

"Tanner," I say. "My name's Tanner, but my friends call me Tan."

"You're early... Tanner," Rachel calls from inside the house, "you'd better come in while I grab my things."

"Thanks." I nod at Megan as she stands back for me to enter. It's a pleasant house that shows two girls live here from the vase of flowers on the hall table and one of those reed things in a bottle that smells. My eyes are drawn to a framed drawing on the wall. It looks exactly like Rachel and Megan in red flight attendant uniforms.

"Did you draw this?" I gesture to the artwork.

"Yeah," says Megan, her cheeks flushing, "I'm an illustrator. I used to fly for Atlantic Airways, the same as Rach, but I left a few months ago when I got a job at a large design company."

"That's incredible; you're very talented," I say sincerely. I mean it, this girl is good. The picture seems so lifelike. She's captured something in Rachel's eyes. It almost seems intrusive to look at it for too long.

Her blush deepens. "Thank you, Tan, that's a nice thing to say."

"It's the truth," Rachel says as she comes down the stairs.

I try not to stare. She's wearing ripped black jeans and a white t-shirt gathered into a knot near her tiny waist. I can just glimpse the dip of her belly button underneath the bottom of her t-shirt and imagine running my tongue up her toned stomach, dipping it in to taste her. Her eyes flash up to my face, and I have to disguise the deep swallow I've just taken, pretending to clear my throat instead.

"Ready?" I ask.

"You bet," she says as she throws on a denim jacket. "See you later, Meg." She gives her housemate a quick kiss on the cheek.

"Nice to meet you again," I say to Megan as we head outside.

"So, how far away is your friend's house?" Rachel asks the second the door closes behind us.

"Not even three minutes in the car," I say as I unlock my black Aston Martin and hold the door open for her. Her eyebrows rise at the gesture as she slides into the passenger seat.

"Just as well, seeing as I don't know you. Less time for you to abduct me in your fancy car. I carry pepper spray, you know. And I fight dirty," she says as I get in behind the wheel.

"Oh, I'm sure you do." I stare straight ahead. I start the engine, and the car purrs to life. I pull out onto the road, stealing a sideways glance at her. Her expression has softened slightly, her eyes are studying me, her red lips slightly parted.

Fuck, she's beautiful.

"What are you looking at?" I ask.

She raises an eyebrow at me. "I'm wondering why you decided to help me after spectacularly fucking me over the other day."

I groan inwardly at the way her lips move when she says the word "fucking". It's almost more than a man can take.

God, I want to fuck you over, Snow, just not in the way you mean.

"I'm disappointed you have such a low opinion of me. It was just business at the auction," I say matter-of-factly as I pull over to the side of the road and park the car.

"What's today then?" she asks, her eyes studying my face suspiciously.

"Today is pleasure," I say smoothly.

She smirks. "I'll be the judge of that."

I feel the corner of my mouth lift in amusement. "You do that, Rachel," I reply, and I notice her smirk fade as she studies my face. "Anyway, you can save your evaluations until later. We're here."

I lean across her to point at the house we've parked in front of—two streets away from where she lives. As I do, I catch a hint of her perfume; jasmine mixed with musk, sexy as hell. I adjust myself in my jeans as I move back to my seat.

Rachel's still staring out the window.

"I can't afford this, Tanner," she whispers as she looks up at the pale-grey painted terrace house, shiny black railings leading up the steps to its front door.

"I know what your budget is from the auction. I wouldn't have brought you here if it couldn't work. I told you, my friend needs a quick sale." I try to sound reassuring. "Come on, I'll show you inside; he gave me the keys." I climb out and make my way around to open Rachel's door for her. She beats me to it and is already standing on the pavement, her eyes still fixed on the house.

I look at her face and its delicate features. Her brow is wrinkled, and her lips pursed. She looks childlike and worried. "Everything okay?"

"Yeah, of course," she answers quickly before turning towards me and giving me a small smile. "Can we go inside now?"

We head up the steps to the front door, and I unlock it, holding it open so Rachel can go in first. As she passes me, I try not to breathe in. The last thing I need is to get a hard-on from the scent of her. She glances at me as she passes. "Thanks."

I gaze at this new, quieter, polite version of her. "You're welcome."

We head through the hallway and into the front room, which is flooded with light from the large window. Rachel walks over the polished floorboards as her eyes dart around.

"It's hard to imagine when it's empty like this." I point over at the wall, "but just picture your sofa over there and a tall lamp. Some bookshelves built into those alcoves over there, on either side of the fireplace. You could make it really cozy."

She says nothing, just nods as she walks into the next room, a dining room, leading into a newly re-fitted kitchen at the back of the house. She's looking out of the window at the garden as I come to stand next to her. She's wearing flat shoes today, accentuating how petite she is next to me.

"It's south-facing; you'll get the sun all day," I say, looking over at her.

"Nigel will love it," she murmurs, lost in thought.

Whoa, hang on. Have I completely missed

45

something here? Nigel? Don't tell me Snow has a boyfriend. *Motherfucker*. My jaw tenses at the idea.

I cough. "Who's Nigel, your boyfriend?" I ask in the most innocent, not-fucked-either-way voice I can muster.

"I don't have a boyfriend. He's our house rabbit." She turns to look up at me for the first time since we came through the front door.

My jaw relaxes. She doesn't have a boyfriend.

"A what? Don't they live in hutches? Or even better, out in a field somewhere?" I say, distracted by her sweet red lips. I wonder what they would look like wrapped around my cock.

"He would hate that. His favorite place is sleeping on the sofa. You should see the size of him; he's practically a cat." She takes one last look at the garden. "Show me upstairs?" she asks, turning back to me.

My cock stirs again as I imagine a very different intention her words could have.

One day, one day soon.

"After you." I gesture politely, following behind as Rachel walks back to the hallway and climbs up the stairs ahead of me. I have the perfect view of her tight little ass in her jeans.

It pays to have manners sometimes.

We look around the three bedrooms and bathroom upstairs. The house is in good shape. It just needs fresh paint and some nice furniture, and it'll look great.

"What do you think?" I ask as we head back out the front door and towards my car.

"I think it's too good to be true. What's the catch?" she says, looking up at me.

"Well, the catch is my friend still has to accept your offer. But I know if you said Three Hundred and Twenty Thousand and could complete the sale in a month, he would probably accept."

She rubs her lips together and looks back at the house. "Okay." She brings her eyes back to mine. "Let's call him now."

I pull out my phone and bring up Rich's number, hitting dial before bringing the phone up to my ear. Rachel takes a step closer to me. So close, I swallow and close my eyes briefly as the scent of her perfume invades my senses. I can practically feel the heat radiating between us as she rises on her tiptoes towards my face.

Holy fuck, yes!

I'm about to close my eyes and lean forward into her kiss when my phone is plucked out of my hand.

"Hello... Rich?" Rachel says as she checks the name on the screen and brings the phone up to her ear, her eyes glinting at me. "This is Rachel," pause, "oh, he did, did he?" She laughs at whatever Rich is saying.

He better not be chatting her up, or I swear I'll kick his ass next time I see him.

"Well," she says, "yes, I do like it, and I have an offer for you."

"Three twenty," I whisper the number to her.

She arches an eyebrow as she looks me straight in the eye. "I'll give you Three Hundred and Fifteen and not a penny more. And I can complete the sale in three weeks. Do we have a deal?"

My eyes widen as she smirks at me. She completely ignored what I said and purposefully did her own thing. Something heads would roll for if it happened at my company. Yet I can't help noticing how fucking turned on I am right now.

She smiles, her eyes never leaving mine. "Thank you, Rich. Speak soon." She ends the call.

"I've just bought a house, I've just bought a house!" she cries and wraps her arms up around my neck, pulling me into an embrace. My hands drop to rest on her waist, and my head gets buried into her hair as she pulls me in close.

She feels so soft and warm in my arms—*fucking perfect.*

Almost as quickly as it started, it's over, and she pulls away from me and takes a step back.

"Thank you, Tanner," she says, looking up at me.

I've regained my composure, but my heart races inside my chest from how good it felt being so close to her. "Don't mention it. Rich needed a buyer, and you were in a position to make an offer. It just made good business sense."

"I thought today was about pleasure," she says, repeating my words from earlier.

I can't help but smile.

She's right; today was a pleasure for me.

She has no idea just how much.

SEVEN

RACHEL

"Cheers!" I clink my champagne flute against Megan and Matt's.

"To making lots of new happy memories in yo͏ new house," Megan says, taking a sip.

"And to the amazing house party we are th͏ when you move in!" Matt says, a devili͏ ͏e spreading across his face.

I raise my eyebrows at him. "As long ͏ ͏u promise not to get so drunk again that you r͏ around naked and slip over. That night in h͏ ͏l with you is one night of my life I will nev͏ ͏ack, and the images are forever burned i͏ ͏ ͏nemory." I shudder.

"Oh, Rach͏ ͏almost forgotten about that, hah!" Matt chu͏ ͏s he leans back into our sofa.

"͏ ͏ will you get the keys, Rach?" Megan asks.

"͏ ell, we're close to officially exchanging contracts ͏ow, so the sale will be legally binding soon. Rich said I can pick up the keys a week on Saturday." I smile as I take a large gulp of champagne, the bubbles fizzing against my tongue. I can't believe I'm here, toasting this moment. I've done it! I've finally bought my house. It's going to be the first proper home I've ever had.

"I still think it's incredible that you're getting all the paperwork done for the sale so fast," Megan says.

"That's all thanks to Holly. She asked her sister Sophie for help. She's a lawyer. She doesn't deal with property conveyancing, but she put me in touch with a friend of hers, who has been amazing. She's pushing it through as fast as she can."

"Aww, our lovely Holly, always there to help, even all the way from LA." Matt sighs.

"I know. I miss her. Although you must see her all the time? I'm sure you've bribed the whole crewing department by now so that you can operate all the LA flights?" I smile as an image of Holly and Jay in their beachfront house pops into my head.

"Of course, I have. What would Stefan do without me if I weren't there as much as possible?" He grins at the mention of his boyfriend—and Jay's best friend —Stefan.

"I'm pretty sure he'd forget about you within a week and be shagging some Californian hunk," I say, keeping a straight face.

Matt stares daggers at me even though I'm sure after all our years of friendship, he knows I'm only teasing him. "Never! He's the one, Rach, I'm telling you. It's incredible between us."

"I'll take your word for it." I roll my eyes. "No strings for me, every time."

Megan leans forward to get a handful of crisps from the bowl on the coffee table, sitting back carefully to not disturb Nigel, who is sprawled out on the sofa, taking up most of the space. "I've tried telling her, Matt," she says between mouthfuls, "all this hot sex is okay, but one day she's going to meet a man who will make her want more."

"Nope, not going to happen." I shake my head firmly.

Matt is about to say something but looks down and raises an eyebrow at Nigel as he shuffles about, his furry tail rubbing against Matt's thigh. "Well, I guess his tail's lucky, isn't it? Even if I do smell like rabbit butt now."

"It's a rabbit's foot that's meant to be lucky." Megan gently places her hands over Nigel's ears. "And that's when it's made into a keyring," she whispers.

Matt's mouth drops open in horror. "That's barbaric! Who'd want to fish around in their pocket for that each time they want to open the front door?"

"I know, horrible, right?" Megan agrees. "Going back to keys and doors, though, has Rach told you about the guy who helped her find the house?"

"You told me it was some stuffy property bore?" Matt says, his eyes rounding on me.

Megan scoffs into her champagne glass. "Rach! You did not?"

"What?" I say, "he is. He's got more money than

sense. He drives an Aston Martin, for goodness' sake. He barely smiles, unless it's for looking smug and annoying, and I bet he has no clue how to loosen up and have fun."

Megan raises her eyebrows at me. "He's totally hot though, admit it, Rach."

When I say nothing, she turns her attention to Matt. "He's got this dark, wavy hair and intense, sexy eyes and an amazing body, from what I could tell, anyway." She giggles.

Matt narrows his eyes at me in suspicion. "How old is this sexy man?"

"I dunno." I shrug. "Mid-thirties, maybe. And he's not that sexy."

"Ah! So, you'll admit you think he's a teeny bit sexy?" Megan says, holding her fingers up in the air an inch apart.

I shake my head as I knock back my champagne. "Don't put words in my mouth."

"The question is, what would you let Mr. Sexy put in your mouth, Rach?" Matt asks with a smirk. "Have you even spoken to him since he helped line up this house for you?" Matt continues, not at all bothered that I'm glaring at him.

"Yeah, he's texted a couple of times to see how it's going. Asked if I needed any help with getting the paperwork sorted."

"And?" Matt coaxes.

"And nothing. The lawyer has it all in hand.

Besides, I like to do things myself. I don't need some man I hardly know sticking his nose in."

"This hot guy, what's his name?" Matt looks across at Megan.

"Tanner," she says.

"Oh, sounds strong. I like it." Matt grins. "So, hot Tanner offers to assist you, after finding you the house in the first place, and you won't accept his help?"

"Exactly." Megan nods at Matt.

"Rachel," he tuts, "where are your manners? You need to thank this man properly."

"I'm not shagging him as a thank you, Matt," I say, rolling my eyes, unimpressed.

"I wasn't suggesting that. But you should show your gratitude in some other way. What does he like?"

"I have no idea." I blow out a breath and shrug my shoulders. "Expensive crap and being nosey. Did you know he asked who you were when I thought it was you on the phone winding me up?"

Matt catches Megan's eye, and they exchange a knowing look. Before I can ask what it's all about, Megan's eyes light up. "He likes whisky! Same as you, Rach. He was drinking it at the nightclub, remember?"

I kind of remember seeing a bottle on the table of their booth. But my main memory of that night is how much I wanted to slap the smug look off his face. That and the heat of his eyes on me all night.

"Perfect!" Matt says as he taps away on his phone. "Take him here." He shoves the screen in front of my face. It's an advert for a whisky tasting night at a nearby swanky hotel.

"Are you serious? You think I should ask him to go there with me?"

"Absolutely, why not?"

"It's not as if you couldn't handle it way better than him anyway, Rach. We've all seen you drink that stuff like water," Meg pipes up.

She has a good point. I *can* hold my drink. It would be the perfect chance to show Tanner that I'm capable of looking after myself. And God knows he could do with loosening up. This might not be such a bad idea after all.

"Okay," I say to Matt, "how do I book?"

I operate a flight to Boston with a one-night layover, and before I know it, it's Saturday evening, the night of the whisky tasting. I wasn't entirely sure Tanner would want to go, but when I texted him, he said he thought he could make time. I mean, come on, like I should feel lucky that he's taken time out of his busy work schedule to meet me. The guy has such a nerve.

"Holls, I think we're almost there," I groan, glancing out of the window, then back to my phone screen. Holly's smiling face looks back at me. "I'd much rather stay in the cab and talk to you."

"Try to have fun, Rach. I'm sure he's not that awful."

"You haven't met him," I say, screwing up my nose. "I swear I'm going to kill Matt. This is such a bad idea."

"Go!" She giggles. "I want to hear all about it tomorrow."

"Yeah, yeah, okay."

"Love you, Rach."

"You too, Holls," I say as I hang up.

This is great. Why did I let Matt talk me into this? Surely a thank-you bottle of whisky would have sufficed. Now I have to spend a whole evening with Tanner. I would rather stick pins in my nails. Ugh, I hope it doesn't drag too much.

I smooth down my knee-length black dress as I get out of the cab. It's one of my favorites, sleeveless, with a high neck and a long, fitted pencil skirt. I've teamed it with pointy black heels. I've noticed how much bigger Tanner is than me, in both height and build, especially at the house that day when I hugged him —*God, what was I thinking?* Excitement does stupid things to you.

I walk up to the hotel in front of me. It's a beautiful old building with a brick pillared entryway that extends out to the pavement. There's a dark grey carpet rolled out, the hotel's emblem sparkling in silver on it. I love central London, especially parts like Knightsbridge, with its history.

The doorman dips his head in greeting as he holds the large, heavy door open.

"Good evening, Madam."

I step inside. It's all black, grey, and silver, with

mirrors everywhere—large, arch-shaped, paneled ones.

Wow.

The building itself may be old, but the inside has been completely remodeled. I make my way over to the reception desk, also made entirely of mirrored glass.

How the hell do they keep it so shiny?

"Can I help you, miss?" the lady behind the desk asks me, smiling, her deep plum lipstick catching my eye.

"Yes, I'm here for the whisky tasting event. I'm meeting a friend."

"Your name, please?" she asks as she glances down at her computer.

"Rachel Jones."

"Oh yes, I see you here, Ms. Jones." She looks up from the screen and smiles. "The evening will take place in the Grayson Bar. Please, if you follow me, I can show you to the bar area. You can wait here for your friend. Then once it's time to begin, one of our hosts will show you to your table."

"Okay, thank you," I say as I walk alongside her.

The bar has the same theme as the foyer—grey, black, and mirrors. The intimate tables in here are marble, each with black velvet chairs tucked underneath them. A few couples stand around talking, and most of the stools at the main bar are already occupied.

I feel the heat of his eyes on the bare skin of my arms before I see him. I scan down the length of the main bar, and there, sitting at the end, is Tanner. His dark eyes catch mine as he runs a hand back through his hair, his mouth in a firm line. He's wearing dark grey slacks and a crisp white shirt, unbuttoned at the neck. If I didn't know better, I would fall into the trap of even saying he looks sexy. In a dark, moody way, if you're into that sort of thing.

"Here you are." The receptionist gestures to a free stool at the bar. "Have a seat here while you wait for your friend."

"Actually, I can see him over there," I say, looking over in Tanner's direction.

"Oh?" The receptionist's mouth forms a small, surprised 'O' briefly as she sees Tanner looking at me. "Well, I will leave you to it then." She smiles. "Have a nice evening."

"Thank you," I reply before walking over to Tanner. His eyes haven't left mine. His mouth is still set in a straight line. Looks like I'm in for a great evening with Mr. 'Can't-crack-a-smile'.

"Rachel," he says smoothly, rising to his feet to greet me. His warm, smooth jaw brushes against my skin as he kisses me on each cheek, one hand lightly holding my elbow. A buzz of electricity runs up my arm where his hand is.

What the hell?

"Tanner," I say in greeting as I slide onto the stool next to him.

"You look beautiful," he says, taking me by surprise.

"Erm, thank you." I clear my throat as I look at him. This is weird, getting compliments from him.

"You seem surprised?" He rests a finger against his lips and watches me, his eyes crinkling with amusement. "Does it surprise you that I find you beautiful?"

"It surprises me you would think of commenting on it to me. After all, this isn't a date," I say, staring straight into his eyes.

"Of course not," he replies, with what looks like the start of a tiny smile forming on his lips.

"Think of it as a business drink. Thanking you for your help with the house."

"As you wish, Rachel," he says. That is definitely a smile he's trying to hide. Smarmy bastard: he thinks I fancy him, and this was a ploy to get him on a date.

"So, are you all ready to collect the keys next week?" he asks.

"Yes." I smile, pleased to be back on-topic. "I don't think I've ever been more ready for anything."

"I've seen a lot of people buy houses; none quite as focused as you. It really means something to you, doesn't it?" he asks, his eyes staring into mine.

"It does." I clear my throat, not wanting to elaborate further.

He narrows his eyes at me like he's trying to work something out.

A male staff member approaches us, "Madam, Mr. —" he begins, but Tanner cuts in, "Tanner, please call me Tanner, and this is Rachel."

"Very well." The young man smiles. "Rachel and Tanner, my name is Samuel. If you would please follow me, I will show you to your table to start the tasting evening."

"Thank you." I slide down off my stool and follow him. Tanner walks behind me. I'm aware of his eyes on me as we cross the room to our table, which is tucked away into an intimate corner of the bar. A single low lamp hangs in its center, giving off a warm glow.

"Here you are. Please make yourselves comfortable," Samuel says as he pulls a chair out for me.

"Thank you, Samuel," Tanner says, taking the chair from him and pushing it in as I sit down.

Samuel smiles as he steps to one side. "I will be back shortly," he says before disappearing back to the bar.

Tanner sits down in the other chair. It isn't opposite me, but at a ninety-degree angle, so he's practically right next to me. His leg brushes up against mine as he pulls his chair in. I swallow at the uncomfortableness of having him so close. I can even smell his aftershave, spicy and warm.

"Have you ever been here before?" I ask.

"I have actually," he says, his voice deep, "more than once. Have you?"

"No, first time. I like it, though. It's very stylish." I look around at the modern décor.

Tanner raises his eyebrows at me. "You like the style of it?"

"I do. It's a bit pretentious, but I think they get away with it."

He smirks as he studies my face. "Tell me, Rachel, how will you decorate your new house?"

"I haven't decided yet. It must feel homely, though. I want my friends to know they're welcome anytime. I want them to come in and help themselves to a cup of tea and make themselves at home."

"What did your family say when you told them your news?" Tanner asks.

"I don't have any family," I say, looking into his eyes. I wait for him to probe, ask what I mean, or say he's sorry. The usual things people say when I tell them. But he doesn't. Instead, he just looks deep into my eyes, as though he's trying to see my soul.

"I think your vision for your new home sounds perfect. I'm sure you'll have plenty of friends wishing to visit."

"You being one of them?" I tease, raising an eyebrow, immediately wondering why the hell I just said it.

"Most definitely," Tanner replies, his dark chocolate eyes glinting.

I feel a rush of heat between my legs at the way he's looking at me. I've never noticed before, but his irises have a circle of fiery amber around the pupil. The effect is mesmerizing. My body feels like a traitor, reacting this way in his company. He is absolutely not the type of guy I usually find attractive. I don't know what's got into me. I'm going to need those whiskeys tonight.

With impeccable timing, Samuel reappears, and I gratefully turn my gaze onto him as he speaks.

"Rachel, Tanner, welcome again to our taster evening. Tonight, we will present you with a selection of fine whiskeys from around the world. Each has its own unique flavor and story of how they are created. They will also be accompanied by small sharing dishes designed to complement," Samuel says as he sets down two glasses and fills them from a jug of iced water.

"Thank you," we both say in unison, and I look up and catch Tanner's eyes. He smiles at me, but I look away quickly and back to Samuel, who is busy setting down a board of smoked fish, cheese, and crackers. He follows that with two long trays, each with ten shots of whisky on. Their various honey colors shine in the lamplight.

Now we're talking.

I smile at the sight of each seductive little glass.

"If you wish, I can introduce each whisky to you. Please let me know when you are ready. Or if you wish for some privacy..." Samuel looks to Tanner, "then all descriptions can be found here." He hands us each a beautiful menu in a black velvet case.

"I think we can take it from here, thank you, Samuel," Tanner says.

Samuel smiles and heads back across the bar to greet an elderly couple who have just arrived. They must be in their eighties and are holding hands.

Tanner follows my gaze to where the older man is now helping the lady take her coat off before passing it to Samuel. "Still having date night, good for them."

"Unless they're having an illicit affair," I say, raising an eyebrow, "would make it more interesting, don't you think?"

Tanner turns his gaze back to me. "Does the idea of romance and loving one person for life not appeal to you, Rachel? I thought that was what all women want."

I snort. "I'm not all women."

He studies me intently. The amber in his dark eyes catches the light on the table and glows like embers in a fire. "No, you're not. Forgive me. I should know better than to make any assumptions when it comes to you, Rachel," he says my name again, taking his time, as though savoring the feel of it on his tongue.

We sit looking at each other for a few moments, my eyes challenging him to look away first. If he thinks he is the one in control here, he's mistaken. I can't quite work him out, but I know he's probably used to getting his own way and being in charge at all his bigwig meetings. Too bad for him, he's spending the evening with me, and I give as good as I get.

"Shall we?" He gestures to the first glass, and I feel a small sense of childish victory that he broke eye contact first. "This is a Scottish malt with bursts of chocolate and fudge," he reads from the menu.

"Sounds delicious," I say as I take the first whisky from the tray and bring it up to my eye level, admiring its warm, honey color. Tanner's eyes hold mine as we both lift the glasses to our lips and take a sip. The warmth spreads around my mouth and down my throat. I can't help but blink slowly as I savor it. "That's one sexy whisky." I smile as I tip my head back and finish the glass, licking my lips.

"Isn't it just," Tanner says darkly, his eyes dropping to my lips as he finishes his.

"Where does the name Tanner come from?" I ask as the whisky's heat spreads throughout my body. "It doesn't sound English."

"I was born in Chicago. We moved here when I was a baby." He leans his chin on his hands and runs a finger along his lips absentmindedly as he speaks. I watch as it glides back and forth.

"Your parents are American?"

"My mom's English. My father is American. Although, I don't remember him. He didn't react well when my mom told him she was pregnant. Stuck around for a bit but left before I was six months old." Tanner's forehead creases and his eyes darken momentarily. "It was just Mom and me growing up."

"What's she like?" I ask, despite never normally caring about peoples' family lives. Maybe because of the complete lack of mine.

He smiles, the most genuine smile I've ever seen. "She's amazing. I never felt like I was lacking anything growing up. She worked three jobs at one point just to make ends meet. Yet she was always there for me." He stares off in the distance as though lost in a memory.

"You didn't grow up with money then?"

He shakes his head as he looks back at me. "You have the wrong impression of me, Rachel."

"What impression would that be?" I ask with a small smile.

"I see the way you look at me. I've heard the comments you've made about my watch and my job. You think I'm some smug wanker."

I widen my eyes and can't help my smile from growing. He's hit the nail on the head. One thing he isn't is stupid. "So, enlighten me," I say, looking into his eyes.

Over the Irish and Indian whiskey, Tanner tells me how he started working as a builder's apprentice. Before working his way up to having his own property development business and living in New York for a year for a contract he won.

The Japanese and American whisky leads to me regaling him with stories about what it's like working as a long-haul flight attendant, including the time I discovered a very well-known actor and a woman who wasn't his wife, joining the mile-high club in the toilet.

Two more Scottish whiskies opens a can-of-worms' story about him and his best friend Drew getting lost at a friend's stag party wearing nothing but homemade togas, not much bigger than a flannel. I throw my head back and laugh at this story, attracting the couple's attention at the next table. The idea of Tanner wearing a toga and being anything other than serious and in control seems crazy.

Two more whiskeys from Taiwan and Ireland, and

my lips have been well and truly loosened by the alcohol, and I'm telling him how Nigel is the only male I would ever want to live with and that I've never had a real boyfriend, just "friends".

"Okay. Okay." I giggle. "This is the last one; you read it." I slap the menu down in front of Tanner, who frowns as he tries to focus on it. He fixates on it, making me think of a schoolboy being asked to read in the class by the teacher. "Here, I'll do it," I say, putting my hand on the menu.

"No, No, I can manage." Tanner smiles and returns to his serious face, his bottom lip pulled in as he stares at the page again. These whiskies are the strongest I've ever had. I would never usually feel this drunk.

"Come on, Mr. Sixty-nine, let me do it." I giggle as I slide the menu over to me.

Tanner puts his hand on top of mine, and warmth spreads up my arm.

"I can do it," he says again.

God, he's even stubborn when he's drunk. He leaves his hand on mine and lifts my fingers up one by one to read the description. "This one is triple distilled and purified. It has the highest alcohol content of the lot."

"Oh, fuck." I snort. "Save the best till last, eh? Let's do it on three." I lift the glass with my spare hand. I haven't moved the other one out of Tanner's warm grip yet. We lift our glasses and clink them together. "One, two, three!" I count and knock mine back in one. Fuck, that was strong. Although, I'm determined not to let it show on my face. I look at Tanner, who hasn't even blinked. *Fucker.*

"You called me Mr. Sixty-nine," he says, smirking. His thumb rubs back and forth across my knuckles.

"I've called you a lot of things since I met you," I say, noticing his pupils dilate as I look into his eyes.

"Have you?" he says, reaching forward and gently dusting the pad of his thumb over my bottom lip, his eyes following its path.

I know I should turn away or move out of his grasp. Do *something.* Yet, I just sit glued to the spot, watching his face as he studies my lips.

"It's time I called a taxi. Shall I order one for you?" I ask, still not moving out of his touch. *What's wrong with me?*

"No, Snow. I've got a room here for the night," he says as he draws his hand back, the warmth leaving my lips.

"Snow?" I murmur.

His lips curl. "You said you've called me all sorts of things. Don't I get to call you something?"

"Why Snow?" I ask, finding myself looking at his hand and wanting to feel it against my lips again.

"You make me think of Snow White. Your dark hair, your red lips," he says, his eyes dropping to them again.

"And the seven dwarves I live with?" I raise an eyebrow at him.

"They'd be seven fucking lucky fellas." His eyes meet mine, and I feel my heart hammering in my chest. Seriously, what the hell is wrong with me? Flirting is nothing new to me. Hell, I'm no saint, but I'm always in control. Somehow here, with Tanner, I can feel it slipping through my fingers. I know I should run, but my body is willing me—No—*begging* me to stay.

"You could be Grumpy," I say. His eyes crease in amusement, but they never leave my lips.

"Come up to my room, Rachel," he says quietly, running a hand through his hair and shifting in his seat so he's closer to me and his thigh is pressed up against mine.

I swallow down the flutters rising from my stomach as I allow my eyes to roam from his face down over his broad shoulders, and muscular arms, and chest.

I know I should say no, but it's not like I haven't done this a ton of times before. It's just sex, and he looks kind of hot tonight. Maybe it will put a stop to whatever this weird feeling is. Nip my growing attraction to him in the bud. I can fuck it out of my system and still be home by midnight.

"Fine," I say, "but I'm not coming just because you want me to."

He grins at me. "We'll see about that."

EIGHT

TANNER

I open the door to my hotel suite and stand back so Rachel can go in first. She looks up at me as she passes, and I breathe in her heady jasmine perfume. My cock hardens as my mind is transported back to when I showed her around the house. I had hoped then that this day would come, but I didn't think it would be so soon.

I'm one lucky bastard.

"Nice," she says, looking around at the suite, her eyes landing on the giant four-poster bed in the middle of the room.

It's sexy and seductive. It's not a room you make love in. It's a room where fantasies are played out, and mine is standing right in front of me.

"Would you like another drink?" I ask her as I open the minibar. I turn to look for her answer and realize she's moved to stand right next to me.

"No, thank you, Tanner; we both know why we're here."

Fuck, my cock hardens more at the way she's looking at me, her glittering eyes confident and determined.

"Maybe I need reminding," I say, my eyes never leaving her face as she reaches up and around my neck and pulls my mouth down onto her warm, waiting lips. I can taste the whisky on her tongue as she opens for me, allowing me to press deeper, exploring her. Holy fuck, her lips are even sweeter to kiss than I imagined. I bring my hands up to her face and tilt her head back, getting her exactly where I want her. She pushes me, forcing my back against the wall as her hand drops to my pants. I let out a low groan as she grabs me roughly through the material.

Pulling her lips back from mine, she looks me in the eye before leaning closer. "It's not just your ego that's big then?" she whispers before nipping my ear between her teeth.

The feel of her breath as she whispers to me unleashes something, and I spin us around hard, so she is pressed against the wall instead. I look down at her, and she gazes up at me wickedly from under her long dark lashes, one hand still on my cock. She wraps her fingers around it and squeezes, her eyes fixed on mine, gauging my reaction.

"Fuck, you could make me come just by looking at me with those baby doll eyes," I growl as I grab a fistful of her hair. I pull her head back sharply so I can kiss her again, deeply stroking my tongue against hers. I'm aware of our breathing growing ragged. I suck on her bottom lip before giving it a slight tug between my teeth.

"Let me see you, baby," I say, reaching my hands down to the hem of her dress. I inch it up slowly over her knees and thighs, my fingers brushing against her soft skin. She draws in a small gasp, and I smile to myself as the sound confirms it—the touch of my hands against her bare skin feels just as good for her as it does for me. I pause once my hands reach her hips, my palms cupping each hip bone gently before my fingers slip underneath the lace fabric of her panties to stroke her skin.

"What are you waiting for?" She moves her hands to her dress to pull it over her head.

"Wait." I stop her hands, and she looks at me in curiosity. But when I drop to my knees, she smiles, leaning her head back against the wall and parting her legs wider.

Fuck, she's opening right up for me, beautiful girl.

"Watch me, Rachel," I growl as I lean forward and press my mouth against the lace, biting her clitoris gently.

"Tanner," she hisses, sucking in her breath as her body bucks forward from the wall.

"I want you to watch as I fuck you with my tongue, Rachel." I look up at her from between her legs.

Her eyes drop to my face, and I watch them darken as I press my face back into her soaking wet panties and inhale deeply. "You smell so fucking delicious." She shudders as I use one hand to yank the lace roughly to one side and press my hot tongue against her skin. She tastes so sweet, even better than I imagined. I groan as I lick her slowly across her lips and up to her clitoris in one smooth motion.

"Fuck, Tan," she says, her eyes burning into mine.

"We're friends now, are we?" I smile against her, sliding my tongue in and around her folds as I watch her eyes roll back in her head. "You just called me Tan."

"You're better when you don't talk," she moans, threading her fingers into my hair and pulling me back against her dripping wet sex. I laugh against her and use my hand to spread her wide, so I can suck hard on her clit, which draws a hiss from her lips.

"Too sensitive, baby?" I tease, pulling back.

"You're a wanker," I hear her murmur, but it sounds as though she's smiling.

I lean back into her, stretching her open as I slide my tongue up deep inside her. Oh man, she really does taste fucking incredible. I feel the end of my cock leaking inside my pants, throbbing at the feel of her on my face. I swirl my tongue around, devouring her, my arousal increasing more and more as her wetness covers my chin.

"Oh fuck," Rachel pants above me. It's just the sound I need to ramp it up, knowing that I'm the one responsible for her moans. I keep holding her wide open with one hand and use the other to lean against the wall so that I can really drive my tongue as deep inside her as possible. I've got my face pressed right into her as she pushes back, grinding against me.

"Oh God," she moans as her legs shake around my ears. I lift one over my shoulder and pin her back against the wall harder. "Oh fuck, oh fuck," she moans above me, lost in her own ecstasy.

I groan against her, diving deeper and rubbing my face against her swollen clit. It's then I feel the fucking perfect moment that she releases, her body sucking my tongue up inside it as it pulses around me and comes undone.

Her grip on my hair tightens. "God, Tanner," she cries as I swirl my tongue around harder, feeling her muscles clamping, holding it tight. I drink up her wetness and bury my head deep between her legs as she shudders and shakes, riding her orgasm down around my tongue.

As her shallow breaths grow deeper and slower, I slide my tongue out gently. I take one more deep breath in, savoring her scent before kissing her tender skin. She shudders in response.

"Get up here," she orders, dragging me up by my hair.

As I stand, there's an unmistakable fire in her eyes as her pupils dilate back at me. "Well, aren't you full of surprises?" she pants, cocking her head to one side, unwittingly exposing her neck. I swoop down on it, kissing it hungrily, biting it gently as she moans.

The sounds she makes speak directly to my cock,

which is straining painfully now. Rachel notices and unfastens my belt and pants, pushing them down my hips with my boxer shorts so that they all fall around my ankles, freeing my cock, which is heavy and aching. Fuck, my balls feel huge and tight, full to the brim, just for her.

"Are you as good at fucking as you are at giving head, Tanner?" Rachel whispers, causing me to tear my lips away from her delicate neck and bring them to rest millimeters away from hers. I glance up into her eyes, which are dark and fiery.

"Maybe you should find out for yourself," I say, leaning down and sucking on her bottom lip. Her lips are swollen and a darker shade of red now.

"I want you to fuck me like you own me, right here, against this wall. Do you think you can do that?" She cocks a brow at me.

I keep my mouth shut as I bend down to my pants pocket and grab a condom.

Fuck yes, I can do that. You'll be begging me to stop when I'm done with you, baby.

"Let me," Rachel says, taking it from my hand, her eyes never leaving mine as she rolls it all the way down onto me. I hiss at the sensation of her fingers around me and glance down to see her red fingernails cupping my balls, giving them a brief squeeze. "Looks like you've got a big load for me." She bites her lip as she uses her other hand to wriggle out of her panties.

Oh fuck, she knows just what she's doing to me.

"You're a naughty girl," I force out through gritted

teeth as I lift each of her legs and wrap them around my waist.

Her eyes sparkle back at me as she snakes one hand around the back of my head and brings her lips to my ear. "You should fuck me extra hard then, Tan; that's what naughty girls like."

The sound of her saying those words is too much for any sane man to take. I line my cock up and let out a deep groan as I slowly sink into her, inch by inch, until I'm balls deep.

"Fuuucckk." I can't help hissing out. She feels incredible, all wrapped around me, so hot, tight, and wet.

"That feels so good," she sighs, leaning her head back against the wall.

"Don't you dare look away," I growl as my cock twitches inside her, already threatening to blow its load. "I want you to watch as I fuck you, so you remember who made you so sore."

Her eyes light up, and she smirks at me. "That's big talk. Do you think you can live up to it?"

"You cheeky bitch," I say as I draw back and slam into her. Her eyes widen before she reaches around my back and pushes her hands up inside my shirt, smiling back at me.

I draw back and slam into her again as she lets out a cry and digs her nails into my skin. It's animalistic and raw. I pull back, again and again, slamming into her harder and faster each time, setting a relentless rhythm.

"Oh fuck, Tan," she cries, leaning her head back, her mouth falling open.

"I said, fucking look at me!" I practically shout as I drive into her, both of us gasping for air.

She drags her eyes back to mine as I pick up the pace again. She's struggling to keep her eyes open.

"Tan?"

"Yes, Snow?"

She smiles briefly at my name for her before her eyes roll back in her head, and she screams, "fuck, I'm going to come, I'm going to come." She drags her nails down my back, and even though I wince as they draw blood, my cock swells even more.

"That's it, baby, come all over my cock, let me feel you," I growl as I watch her explode in my arms. The sight of her coming hard because of me, the feel of her muscles clamping down around my cock, is too much, and I release violently inside her. "God, fuck!" I moan as I keep hammering into her, my cock going wild, pulsing out with each thrust. "Fuck, Rachel," I pant, as I feel all my sense of control gone. I slow my body down until we are both panting, a sheen of sweat where our skin meets.

I lean my forehead against hers, closing my eyes briefly, still trying to catch my breath. "You're fucking incredible," I whisper.

When I open my eyes, she brings her hands to my face, pulling me into a slow, deep kiss.

Fucking hell, I knew this woman would be trouble.

NINE

RACHEL

MY EYELIDS FLUTTER OPEN TO THE SOUND OF GENTLE breathing. Glancing over my shoulder, I see Tanner. He's laid out on his back, his exposed chest gently rising and falling with each sleepy breath. *Oh, fuck! Fuck, fuck, fuck!* I throw my arm across my face and groan inwardly as I recall last night; the hot as hell sex against the wall, followed by another two equally hot times. What the hell was I thinking? I've never spent an entire night in bed with a man in my entire life, certainly never fallen asleep next to one, and I don't even like him! I've really fucked up now.

I look back at Tanner's peaceful face, his dark hair messy in that sexy, just-fucked way. His firm jaw leading to those soft, kissable, and ridiculously skilled lips. His chest is muscular, toned, and broad, much like the rest of his body. I suppose I at least chose well for a one-night stand. I finally see what Megan's been telling me. His hotness is off the charts. Too bad he's still the most irritating man I've ever met.

Glancing around the room, I mentally tally up my clothing. I see everything apart from my knickers. Fuck it, I can do without them. I slide out of bed as gently as I can and silently tiptoe around the room, pulling my clothes on. With one last look at Tanner's sleeping face, I open the door into the hotel corridor and step out, gently clicking it shut behind me.

"I bet you can't wait to get home?" Matt nudges me as we walk along the Las Vegas strip, sipping our lattes.

"You're right; I can't." A smile spreads across my face. "Soon I will hold the keys to my very own house in my hands!" I bounce a little as I walk.

"I like this new, bubbly Rachel," Matt says, grinning at me. "Are you sure it's all the house's doing? Or might it be what else you got your hands on last weekend?" He raises his eyebrows at me as he sips his drink.

"Don't you start as well." I feel my shoulders tense up. "It's all Megan keeps talking about. I wish I hadn't told you both."

"What? that Tanner, the property mogul," Matt emphasizes his name, "is now to be known as Tanner good-with-his-hammer." He titters, laughing at his own joke.

"Piss off," I fire back.

"Oh, come on, Rach, you know I love you. I'm just

teasing. I'm pleased that you got the hottest sex you've ever had with a man you hated just one month ago." Matt smirks as I look sideways at him through narrowed eyes. "Maybe that's why it was so hot," he continues, "all that burning hate inside, fueling the passion."

"Stop." I hold up my hand. "Unless you want to spend the rest of this trip alone," I look at him pointedly, "then you'll drop it and just let me focus on getting my new keys."

He looks disappointed for a moment, and I almost feel sorry for him, but then I remember this is Matt. He's spent years perfecting the kicked puppy look to get himself out of trouble, which has found him regularly in the past.

"Okay, fine," he huffs like a child that's had their playtime cut short. "So, which room are you most looking forward to decorating first?"

"Easy. The bathroom."

"Really?"

"Yep. It's got the original roll-top bath in there! I'm going to turn it into a peaceful haven where I can soak for hours." I smile, feeling more relaxed at the thought of sinking down in a mound of bubbles.

"Oh, I forgot, you and your baths." He rolls his eyes. "I've never understood why you like them so much. I am partial to bubbles, especially those posh ones that Stefan has at his house." He trails off, clearly distracted by the thought of his boyfriend.

"Are you seeing him again soon?"

"Yep, next flight, and I can't wait. You need to get on an LA flight soon and visit Holly and Jay. You can see her bump now." Matt uses one hand to simulate a tiny baby bump against his stomach.

"I know, I know. I can't believe it's been more than a month since I last saw her in person. I obviously don't bribe the crewing department as well as you. I've had all East Coast USA flights until this Vegas. I video called her again this morning, though. She's totally glowing; pregnancy suits her."

I tilt my head back and drain the last of my double espresso caramel latte. God knows I need the caffeine. I'm not used to the eight-hour time difference between London and the West Coast.

"Oh, look," Matt says, stopping and looking up at the building site off to one side of the strip. "They're re-modeling one of the hotels. Looks swanky." He points to the large photographs depicting the finished design, which cover the surrounding fence.

I cast my eyes over the designs; they look familiar, dark greys and black, with a very stylish, contemporary vibe. "These are like the hotel in London where I met Tanner."

I shoot Matt a look as he opens his mouth, thinking that he's about to turn the conversation back to that night again. Instead, he closes it again and just nods.

"Do they? Must be a coincidence."

I look at the posters again, the company logo and motto visible in the top right corner.

'Grayson Designs, building visions together from the ground up.'

"No, I don't think so. The bar at that hotel was called the Grayson bar. I'm sure I've heard of the company before." I shrug as we carry on with our walk. "You know one thing that's definitely better about the West Coast?" I turn to Matt. "Not having to pack huge winter coats at this time of year. I'll be freezing my tits off on my next New York flight. It might even snow."

"You love it." He nudges me. "All those hot businessmen in suits, with their smart coats and scarves on, hiding hard, toned bodies underneath."

It's no secret to my friends that I've always loved a man in a sharp suit.

"Yeah, okay, there is that. I suppose I can make do with taking a larger case to fit my coat in."

"Oh, it's such a hardship being Rachel Jones." Matt sighs dramatically. "It's not as if you've had to fight for everything by yourself growing up." He eyes me sideways before pulling me into his side. Matt is the one of the few people who can joke about my upbringing in foster care and not expect a smack in the face. He gets away with it as we've been friends for so many years, and I know he loves me.

"Okay, that's enough cuddling for one week." I slip out from under his arm and pretend to shudder at the physical contact.

Matt smiles at me. "I'll make a hugger out of you yet, Rach."

"No. You won't." I smirk. "Come on, let's get some lunch. I'm starving."

The day after landing home from Vegas, I'm standing in line at our local coffee shop with Megan. We've just come out of the early kick-boxing class. I will collect the house keys later this morning and was too excited to sleep, hence the early attempt at releasing some excited energy.

"I can't believe I let you talk me into that," Megan moans, stretching her back out. "I swear I'm going to ache forever."

"Come on, you do your barre class all the time. I've seen the strength you need to do that. It's amazing and so graceful." I smile at her as I pull my card out of my purse.

"Yeah, but I think I've just discovered a whole new load of muscles that I didn't even know existed. How do you do that class so often?"

"I like it. It helps keep me calm."

"That..." Megan points back towards the street outside. "That keeps you calm? You're like a flipping assassin in there. I was scared for my life." She laughs.

"Didn't it help you? Imagining your idiot boss on the receiving end?" I ask, turning to her.

"Don't remind me." She groans. "You know, he asked me to move his car for him yesterday so that he wouldn't get a ticket. I had to circle for twenty minutes during my lunch break to find another spot. *And* I hit a traffic cone." She lowers her voice at her confession.

"You what?" I smirk.

"Totally crushed it. It was stuck under the wheel and everything. Luckily, the guys doing the roadworks saw the funny side. I could see them trying to straighten it back out again when I finally parked up."

I laugh. "Megan, he's such an ass. He's lucky you returned his car in one piece. You should have crushed it, not the cone."

We move along to the head of the line. "One cappuccino and a double shot caramel latte, please," I say to the woman behind the counter as I reach over to the payment machine, ready to tap my card.

"Let me get those," a deep voice cuts in. A hand reaches forward, giving a note to the woman behind the counter. "Keep the change." She blushes as she takes it. If I didn't recognize the voice, then the Rolex watch on his wrist would give it away. I turn around and stare straight into the dark, glinting eyes of Tanner as he removes his sunglasses.

"We can buy our own coffee, you know," I say. It comes out harder than I intend it to, but Tanner doesn't flinch.

"Or you could just say thank you," he says, studying my face with a smirk. God, I want to slap it off his face. I bet he thinks I'm happy to see him. The fact I haven't called or text him since that night together should tell him I'm not.

"Thank you." Megan smiles, looking up at him. I scowl at her quickly. *Traitor.*

"You're very welcome, Megan." He grins at her before turning his gaze back to mine, one eyebrow raised, as though he finds something amusing. I will the woman behind the counter to hurry with our drinks so we can get out of here.

"What are you doing here, anyway? I'm fairly sure there are no fancy, smug apartment complexes around here like the one you must live in."

Despite being used to my bluntness, I see Megan glance between us warily.

"Early business meeting," he says smoothly, unaffected by my tone. I look down and swallow hard as I take in his charcoal grey suit, white shirt, and deep red tie.

He wears it well, *very* well.

"Well, got to be going," he says as he runs his hand through his dark, wavy hair. Hair that I held in my fists as he fucked me with his tongue just days ago. I shake the thought from my head as I frown at him. His eyes flash darkly, "You going to thank me for your coffee, Snow?" He rolls the last word off his lips purposefully so that I look at them, once again reminded of just how skilled his mouth is.

"No," I say childishly, crossing my arms over my chest.

"Too bad," he says as he plucks my takeaway cup off the counter and takes a sip. "Mmm, caramel latte.

Not had one of these in a while." He winks at me as he walks off with it in his hand.

"Nice to see you again, Megan. Oh, and happy key day!" he calls over his shoulder as he walks off.

"Rach, did he just...?"

"Yes," I reply, "he just signed his own death wish."

TEN

TANNER

"I've missed you, Tan," Mom says as she wraps her arms around me, planting a kiss on my cheek. "And what have I told you about wasting your money on me?" She tuts as she takes the lilies out of my hand.

"It's never a waste if it makes you smile, Mom," I say, following her through her hallway into the kitchen.

"Charmer," she throws back over her shoulder. She heads to the cupboard under the sink and takes out a vase, filling it with water before she arranges the flowers inside it. "So, what's the special occasion?"

"No special occasion." I smile, watching her tuck a piece of her hair behind her ear.

"Nonsense, you can't lie to me, you know. I know you better than you know yourself." She chuckles. "This is the second time I've seen you this week, not that I'm complaining." Her green eyes sparkle at me.

"Can't a son come by to visit his beautiful Mom?" I say, pretending to look hurt.

"It's a woman, isn't it?" Her complete focus is now on me, the flowers forgotten. "You've met someone, Tan? I can see it in your eyes." She clasps her hands in front of her, grinning. She looks so much younger than her age. She's always had this youthful girliness about her, full of mischief, despite how hard it was for her, struggling as a single mom. She's never lost her sense of fun, her magic gift that means any child who meets her loves her instantly.

"Come on then, tell me about her. What's her name?" She grins, finishing the flowers but keeping me firmly in sight, unable to escape her interrogation.

I take a deep breath. "We're not even... I mean, she's... we're not even friends, really," I say, unsure how to describe what I have with Rachel.

"She must be something special if you're getting all tongue-tied over her. That's not like you at all." Mom can barely contain her grin as she fills the kettle.

"She's certainly something, Mom." I look up at the ceiling, trying to find the right words. "She's the most stubborn, infuriating woman. She always wants to be right. And she's so hell-bent on being independent that she's practically outraged at the offer of any help like you're saying that she's not capable of doing it by herself." I sigh as I bring my eyes back to Mom.

"She sounds an awful lot like someone else I know," Mom says as she turns to make the coffee. "You know what I think?" she says a moment later as she passes a steaming mug to me.

"You're going to tell me, anyway." I smile.

"Cheeky!" Mom bats me on the arm. "I think she just hasn't met a person she feels she can really trust yet. I was a lot like that when you were a baby. Before I met Peter, I was always fighting for us on my own. You learn how to not rely on anyone but yourself when you have no choice. Of course, moving back here and having your Nana close by was a Godsend—while it lasted," she says sadly. We lost Nana when I was young. It's just been Mom and me for years.

"You did so well, Mom," I say, reaching out to squeeze her hand.

I remember all the years she worked so hard, taking on extra shifts, fixing the same dress over and over so that she could afford to buy me new school shoes. She's the most selfless person I've ever known. Even now that my company is doing so well, I have to practically force her to accept anything from me. I'm happy she met Peter, her partner of four years. He's a good man, although I wouldn't hesitate to floor him if he ever hurt her.

"It might take time to earn her trust, Tanner. But if she's got you smiling like this, then she's worth it. Goodness knows you need someone with a strong backbone who will stand up to you. I know how stubborn you can be too." She chuckles. "Remember what I always used to say to you growing up?"

"How could I forget, Mom?" I roll my eyes jokingly. "You only said it like every other day."

"Difficult roads lead to beautiful destinations." She smiles as she pulls me into a hug. "It was your Nana's saying, Tan. She was made of tough stuff and knew what she was talking about. I like to think she watches over us and helps where she can. Well... meddles." Mom laughs.

"I know, Mom," I say, hugging her back. "I'm sure she's up there, wreaking havoc." I'm convinced of it.

I climb the steps and wrap my knuckles against the door, juggling the two takeaway cups in one hand. I wait a few moments and wonder if I've made a mistake. Maybe she's away on a flight? No, she told me at the whisky night that she had a flight to Vegas and then a week off after collecting the keys.

Suddenly the door opens in a rush, and I'm greeted with the sight of Rachel in a pair of faded, torn jeans and a tight grey t-shirt, both splattered in paint. Her dark hair is tied up messily on top of her head. She's never looked sexier. Her eyes drop down my body, taking in my suit before coming to rest on my face. She wrinkles her brow, clearly not expecting me.

"Peace offering," I say gently, holding one cup out towards her. She eyes it suspiciously. "There's no poison in it, promise." I smirk.

"Thanks," she says, reaching out. Her fingers bump

against mine, and she looks as though she may jump back as if I've stung her.

I watch her take a sip of her drink. I'm sure her eyebrows raise as she realizes it's a double shot caramel latte.

"I suppose you'd like to come in?" she says finally.

"Well, seeing as you're offering," I say as I quickly squeeze past her through the doorway before she can change her mind. I walk through into the living room. It looks the same as the last time I saw it, except now the floor has various paintbrushes and tester cans on it. The wall behind them has four different dark blue paint patches on it, with names written in pencil underneath.

"One on the right." I gesture towards the blue paint patches. "Midnight Lover," I say, reading the name below.

Rachel smirks. "That's my least favorite."

"Why doesn't that surprise me," I murmur to myself, taking a sip of my coffee. "Looks like you're busy getting things done." I look at her paint-covered clothes. I can't help pausing for a split second as my eyes reach her breasts, round and full under her tight t-shirt. I swallow, remembering all too well what they felt like underneath my palms—how her nipples hardened as I ran my tongue over them.

"Yeah, I thought I should. I've only got this week off work, and then the contract ends on our rental, so we'll be moving in. I need to get all the painting done so the house can air before Nigel comes."

"Are you doing it by yourself?"

Rachel shrugs. "Yeah. Megan got offered a really great contract for a special edition comic, so she has to work flat out as it's got a tight deadline."

"How many rooms are you planning on doing?" I ask, looking around.

"All of them," Rachel says without missing a beat.

I snap my eyes back to her. "You're going to paint every room in this house all by yourself... in a week?"

"Yeah," she says, "So?"

I blow out a breath. "Rachel, you'll never get that all done by yourself."

She frowns as she looks at me. "Don't tell me what I can and can't do."

"Hey." I hold my hands up. "I know you're more than capable of doing a hell of a lot by yourself. But this, Rachel..." I shake my head as I look around, "this is just too big of a job to do alone."

She avoids my eyes as she shrugs. God, she's like a petulant teenager.

"Listen, I can get a couple of guys over here, professional painters. They'll get it done in no time." I pull my phone out of my jacket pocket.

"No!" Rachel snaps, glaring at me.

"Why not?" I glare back.

"You are not throwing your money at a problem that isn't yours. This has got nothing to do with you. I don't need professional painters swooping into my house."

"Fine," I mutter to myself, bringing my PA, Penny's

number up in my phone and hitting dial, "no paying anyone."

Rachel's eyes study my face as I bring my phone to my ear. "What are you doing?"

I hold a finger up to her to indicate to her to keep quiet while she glares at me like she might rip my hand off.

"Hi, Penny," I say as she answers, my eyes glued firmly to Rachel's. "Listen, I need you to reschedule everything for this week. I'm taking the week off."

Penny's silence tells me how shocked she is. I never take time off at short notice. Hell, I hardly ever take time off full stop. All credit to her, though, she quickly recovers and assures me she has it all in hand before I end the call. I'm giving her a bonus when I go back.

Rachel's eyes widen. "What the hell did you do that for? I said I don't need your help."

I look at her eyes burning into mine—all that fire and passion in them.

Snow, baby, why won't you let me do this for you? I want to do this for you.

"I'm not doing it for you," I lie smoothly as she gives me a "that's bullshit" look. "I'm doing it for Nigel."

"What?"

"You heard me. I can't stand by and do nothing, knowing that an animal's well-being may be at stake." I stare back at Rachel, my face serious, neither one of us wanting to back down first. Finally, she narrows her eyes at me, and I swear there's a trace of a smile on her lips.

"Fine," she huffs, "but you can't paint in that." Her eyes roam up and down my suit.

"I could take it off." I smirk.

She sighs. "Just come back in the morning, Tanner. I've almost finished for today anyway, and I have to get some more paint for the morning."

"Whatever you say, you're the boss." I grin. "I'll be here first thing."

This time I'm sure she smiles.

"Let me get this straight. You've taken a week off work to help this woman paint her house?" Drew looks at me as though I've grown another head. We're sitting in our favorite after-work bar, a converted basement with a modern, industrial feel.

"Yes, for the tenth time." I sigh, wondering how many more times we are going to go over this. "You'll cope without me at work, and Penny has moved all my big meetings until next week," I say, swirling the dark amber liquid in my glass. It was a poor choice of drink. The whisky just makes me think of that night.

"She's hot, I'll give you that. But you, missing work for a woman?" Drew shakes his head. "I never thought I'd see the day."

"She's not just the hottest woman I've ever met," I say, searching for the right words to describe Rachel.

How can you describe an attraction to someone that is so strong no amount of logic you use could ever help you understand it?

"There's just something about her." I blow out my breath and stare into my glass. "It doesn't make sense. She acts like she hates me most of the time, but I can't stop thinking about her."

"Tan, you've got it bad." Drew chuckles, slapping me on the back. "The sex must have been awesome."

I swallow, remembering the way her skin tasted. "The way she's acting, you'd think it never happened."

"Women." Drew rolls his eyes. "Never know what goes on in those minds of theirs," he says as he takes a mouthful of his drink.

I look across at him. "You never told me how that blind double-date you went on was."

"Ha! Yeah, that." He smirks. "Turns out, my date was... not the sharpest knife in the drawer, shall we say? I don't fancy spending my days talking about the latest celebrity wedding and nothing else."

"Sorry to hear that."

"Don't be." Drew's eyes light up. "The other woman, Sophie, her name was—absolute knockout!"

"The one that was there with another man?" I ask, not sure where this is heading.

"Yeah, but she wasn't interested in Logan. Not when he spent half the night looking down my date's top, anyway."

I shake my head, smiling; that sounds just like our

mate Logan. Unfortunately, subtlety isn't one of his strengths.

"So, this Sophie," Drew continues, "was just up in London visiting her friend. Turns out, she's a lawyer back in Bath. I'm telling you, Tan. You should have seen her. Absolutely gorgeous and so intelligent. Almost cleverer than me."

My shoulders shake as I laugh into my glass. "Too clever for you, don't you mean? And a lawyer. What the hell? I take it you didn't tell her about your less than squeaky-clean past then?"

"Plenty of time for that," Drew says smoothly. "I'm taking her out for dinner at the weekend in Bath."

I can't hide the surprise in my voice, "really? That was quick work."

"Yeah." He leans back in his chair. "She doesn't know it yet, but we're going to have a great night."

"She doesn't know she's going for dinner with you yet?" I ask, looking at Drew.

"Minor details, Tan." He waves his hand in the air dismissively. "We'll have a great time. She will be glad she went."

I raise my eyebrows. "Is this before or after you tell her about your criminal record? I'm sure a lawyer may have a thing or two to say about dating an ex-con."

"Hey, don't piss on my parade, Tan. I'll tell her when the time's right. Besides, I'm a reformed man, you know that. All that shit happened years ago."

"I know, Drew. I'm just messing with you," I say because it's true. Drew is nothing like the bad boy he used to be growing up. He just got in with the wrong crowd for a bit. Ended up doing some time in a young offender's institute for car theft. But now, he's one of the straightest guys I know. Plus, he can't lie for shit. It's written all over his face when he tries.

"Oh, and it's *rain* on my parade," I say, "not piss."

"Could have fooled me, mate. Besides, you're one to talk. When are you going to tell Rachel about your secret, eh?" He eyes me over his glass.

I groan and lean back, loosening my tie. "I don't know. Soon, real soon. Just not this week. If she flies off the handle like I expect she will, then I want to at least have been able to help her out this week first."

Drew shakes his head again. "Fucking hell, man. You've got it bad. One night with this woman, and you've turned into a pussy."

I stare straight ahead as I drink. What can I say? He's right. One night with Rachel, and I'm all over the place. Doing things I wouldn't usually do, losing focus at work. I need to get a fucking grip. The problem is all I can think about is getting a grip on her.

ELEVEN

RACHEL

I'M AT THE NEW HOUSE GETTING SET UP FOR THE DAY. It's only eight in the morning, but there's so much to do that I wanted to make an early start. At this rate, I will work all night too.

I won't admit it to Tanner, but he was right; I would never get the entire house painted by myself in just a week. I can't say I'm looking forward to spending an entire week with him, even if it means the house might be ready for us to move in at the weekend.

My phone beeps in my pocket with a message.

Megan: Is he there yet?
Me: No, Meg. It's far too early. He's probably
still styling his hair!

I smirk at the thought before the mental image changes to my hands running through his thick, dark waves as his mouth explored my body that night.

Ugh!

Why can't I forget about it? It's not like I haven't had meaningless sex before.

My phone beeps again.

Megan: I wonder if he'll paint without a shirt on???
Me: You're not helping!
Megan: Sorry. Have fun! I wish I could help, but they're already pushing me for sketches I'm only halfway through.
Me: Honestly, I told you, don't worry. It'll be fine. It will all be done in time. You, me, and Nigel will be in our new home soon!

I can't help but smile as I look at the paintbrushes and cans. I can't believe I'm standing here, in *my* house. I never thought this day would come growing up, having something that is just for me, that no one can take away.

All those months of doing extra flights, saving my crew allowances, and of course, Mr. X was all worth it. He seemed strangely happy about it when I told him I was closing my website, *Scent from Rachel.* Although, saying that, I barely used it in the end. Mr. X contacted me within the first month and offered me a deal I couldn't refuse—send everything on the website to him, and he would pay double for it, on the understanding that he was my only client.

I'm kind of sad that I won't be emailing him

anymore. He usually had something funny to say. The fact he wasn't bothered about our arrangement ending probably means he has already moved on with someone else. When I spoke to Holly earlier, she said she thought it was for the best. New house, new start. I guess she's right. Living in the past never gets you anywhere.

A knock at the door brings me back to reality. It's not even eight-fifteen; surely that isn't Tanner already?

As I open the door, a coffee cup is thrust into my hand.

"Your favorite." Tanner smiles warmly as I take it from him.

"Thanks," I say, my eyes taking him in. He's wearing an old pair of black cargo pants and a slim-fitting pale grey t-shirt, the muscles in his chest clearly visible. Both are already covered in paint splashes of varying shades. I bite down on the inside of my cheek. Suits have always done it for me before but seeing him standing there right now sends my pulse racing. He looks like he's stepped off some hot calendar shoot.

"Sorry I'm a bit late," he says, watching me carefully. "I meant to be here by eight but wanted to bring you coffee, and the line was ridiculous."

"Yeah, well, you're here now, I suppose." I stand back so he can pass me to come inside.

A hint of soap accompanies him. He smells like he just stepped out of the shower—clean, fresh skin mixed with a masculine edge. He smelled amazing that night at the whiskey tasting; some expensive cologne, no doubt. But this, his own unique scent, is something else. I shut my eyes briefly as I try to squash down my growing arousal.

"So where are we starting?" he asks, turning to look at me.

"In here." I lead him into the lounge. "I did the bathroom yesterday, so we've just got in here, the dining room, and three bedrooms to do. I figured the kitchen doesn't need it as it has just been re-modeled anyway, and the hallway I was going to keep white like it is."

Tanner's eyes scan the room, and I find myself mesmerized by his Adam's apple moving in his muscular neck as he takes a drink of his coffee.

"Better get started then," he says.

"Okay, you stir the paint." I point to the can I picked up last night. "And I'll put some music on."

I head to the kitchen and pick up my speakers to plug my phone into. When I come back, I pause in the doorway, watching Tanner. He's shaking his head, smiling to himself as he reads the label on the paint can. *Midnight Lover.*

"Problem?" I ask, feeling my stomach leap as his eyes meet mine.

"Nope," he says smoothly, picking up a screwdriver.

I watch the muscles in his biceps as he levers the lid off with ease. It makes a satisfying "*pop*" before he looks up at me again, his eyes glinting.

"Don't just stand there looking pretty, Snow. Grab a brush."

That kind of smart-ass comment would usually earn a quick-witted remark, but I find myself picking up a brush and kneeling next to him, a hint of a smile on my lips.

"I didn't have you down as a rock chick," he says, as the speakers blast out a guitar solo from one of my favorite bands.

"You don't know much about me at all," I say matter-of-factly.

"Why don't you tell me something then?" Tanner says, his brows pulled together in concentration as he pours the paint into a roller tray.

"I'm good," I say as I pick up the tray.

"It's going to be a long week if we don't talk to each other."

"I told you, I prefer you when you don't talk," I say with a straight face.

Tanner chuckles. "And I prefer you when you're screaming my name. But we can't always get what we want, can we?"

I snap my eyes up to his. I can't believe he just said that. He's looking at me darkly, a smile playing on his lips. And I know the bastard is remembering what I look like naked by the way his eyes drop to my breasts and back up again quickly.

He thinks I didn't notice.

I huff, pretending to be bored with this little game already when, in reality, my pulse is throbbing between my legs at the way he just looked at me. He wants me, and he's not afraid to admit it. Too bad for him; I don't want seconds, despite my body's reaction.

"Fine, what do you want to know?" I ask as I pick up a brush and dip it into the dark, inky paint.

He smiles as though he's won a minor victory. "Why did you call Nigel, well, Nigel?"

I stare at him, possibly with my mouth wide open. "You can ask me anything, and you choose to ask me that?" I shake my head in disbelief as I cut in along the woodwork with my brush.

"You never said I could ask you anything." He raises a brow at me. "But I will remember that for question two." He smiles as he expertly runs his brush in one swift move along the edge of the doorframe, cutting in with a perfectly straight line. "I told you, I started as an apprentice," he says when he sees me watching his progress. "I know my way around a paintbrush, Rachel."

You know your way around a woman's body too.

I shake the thought out of my head angrily. Now is not the time to get distracted. I glance back over at Tanner. The muscles in his shoulders and back ripple under his t-shirt as he paints higher up the wall.

"You still haven't answered me," he says, keeping his focus on his painting. His dark eyes narrow as he presses a new brush-load of paint to the wall. As he strokes it up the wall, a small look of satisfaction crosses his face. It's sexy to watch. *Shit.* It's an unnerving thought, admitting to myself that I find him sexy.

"He's named after a politician."

Tanner's eyes break their focus and round on me. "You named your rabbit after a politician?"

"It was Megan's idea."

"Why would she suggest such a bizarre thing?"

"Because I have this thing where I dream about politicians when I'm aroused," I say quickly, glancing at Tanner's puzzled face.

He stays silent for a long time before turning his attention back to the paint. Hopefully, that's the end of it.

I pick my brush back up to carry on.

Tanner clears his throat. "You know, as far as first questions go, I would say that was an excellent choice. What an insight into the inner workings of Rachel Jones' mind," he says, amusement clear in his voice.

I turn to look at him, and he's wearing a stupid grin, no doubt delighted at my embarrassing confession.

"So, the night before our whisky date, did you, erm... dream about a full-on general election or something?" He winks.

I feel my blood boil. *Who does he think he is?*

"You've already had your question," I snap. "My turn now."

He shrugs his shoulders at me. "Bring it on."

God, he's so annoying and sure of himself.

"What are you doing here? Really? I'm sure there are loads of women who will fall for the hair and the car, and...," I gesture up and down his body with my paintbrush, "... all this. So why do you keep turning up here like a bad smell when I think I've made it quite clear that the other night was a one-off?"

He turns and looks at me, cocking his head to one side, before walking over slowly, closing the distance between us.

"Was it? Was it a one-off?" he asks as he stops in front of me. He's so close that I have to tilt my head back to look up into his burning gaze.

"Because, the way I see it," he says huskily as he raises his paintbrush and holds it over my chest, "is that your body is telling me that night was only the beginning."

He gently runs the brush over my t-shirt, where my hardened nipples are now straining against the fabric. The rough drag of the brush's bristles sends a shiver down my spine.

"You did not just paint me," I say, glaring up at him.

In case there was any doubt, he raises the brush again and slowly paints across my other nipple, his eyes blazing into mine, taunting me.

"You're an asshole," I say as my body takes over, reaching my hands up and digging them into his hair, pulling his head, so his mouth crashes down onto mine.

I kiss him hard, delving deep and pulling him against me. All the air leaves my lungs before I gasp as I pull away for a second. He pants, pressing his forehead against mine.

"If you need an asshole, Snow, then I'll be one. I

will be whatever you need," he growls, wrapping an arm around my waist and pulling me back into the kiss. His tongue swirls against mine with the perfect pressure.

Fuck, can he kiss.

"Let me take that," Tanner says, pulling back from our kiss to remove the brush from my hand. He places them down carefully in the roller tray. "We don't want to get paint on the floor and give you any more reason to hate me, now do we?" His eyes flash with desire as he rises back to his feet.

I can't tear my eyes away from his. He looks at me like he's been starved, and I'm the most delicious thing he's ever laid eyes on.

"No, don't give me any more reasons," I smirk.

"It's like this t-shirt of yours that I've got paint all over," he says as his warm fingers inch up underneath the fabric, exposing my stomach, "I should take it off before you notice just how ruined it is."

I shudder as his fingers brush higher up the side of my ribs, and then the underside of my arms as I raise them in the air for him to pull it off over my head.

"So much better," he murmurs as his hands come to my breasts, cupping them through the sheer fabric of my bra. He rolls my nipples between his thumbs and forefingers as he lets out a low, involuntarily moan of appreciation. "It's cruel of you to keep these pretty tits from me for over a week, Rachel." He reaches behind my back and effortlessly flicks the strap, so it comes undone.

I lean back against the wall as he lowers his mouth onto me, my nipple engulfed by his hot, wet lips. Fuck, it feels so good. A small whimper escapes my lips before I reign it back in.

I'm too late. He heard it.

"See, Rachel, you say you don't want this, want me," Tanner murmurs as he switches his attention to my other nipple, "but your fucking delicious body tells me otherwise," he growls, nipping me between his teeth.

A rush of arousal soaks my panties, and it takes all my self-control not to grab his strong, thick fingers and force them inside my jeans to where I want them.

"So why don't you tell me? Which should I believe?" he says, bringing his mouth to mine once again and catching my lips in a heated kiss.

"I think you're deranged," I pant between kisses. "The paint fumes must be getting to you." He smirks against my lips as he presses his body against mine. I feel his erection pressing into me.

"I think you're the one who's fucking deranged, Rachel, if you can't see just how good we can be together." He spins me around, so my face is against the wall. His hands undo my jeans, and he slides them down to my ankles, dropping to his knees behind me. He plants one hand against my bum, holding me in place as the other slips my shoes off and helps me step out of my jeans.

"You know, I love these sexy panties you always wear," he hisses.

He tugs and releases the fabric, and a sharp sting lands across my skin. I swallow hard as I try not to writhe back against his fingers. I don't want him to know how much his words and touch are affecting me.

"I've got the last pair you left behind. They still smell like you," he says darkly, his fingers kneading into my buttocks.

"I didn't intentionally leave you a free gift." I gasp as he pulls my cheeks apart and buries his face against the lace of my thong, soaking wet from my arousal. "I couldn't find them in the morning." I shudder as he pulls the fabric to one side, and the warmth of his tongue slides against my skin.

"A small price to pay for my disappointment at finding you gone when I woke up, then," Tanner growls. He pulls his tongue back and moves one hand between my legs, sliding two fingers up deep inside me from behind.

I hiss at his roughness, although I can't help my body screaming out for more as I grind back against his hand.

"Such a greedy little thing, aren't you?" he says, pulling his fingers out and sliding my thong down my legs. "Spread your legs, Snow. Let me really taste you."

"We're back on the Snow thing, are we?" I smirk, but I do as he says and spread my legs as I lean against the wall, my hands on either side of my face and my bum pushed back on full display for him.

"Yes, we're back on the Snow thing," he growls as he pulls my cheeks apart again. "I'll call you whatever the fuck I want when I'm drinking up your greedy little pussy's orgasms."

I smile at his words and let out a low moan as he leans forward and buries his mouth and tongue into me. I'm not used to someone calling me out on my shit. I know I have an attitude and can be a handful. Most guys just take it, but not Tanner. He loves to give it back, and fuck is he giving it back right now.

"Oh, yes, just like that," I cry as his tongue speeds up, circling over my clit repeatedly. "Fuck, you do that so well," I moan, pushing back into him.

His fingers reach around and take over, stroking my clit as his tongue slides up deep inside me.

"Oh, fuck yes! Give me more. I need more," I plead, feeling the familiar pressure growing.

Tanner pinches my clit, and it's the final push I need. I cry out as I come hard against him, his tongue swirling deep inside me, lapping it up. I hear a deep moan coming from his throat, but it sounds far away with all the blood that's rushing in my ears.

"Tan," I pant, "fuck! that was good." I try to get my breath back as he stands up behind me, easing me back around, so I'm facing him.

His dark eyes look wild as he strokes one side of my face with the back of his hand. "You're so fucking beautiful right after I've made you come."

The intensity he's looking at me with is too much, so I lower my eyes to his pants and unfasten them.

"I think it's time we play fair for a bit, don't you?" I say as I smile at him, pushing them down, along with his boxers. I move in front of him so that he can lean back against the wall.

"I think that sounds like a good idea," he murmurs, pulling his t-shirt off over his head.

My eyes roam over his broad, muscular chest. He really is a fine example of a man.

I drop to my knees at his feet before looking back up at him from underneath my eyelashes. His cock hangs between his legs, a bead of wetness glistening on its tip.

"Fuck yes," he whispers as he reaches down and rubs his thumb across my bottom lip before bringing his other hand down to my hair, gathering it gently away from my face. He looks like he's lost in his own fantasy. His eyelids are heavy and his breathing deep, anticipating my next move.

I reach both hands out and run them up his thighs. He hisses, and his eyes darken as I wrap one hand around his smooth balls and the other around the base of his thick cock.

"Have you ever thought of me, kneeling in front of you like this, ready to suck on your cock?" I say in mock sweetness as I look up at him and lick my lips.

"Only since the first time I ever fucking saw you," he says through gritted teeth, his voice strained.

"I guess I shouldn't keep you waiting any longer, then?"

Tanner sucks in a breath and gently tugs my hair. I look up at him and watch his eyes widen as I extend my tongue and lick the bead of wetness off the end of his cock.

"Mmm, you taste good," I say before leaning further forward and wrapping my lips around his smooth head.

I don't dare tear my eyes away from him as I slowly sink down, relaxing my throat so I can take every inch of him in. He's looking at me like I'm the only woman in existence, made especially for him. It's so strong and territorial—like he's claiming me as his.

I can't get enough.

I moan deep in my throat as I pick up the pace, moving my hands onto his thighs so I can draw him in deeper each time before sucking right back to his tip. Twice, I lose him as I pull back, but his spare hand grabs the base, and he taps the end of his cock against my lips before feeding it back into my mouth again.

"You're such a good girl, Snow, swallowing down my cock like that," he says, his eyes glued to where my lips are wrapped around him. "You do not know how fucking hot you look right now, with me in your throat."

I murmur around him and suck harder. "Fuck," he hisses, "I don't want to come yet. You need to stop."

I increase my pace and hold his gaze.

"I said stop," he growls, pulling away from me and grabbing both of my arms, pulling me to my feet. "God, woman, don't you ever listen?"

But before I can answer, he's kissing me again, his

fingers sliding back up inside me and rubbing against my G-spot.

"Tan." I shudder, feeling another orgasm building up. He's in exactly the right spot.

"I love it when you say my name," he growls, dipping his head to kiss and bite my neck.

My hands find his hair, and I run them through his thick, dark waves. Considering how much it irritated me seeing him run his hand through it when I first met him, I find myself not being able to stop doing the exact same thing.

"I want your next orgasm on my cock," he growls, "I want to watch you ride me."

He leans down to pull his shoes off, followed by his pants and boxers that are around his ankles. When he's completely naked, he pulls me down on top of a pile of clean, folded-up dust sheets I'd brought over to cover the floor with during painting. He smiles at me as he lays back against them, lifting me easily and positioning me with one leg on either side of his hips.

There's a deep pulsing between my legs, my arousal almost more than I can bear. No one has ever turned me on as much as him. What the hell is going on? The way he speaks to me, so commanding, not at all worried about challenging me, so he has a turn to be in charge. Fuck, it's hot.

I look down at his expression, and he's smiling to himself, one hand stroking his cock, the other gently running up and down over my waist and hip. "Give me what I want." He smirks at me.

Oh, I'll give it to you, baby.

I'll wipe that smug smile right off his face until he's begging me to stop.

He reaches one hand over to his pants and pulls a condom out of the pocket, expertly tearing the foil between his teeth and rolling it down onto himself. He's obviously used to doing it, judging by his ease.

I don't know why that bothers me.

I stare into his eyes as I rise over him. He holds the base of his cock, positioning it perfectly for me to slide down onto it in one smooth movement until he's deep inside me, filling me completely.

He sucks his breath in. "Fuck, Rachel, you feel so good."

Hell, he feels good too. No one has ever seemed to fit so perfectly with me before.

I rise slowly and sink back down onto him.

"You know, when you're like this, you're not nearly as annoying." I sigh as I savor the fullness from him.

Tanner smiles up at me. "Better do all I can to maintain my winning streak then."

He brings his hands up to cup my breasts. I arch my back and push them further into his large, warm hands, gasping as he squeezes my nipples. Wow, that feels so good. How can he make something that's been done to me many times before feel so much more intense now? So much better, so much… more.

I drop my hands to his shoulders as I lean forward so I can really ride him hard. I slide up and down, finding my rhythm, my eyes fluttering closed as I get lost in my pleasure.

"Rach," Tanner groans as he brings his legs up for leverage. His hands drop to my hips, and he digs his fingers into my skin as he drags me back and forth faster.

I can't help but moan out loud with each delicious thrust—my senses overloaded with pleasure. I open my eyes and look down at Tanner, who bites his lip with a smile, holding my gaze as he pulls me back down onto his cock again and again. His pupils dilate as I stare back into his eyes.

"Come for me, baby," he whispers, lifting his chin, his eyes delving right into my body, deep into my soul as though to extract my pleasure from deep within. I hate being told what to do, but somehow, I can't deny his command; he's got something over me. I don't know what the hell it is, but I feel myself unravel under his intense gaze.

"Tan," I moan, throwing my head back as the first intense wave rips through me.

It takes all my strength to keep riding him, each contraction grabbing my breath and threatening to force me to stop, the pleasure almost unbearable. I do, though. I keep sliding back down onto him, again and again, crying out as each fresh jolt of my orgasm hits me.

"Don't," pant, "fucking", pant, "stop." Tanner forces out each word as his grip on my hips tightens.

His eyes have left my face and are watching his

cock sliding in and out of my body. I clench hard around him, and he loses control, coming hard, his arms shaking as they hold me tight.

"Fuck... Rachel," he groans loudly, his eyes rolling back in his head.

With each strong pulse inside me, I feel whatever this thing is that he has over me growing stronger. It's sinking teeth and claws into me, pulling me under.

It scares the hell out of me.

Our bodies slow down until, finally, we stop moving. I stay still, holding him inside my body as we catch our breath. Beads of sweat run down my back, and there's a sheen of perspiration along Tanner's hairline. His dark waves now perfecting a sexy, just-fucked style.

He locks his eyes onto mine, a sexy smile spreading across his lips as he tenderly strokes the now red skin on my hips.

"In answer to your question. I keep turning up, 'like a bad smell'," he raises his eyebrows at me, "because I'm a sucker for being insulted and then fucked better than ever before in my life."

A pathetic sense of happiness creeps in hearing him say I'm the best sex of his life.

What the fuck is wrong with me?

But deep down, I already know the problem. He's the best sex of mine too. He's ruined any other men for me now. They could never compete with Tan.

I pull back from him, aching instantly from the loss of his body in mine, as I sit down beside him.

"That wasn't meant to happen—again," I say, not able to look him in the face.

The sound of him pulling the condom off and tying it into a knot echoes around the room before he sits up next to me.

"What if it was meant to?" he whispers.

He presses a gentle kiss to my shoulder, and my body stiffens as I stare straight ahead. He seems to sense not to push me.

"Here." He reaches across the floor to our discarded clothes and hands me his t-shirt.

"That's yours, not mine."

"I know, but yours will still be wet. Wear mine until it dries."

I turn and finally look back into his eyes, their beautiful amber flecks catching in the light. I nod and take his t-shirt gratefully, pulling it down over my head.

It smells of him.

Maybe accepting it wasn't such a good idea.

"Thank you," I whisper.

He says nothing, and I wonder if he heard me, but I know he must have.

I swallow the growing lump in my throat and watch as he stands and pulls his boxers and pants back on.

I never stay to cuddle. I'm always straight out the door after sex.

So why do I feel like I've just made a huge mistake?

TWELVE

TANNER

I TURN UP AT EIGHT O'CLOCK EVERY MORNING FOR THE rest of the week, always with Rachel's double-shot caramel latte and my coffee. We've almost finished painting now, and the house is looking great. We've spent all week chatting about her flying and the places she's been, about my mom and growing up, yet Rachel never mentions her past. She talks more about the fucking rabbit. I must meet him soon. I've heard more about him than anything else. She may not show her emotion to people easily, but it's obvious she adores him.

Neither of us talks about the other day, how we just got dressed and carried on painting like nothing had happened, except I had no t-shirt on. Rachel wore it, and hell, she looked great in it. It swamped her and made her seem delicate and vulnerable. I wanted nothing more than to wrap her in my arms, but I know that's not what she would have wanted.

My mom's words keep repeating in my head.

It might take time to earn her trust, Tanner.

I've never wanted to invest time in someone else before, not romantically, not like I want to with Rachel. Most guys would have probably given up by now, but not me. I can't keep away from her. It's physically impossible. The more she pushes me away, the more determined I am that I will be the one she lets in.

She will let me in.

She has to.

"It looks great!" I say, meaning it as I stand back with my hands on my hips to admire our hard work.

"I can't believe it's actually finished." Rachel smiles the easiest smile I've seen on her face this week, her eyes sparkling with joy.

She looks so beautiful.

"Someone," I point at her, "thought she could do this all by herself."

I pull my phone out of my pocket to look at the time.

"It's ten past six in the evening, and it's only just finished, with two of us going at it." I emphasize the word *two* as she narrows her eyes at me.

"I could have finished it before midnight by myself." She shrugs her shoulders, but there's a small smile on her lips as she takes my brush from me and heads into the kitchen to wash the paint out at the sink.

"Of course, you could." I smirk, following her and

leaning against the doorframe as I watch her. "So, what's the plan for tomorrow?"

She pauses from washing the brushes. "I've hired a small van for the day. I was going to move some furniture over, but we aren't spending the night here until Sunday. I want to air it all out for a couple of days first."

"Can I help?" I ask, noticing she's scratching her wrist under the running tap water.

"There's no need; you've helped enough," she says quickly, not meeting my gaze.

Fucking hell, it's like getting blood out of a stone, getting her to accept any assistance.

"Rachel," I say sternly, "I'm here. I'm offering. Let me do something."

She raises her eyes to meet mine, a frown on her face as she shakes her head. "Fine, you'll probably just turn up, anyway."

Yes, Snow. You know me so well.

"As if I'd do such a thing," I retort, pretending to look outraged, "show up where I'm not wanted. I'd have to be a fool!"

"I can think of other things to call you." Rachel smirks.

"Careful, everyone, she's made a joke! Must be an imposter." I smile at her.

"You're…" she starts.

"I'm what?" I stare at her, a smile playing on my lips as I run a hand back through my hair. What insult is she going to throw at me? I love it when she's feeling feisty; it's when it leads on to the incredible…

"You're hungry. I can hear your stomach rumbling from over here." She arches an eyebrow at me.

Despite my disappointment that I'm not about to have a spectacular fucking session, I chuckle at her response.

"Guilty." I hold my hands up in the air. "It's my new female boss. Fucking slave driver, she is."

"Enough," Rachel says as she puts the clean brushes and rollers up on the draining board and dries her hands on a towel. "I'm not that cruel that I will watch a grown man starve. You can come back to our house. We can order takeout."

I do a good job of hiding the surprise on my face. "Sounds good to me."

"Come on, then." She squeezes past me in the doorway.

Is it me, or did she just brush her breasts against me on purpose?

Either way, I'm not going to stand here and miss finding out.

"Right behind you," I call as I follow her out of the house.

"Another bonus that the new house is only a couple of streets away is you get to keep your regular Thai restaurant. That was so good," I say, putting my empty plate down on the coffee table and leaning back into the sofa.

"I know, nice, isn't it?" Rachel says as she leans back next to me.

Well, I say next to me, but there's a rather large rabbit spread out in-between us. If you can call him that. He's a beast—the size of a fat cat. The fucker has been watching me with one beady eye the entire time. Plonked himself right down next to me as soon as I sat down, and he hasn't moved since. I swear he's cock-blocking me on purpose.

Rachel strokes her hand over him, and he closes his eyes; one back foot thumps as she hits his sweet spot. I see this as my moment and casually stretch my arms up, planning to drape one across the back of the sofa, closer to Rachel. It's like the giant fur ball knows what I'm doing as his eyes snap back open, and he eyeballs me again. Rachel turns to look at her phone, and I point two fingers at my eyes, then back at Nigel.

Yeah, I'm watching you, fucker.

"Megan says she's having a good night." Rachel reads her text out loud. "I'm pleased the new team she's working with seems friendly. I was worried she would get lonely when I'm away flying."

"She's a big girl. Maybe she has a different bloke here every night when you're away," I joke.

"You have met Megan, haven't you? She would never do that. Her morals are far too high. She's waiting for the guy who writes the hallmark greeting cards to sweep her off her feet," Rachel says, stretching her feet up onto the coffee table. Her bright red toenails draw my gaze. Who knew feet could be so damn sexy?

I shrug. "Good for her. Passing the time with the wrong people isn't for everyone," I say casually, taking a drink of the whisky Rachel's given me. I wish I could look over and gauge her reaction without it being obvious.

"It's getting late. I better tidy up," she says, rising to her feet and gathering up the take-away boxes and our plates.

"I can do that." I sit forward and rise from the sofa.

"It's fine, sit," she instructs as she piles everything up.

"Ouch! What the fuck!" I shout, jumping up as pain spreads across one of my ass cheeks. I turn around and see Nigel staring at me. "That little fucker just bit my ass!" I shout, pointing at him as he stares back at me.

"What? Let me see?" Rachel abandons the plates and turns me around. "I can't see anything."

"I'm telling you, I felt it. Rabbit fucking stew tomorrow!" I glare at Nigel. I swear if he could stick a finger up to go with the way he's looking at me, then he would.

"That's not like him at all," Rachel says, scooping the beast up into her arms and kissing his nose. "You must have sat on him, and he got scared."

"I hadn't even gotten fully out of the seat! He knew exactly what he was doing." I scowl. Nigel looks at me smugly from his cozy place in Rachel's arms.

Motherfucker.

"Nigel, that's not how we treat our guests, is it? I think it's time you went to bed. You get cranky when you're tired." She carries him over to a large beanbag-style cat bed and lays him down onto it, stroking him as she says goodnight.

I gather up our plates and follow Rachel out of the room, glaring at Nigel one last time before shutting the door behind us.

I help Rachel load the dishwasher before we talk again.

"See you in the morning, then. You can show me what you want to take over."

"You're leaving?" Rachel asks, sounding—dare I hope—disappointed?

It would be so easy to pull her into my arms right now, suck on that sweet bottom lip.

Fuck! Grant me strength, God.

I saw too easily this week how she pulls herself away. There's no way I want to lose her again by thinking with my dick. No, the next time something happens, I want to know for definite she wants it as much as I do.

"Yeah, it's late, and you've been working hard all week. You need a good rest if you want to cart furniture around all day tomorrow," I say, my considerate friend hat firmly on.

"See you in the morning then," she replies, her eyes holding mine long enough that I know she feels this between us.

There's no denying it. Hell, I can practically hear the crackling in the air.

"Yep, see you tomorrow." I smile.

"Can we just try it over there again?" Megan points across the room as I rest my hands on my knees, taking a break.

"Yeah, of course, never mind the fact that you're killing me here," I pant, wiping sweat off my brow with the back of my hand. "What the fuck is this thing made of?" I ask, reaching down to lug the grey mass to another corner of her bedroom for the third time.

"Oh, concrete. I made it on a sculpting course I took." She looks at where I've placed it. "Great! Thanks, Tan. I think right there is good."

Thank fuck for that.

"What's it meant to be, anyway?" I tilt my head, hoping its true identity emerges. I got nothing, though. It just looks like a lump of concrete.

"It's modern art. It's supposed to be an expression of the changing seasons."

I obviously don't hide the look on my face very well as she giggles. "I know, it's crap, but I like to keep it as it reminds me of one of the first arty things I did after leaving flying. My passion is drawing, but I thought I would try something different. It doesn't always work out." She shrugs good-naturedly.

"Hey, guys," Rachel calls up the stairs, "I'm just

going to head back quickly. I forgot to give Nigel a snack. He'll be in a right mood later if I don't."

So, last night was him in his usual mood?

"I'll do it," I call back, surprising myself. Why the hell did I just say that?

There's a pause before Rachel calls back, "Actually, Tan, yes, please, that would be great. It means I can finish what I'm doing down here."

Tan, she called me Tan.

A sense of satisfaction settles over me. We're getting there.

I jog down the stairs, picking up Rachel's keys, which are on the bottom step, and glance into the living room where she's drilling some shelves into the recesses on either side of the fireplace. She point-blank refused to let me do it. I smile; she's doing a great job.

"Back soon," I say.

She turns to face me as my eyes drop down her body. I can't help myself. I am a man, after all, and she looks fucking edible in another tight t-shirt knotted up around her waist and a pair of slim-fitting jogging bottoms.

"There's a special oat chew for him on the kitchen side and some spinach in the fridge. Just give him a handful."

Christ, this rabbit is a spoiled little wanker.

"Sure." I nod, glancing at Rachel's lips one last time before I head out of the door.

I drive a couple of minutes to Rachel and Megan's

house and park up before heading to the front door, letting myself in.

"Daddy's home," I call sarcastically, instantly wondering why I'm calling out to a rabbit, for fuck's sake.

I head into the kitchen and open the fridge, grabbing out a bag of spinach leaves before I pick up the oat bar in a wrapper. "*Organically grown and ethically sourced*," I read off the label with a snort. "Nigel eats better than me." I shake my head as I walk through the hallway and open the door into the living room.

He's sitting on the carpet, already eyeballing me as I walk over to him.

"Now listen," I say as I take a seat next to him on the floor. "You don't like me, and I don't like you." I open the bag and pull out a spinach leaf, offering it to him. He eyes me warily before leaning forward and snatching it from my fingers, nibbling it down quickly. "But," I continue as I hold him out another one, which he takes more gently, "we both like it when your mommy smiles, and I know that sometimes I'm good at making her smile."

Nigel eyes me again, then slowly hops up onto my legs. I don't dare move.

"You aren't about to launch another attack on me with those teeth, are you?" His nose twitches, and he sniffs towards the other side of my legs where the treats are. "Oh, I get it, keeping your enemies close, eh? Especially when they have the food." I chuckle as I hold the oat stick out to him, and he grabs it, nibbling enthusiastically in my lap. "Smart move Nigel, you'd make a good entrepreneur."

Tentatively, I place a hand down on his back. He pauses, eating to look at me for a brief second, before continuing his attack on the oat stick. I stroke him gently. "You're soft; what the hell do you wash in? I could do with some," I joke.

Actually, this feels really relaxing and explains why therapy pets are a thing. My eyes close before my phone vibrates in my pocket with a message.

"Sorry, mate," I say to Nigel as I reach into my pocket to get it. He hops off my lap, taking his treat with him.

Drew: Hey Tan, how's all the moving going?
Me: Yeah, good. Almost done for the day. Just come to feed the rabbit.
Drew: What the fuck you talking about? Is that some new kinky shit?
Me: I wish. I'm feeding their house rabbit, Nigel.
Drew: She's got you by the balls, man! Lol. Best fucking thing I've heard all week. Tan the man is getting all sappy over some chick's rabbit.
Me: Fuck off!
Drew: Ha!
Me: You still okay for Sunday at the office? I

want to go over those contracts again before I
go to New York.
Drew: Sure thing, Dr. Doolittle.

We spend the rest of the day sorting things out at the
new house. Rachel's kept the van for tomorrow to
move the beds and sofa and the last few items. She
doesn't know I'm planning on coming back again in
the morning to help, but I doubt she will bother
arguing now. She knows it won't do any good. Megan's
nipped over to see a friend from work, so it's just
Rachel and me at the old house, packing up a couple
of things before calling it quits for the day.

"Did you want to take a shower while you're here?"
Rachel asks as she bends over to tape up a box.

My eyes drop to her bum, and I run a hand through
my hair.

"Sorry?" I ask, completely missing what she said.

"If you're going to check out my bum, then at least
make sure you're listening to me, so it's not so obvious,"
she says with a hint of amusement in her voice as she
glances back over her shoulder at me.

"As if I would do such a thing? Doesn't that infringe
your equal rights somehow?" I fire back.

I love it when she's in a playful mood. She's seemed
closed off all week. Maybe the relief at getting the
painting finished and most of the furniture moved has
loosened her up.

She stands back up and turns to face me. "I said, do you want to take a shower while you're here? You've got dust in your hair." Her eyes glance up to my head as she smirks.

"I've got a shower at my house, you know?" I say, testing her invitation to see if it's some roundabout way of asking me to stay the night.

She shrugs. "I just thought you might want to have one sooner rather than later."

Bingo!

She could have just said "fine" and let me leave.

"Well, now that you mention it, it kind of makes sense. I might be too tired when I get back home." I backtrack shamelessly. "I'll just grab some clean clothes from my car."

"You carry clean clothes around in your car? Is that just in case you don't make it back to your own bed?" Rachel asks without looking at me.

I study her face as she busies herself with some post on the kitchen side. I'd say she's trying not to sound interested when, really, I can practically hear the cogs turning in her head. She's wondering just how often I spend the night in beds belonging to other people. Or other women, should I say? I hold back my smile—it bothers her.

"I went to the gym on the way to you this morning. I've got clean clothes and a gym kit in there."

"Oh," she murmurs.

Yes, oh. My Snow is getting jealous, and I fucking love it!

"Back in a minute." I head out to my car to get my bag.

I went to the gym this morning. That wasn't a lie, but this bag has been in my car all week, in the hopes that she may thaw out towards me. I grab it out of the boot and head back inside.

The sound of running water greets me as I enter the hallway.

"Rachel?"

No answer.

Either she's started it running for me, or she's in there waiting for me. I kick off my shoes and take the stairs two at a time, hoping it's the latter.

As I reach the top, Rachel comes out of the bathroom. "I turned it on for you. Sometimes the hot water takes a minute to come through," she says as she goes to walk past me.

I drop my bag at my feet. She's not seriously going to leave it at that, is she? I know she wants more, else why ask me to shower here? I sense she's teetering on the edge of admitting to herself that it's no use fighting this attraction between us any longer. She just needs a little push to sway her.

As she passes, I gently grasp her arm, stroking over her soft skin with the pad of my thumb. She stops, and I hear her suck in her breath, but she doesn't look at me. Leaning down so my breath will be felt on her neck, I whisper, "thank you," before stroking her skin one last time and heading into the bathroom. I'm careful to leave the door open, so there's an unobstructed view from the hallway.

My heart's thumping in my chest as I keep my back to the door, peeling my t-shirt off over my head.

Will it work?

My dick twitches in anticipation. If it doesn't, I'll have no choice but to be a terrible guest and have a wank in her shower.

I lean down and pull my socks off, rising again to undo the button on my jeans. I can't hear her; maybe she's gone back downstairs. I slide my jeans and boxers off, dropping them in a pile on the floor on top of my t-shirt.

My shoulders sag.

It didn't work.

"I know what you're doing?" a sweet voice breaks into my moment of self-pity. I turn. Rachel is standing in the doorway, one eyebrow raised as she looks me straight in the eyes.

"What are you talking about?" I force my eyes to stay focused on her face. One look down at her in that tight t-shirt again, and my dick will surely give the game away about exactly what it is I'm thinking about right now.

She walks over to me slowly, stopping toe to toe with me before she raises her chin, her eyes bright with amusement.

"You didn't shut the door on purpose, hoping I would see you get undressed and come in here, didn't you?"

Well shit. There's no getting anything past her. It worked, though. I hold back my smile.

"Why would I do a thing like that?" I ask seriously.

Her eyes gaze into mine before dropping to my lips. I run a hand back through my hair. Fuck, I love when she looks at me like that.

She smirks. "You just did that thing with your hair again. You do it when you're turned on."

Hang on, I do what?

"I think you hoped that you'd be able to persuade me to come in here and join you," she continues, her eyes focused on mine in a silent challenge. "Tell me I'm right?"

I gaze into her eyes. "You're wrong," I murmur. "That is not what I wanted at all."

Her brows pinch together.

"I'm not going to persuade you to do anything. I'm not even going to hint at it." I take a breath and lean in closer, so my words are almost spoken against her lips. "I want you to do exactly whatever you want to do, Rachel." I pull back slightly, my eyes searching hers.

Just say it, Snow, tell me you want this as much as I do. Stop. Fighting. Us.

She looks down, and I hold my breath.

Please...

Finally, she lifts her eyes to mine, and they're dark with desire. She snakes her arms up around my neck, standing on her tiptoes, so her lips are close to mine. I can smell the perfume on her skin, mixed with the heat of her body. It takes over my fucking head as blood rushes to my cock. I still haven't laid a finger on her. I won't. Not until she tells me exactly what she wants.

"I," she whispers against my mouth, her eyes never leaving mine, "want you." She presses her body firmly against mine, and I clench my fists by my sides.

"You want me to what?" I ask, my voice strained.

She presses a light kiss against my lips. "I want you to make me scream out your name as you say the filthiest things to me you can bear. I want it fast, and I need it hard."

Fucking Hell.

I groan like a tormented animal as I tear her t-shirt up over her head and reach around to unclasp her bra, pulling it off roughly, my hands grabbing her tits at the same time my mouth claims hers.

Fuck, she tastes so good.

My tongue dives deeper into her mouth, meeting her own as we drink each other up. I rub and squeeze her tits with both of my hands, her nipples rising into tight little peaks.

"I'm going to fuck these gorgeous tits of yours one day," I growl against her lips.

Now is not that day, though. She said she wants it fast and needs it hard. Who am I to deprive her? I stop kissing her and reach down to my jeans on the floor to get a condom.

"Take the rest of your clothes off so I can fuck you just like you want it, naughty girl."

Her eyes hold mine as she pulls her pants and panties down and stands in front of me, naked.

Fuck. I will never tire of this sight—her smooth skin, tiny waist, incredible tits, and light pink nipples.

She's fucking sensational.

I roll the condom down onto my stiff cock, the brush of my hands causing my balls to tighten.

Hell, it is going to be fast.

I pull Rachel towards me, grabbing a fistful of her hair in one hand and tipping her head back so I can kiss and suck my way down her neck.

With one hand, I lightly slap across her nipples. She arches into me, sucking in her breath before letting out a moan that almost makes me blow my load on the spot.

"Turn around," I say, twisting her hips, so her back is to me. I position her in front of the sink. Thank fuck they have a self-clearing mirror, and it's not steamed up from the running shower.

"You want it fast and hard, baby," I say through gritted teeth as I bend her forwards, so she's gripping onto the sink, one hand on either side.

"No. I said I want it fast, and I *need* it hard." She fires back, her eyes catching mine in the mirror.

My cock swells even more at her snarky attitude. My girl is back doing what she does best, and she said she wanted filth.

"You're a cheeky bitch, aren't you?" I say as I grip onto her hips and push deep inside her, circling my hips once I've sunk all the way in. She moans as I draw back. "Your greedy pussy is already pulling me back in," I say, thrusting back inside her, so my balls hit her skin. "Admit it, you love me fucking you," I hiss, drawing back and slamming back into her.

"Fuck you," she says, looking at me in the glass.

"You're going to regret saying that." My eyes hold her gaze as I drive into her with such force she's thrown forward towards the sink. I dig my fingers into her hips harder and drag her back down onto me, banging into her with relentless, punishing force.

"I know you love the feel of my cock deep inside you, filling you up, stretching you. Your pussy is mine now, don't you fucking forget it," I hiss as I pound into her.

"Fuck, Tan," Rachel moans. Her eyes are half-closed, her mouth hangs open, and her tits bounce as I fuck her.

It's the best thing I've ever seen.

"Come on, baby, show me what your greedy little pussy can do."

She tenses around me in response.

"Fuck, yeah," I groan loudly. "I know you want me to fill you up, don't you? You want to feel my cock jerking as I blow my load inside you. Don't you, baby?" I look at Rachel's face, and her eyes hold mine. "Fucking say it, Rachel!" I shout, sucking in big, deep breaths.

"I—" She's struggling to talk, her breath coming in ragged pants. "I want you to—Oh, fuck, Tan!" she cries. "I'm going to come."

"That's it, baby, come all over my cock. Your orgasm is mine. Squeeze me, baby, let me have it all," I pant as she opens her mouth and screams, her cheeks flushed, her eyes wild.

She's fucking *beautiful*.

"That's it, Snow," I say as I ride it out with her, feeling her contractions hug my cock. God, it feels so good.

"Tan!" she cries, screwing her face up, and her contractions quicken and intensify again.

Fuck yes! She's coming again.

It's more than I can bear, knowing what she's doing, what I'm responsible for. My cock swells almost painfully, and I come violently, my balls slapping against her as I fuck out every drop.

Oh God, oh fuck. Fuck, fuck, fuck!

I bite my lip as the last wave of pleasure rolls over me, and my body comes back down.

That was intense. I gently ease out of her and bring her upright, pulling her back against my chest, one hand turning her head to the side, so my lips graze hers in a kiss.

"Remember, I said I prefer you when you don't talk?" she murmurs against my lips.

"Mmm." I kiss her again, gently sucking her bottom lip, my fingers stroking her soft cheek.

"I think I like it even better when you talk to me like that," she whispers, kissing me back deeply.

I chuckle. "You like a bit of filth, huh?"

"Only the talking kind." She smirks as she slides

her back against me, and the sweat we are both covered in makes our skin stick together.

"It's a good job you heated the shower for us then, isn't it?" I smile as I take her hand and lead her in under the hot spray with me, claiming her mouth again as I wrap her in my arms.

THIRTEEN

RACHEL

"Why don't we just stay here all night?" Tanner murmurs, his lips against my neck, the cold tiles of the shower hard against my back.

I smile as his kisses trail up over my chin and back onto my lips.

This man can kiss.

I sink into him for a moment. I'm floating somewhere between a dream and reality. Maybe I can stay here after all.

He draws back, gazing at me.

Fuck, this isn't going to turn into one of those deep after-sex talks, is it?

"So, what's this thing I do with my hair?" he asks.

I laugh, relaxing again. "Has no one ever noticed before?"

His raised brow confirms it's a 'no.'

"Really?" I shake my head with a sigh. "You run

your hand back through your hair when you're aroused."

"I do not!" Tanner smiles, tightening his grip on my waist.

"You so do!" I laugh, my palms resting against his warm, hard chest. "I can't believe I'm the first person to notice."

"Maybe you're the first person who's noticed because you're the only person who's seen it every time we are together?" he says, pulling me closer so my breasts press against the back of my hands. I move them up around his neck, and his eyes widen as my nipples take their place against his skin.

"Maybe that's it." I roll my eyes as he lands a playful slap across my bum.

"Hey, I'm serious, Rachel." Tanner's eyes hold mine intently.

I slide my arms down and slip out of his grasp.

"And I'm seriously going to wash away if I stay in here any longer."

I open the door and reach out to grab a towel, wrapping it around me as I step out.

There's a pause before the water is turned off, and Tanner steps out behind me. I pass him another towel.

He clears his throat. "Thanks."

I glance back at him; he's wrapped the towel around his waist, water droplets still cover his perfect abs. He's staring off into space, his jaw tight.

God, he's a fine specimen of a man.

"I'm just going to get dressed," I say, inclining my head towards the door.

Tanner doesn't meet my gaze. "Sure," he says as he bends down and picks up the discarded condom from the floor.

"I'll see you downstairs?" I pause for a second, but he's already got his back to me, pulling on his clothes.

What's got into him suddenly?

I head into my room and pull on some clean joggers and a t-shirt, quickly towel drying my hair and running my brush through it.

Before I'm ready to go downstairs, there's a soft knock at the door.

"Rach?" My stomach lifts at his voice. "I'm heading off."

What? I rush to the door and fling it open.

"No!" I say in a rush.

His eyes rise to meet mine, his face serious. "No?"

"You don't need to leave."

What the hell am I doing?

"Not yet, anyway. I mean, it's not that late."

"Rachel." He looks off towards the stairs, letting out a sigh before his eyes come back to my face. "I don't enjoy the feeling that me still being here makes you uncomfortable."

I fold my arms across my chest. "It doesn't."

"Really?" Tanner says, raising a dark brow.

"Don't be ridiculous. You've seen every part of my body from all sorts of angles. How could you being here make me uncomfortable?" My voice spills out quickly, defensively.

The corners of Tanner's mouth turn down, and his shoulders drop. "We both know that's not it, Rachel."

I'm stumped over what to say. He's right. I am uncomfortable with the idea of him being here after sex at night. I mean, am I supposed to cuddle up in bed and bare the darkest parts of my soul to him, wake up in the morning and make waffles together? The thought makes my chest tighten.

"I'll let myself out," he says as he turns to leave.

"Wait, Tan, please," I whisper.

He turns his eyes back to me, and more than anything, I want to be normal, to not feel this overwhelming urge to turn and run like hell.

"I would like it if you stayed. We could put a movie on?" I look up at him, holding my breath.

He puts one arm up against the doorframe, leaning his head against his fist. His bicep stretches the fabric of his white t-shirt. I drop my eyes to his grey jogging bottoms and swallow the lump in my throat.

"You sure about this?"

"Yes." I nod.

He looks away again before his eyes return to mine, a hint of their usual brightness back. "Fine, but I get to pick which film."

"Sure." I smile.

"Hey, Rach. Psst! You awake?"

"Huh? Meg, what time is it?" I groan, pulling the pillow over my head.

Cool air whips across my face as Megan flings my pillow onto the floor.

"Hey! What was that for?" I look over to the gap in the curtains. The sun is barely coming up; it must be early.

"You need to see this!" Megan whispers.

Her face looks like a kid's on Christmas morning. Well, the ones I saw on toy adverts growing up.

"What is it? Hang on…" I look at the empty space in the bed next to me. I don't remember getting in here, and I'm still wearing my joggers and t-shirt from last night. That must mean… "Where's Tanner?"

"That's what I've been trying to tell you." Megan rolls her eyes as she grabs my hand and hauls me out of bed.

"Shh, be really quiet." She motions for me to follow her downstairs, stopping at the living room door. She holds a finger up to her lips before she slowly opens it.

We both peer our heads around the side of the door, looking into the darkened room. I can hear slow, rhythmic breathing, in and out, in and out. Megan pokes me in the side and points. One look at the sofa tells me where it's coming from.

There, laid out on his back, eyes tightly shut, is Tanner. He's got one arm slung behind his head and—*I don't believe this*—his other arm gently cradling a large, grey mass, which is sprawled across him, Nigel.

Megan clasps her hand over her mouth, but it's too late. A snort escapes, and she grabs my hand and pulls me into the kitchen.

"Oh my God, Rach! Did you see Nigel?" Her shoulders shake as more giggles threaten to erupt. "I'm sorry, it's just, they look so cute together."

"Where's your phone?" I ask quickly.

"Here." She pulls it out of her dressing gown pocket.

"Gimme." I pluck it out of her hand as I sneak back to the lounge door.

I turn the phone torch on, reasoning it will be less obvious than the flash and snap a picture of the two of them together.

"Thank you, send me it," I say, handing Megan back her phone in the kitchen. She taps the screen a few times.

"All sent." She smiles.

"I can't believe that little floozy, Nigel. Tanner feeds him one time, and now they've got their own little bromance going on."

"I know! Crazy, isn't it? He usually hates new people for ages. Don't you remember how long it took him to get used to Matt?"

"Yeah, I do." I lean back against the counter. "He had to bring him at least four sets of treats before Nigel would even let him stroke him. They were the really good ones too."

"Well, looks like he's accepted Tanner into his

club." She laughs. "What the hell's he doing on the sofa, anyway? Did you spend all night together again?"

"Yes, well, no," I say.

Megan's watching me, spinning her hand in front of her stomach, urging me to go on.

"The last thing I remember is watching a movie together. I don't even know how I got to bed."

"He must have carried you up there like Sleeping Beauty!" Megan exclaims, grinning at me. "Wait until we tell Matt!"

"Hang on a minute." I hold my hands up, moving them up and down like I'm trying to talk down a crazed attacker. "We are not telling Matt anything. He will totally get the wrong idea and get carried away."

"The right idea, don't you mean?" Megan says, the grin still firmly plastered on her face.

"What are you talking about?"

"Come on, Rach, are you kidding me? That guy is so into you."

"No, he isn't. He's just a friend."

"A friend that gives you toe-curling orgasms and sleeps on the sofa with a twenty-pound rabbit on his chest because he's already noticed how fucked up you are about actual intimacy, like sleeping in the same bed!" Megan cries.

"Megan, keep your voice down," I hiss.

"Rachel, wake up. He isn't the same as your other 'friends', like Chris—who was at the same bar as me last night and asked after you, by the way."

"Ugh," I groan. I haven't called Chris in weeks. He probably thinks it's strange. "What did you tell him?"

"I told him you'd been busy getting the house ready."

"Thank you." I blow out a breath. We've never pried into each other's lives before. The less he knows, the better.

"Honestly though, Rach, I should have told him the truth."

"Which is?" I raise an eyebrow at her.

"That you've met a great guy who is good for you and that you won't be calling him ever again! It's not like he hasn't got a load of other girls he can call to keep him company."

"I thought you liked Chris?" I look at her.

"He's nice enough. But he isn't Tanner," she says pointedly.

"Meg." I sigh, tipping my head back to look at the ceiling, "this thing with Tanner, that's just sex too," I say, although even I don't believe myself.

A sound at the door makes us both jump.

"Tanner!" I say.

Fuck! How long has he been standing there?

"Good morning." He nods to Megan before his eyes lock onto mine. His dark hair is tousled from sleep, a dark shadow of growth running along his firm jaw. My heart leaps into my chest.

"Morning, Tan. I'm grabbing a shower," Megan chirps at us both before passing him in the doorway and retreating upstairs.

"You slept on the sofa?" I say, more like a question.

"I did." He keeps his eyes on mine, not giving anything away.

Oh, he has a good poker face.

I narrow my eyes at him. "Why?"

"Why what?" he asks, his eyes dropping to my lips.

"Why did you sleep on the sofa?" I ask, studying his face.

I don't know what it is I'm waiting for. For him to admit that he was thinking of my feelings? Didn't want me to feel uncomfortable in the morning? What will I say if he admits to it? Why would he put so much thought into something like that when this is just sex? And it is just sex; it can't be anything else.

"I was thinking about someone else's comfort," he says smoothly.

Oh, fuck.

"Oh?" I say, trying to keep my voice steady as my chest tightens.

"Yeah. I think Nigel gets lonely at night. You ever thought about getting him a girlfriend?"

"A girlfriend?" I smirk, relief washing over me.

"Yeah. He could have a friend to play with when you're out. Someone to sleep next to at night." Tan's eyes are studying me carefully.

Are we still talking about Nigel?

"He's a rabbit. He would spend all night shagging himself to death if he had a girlfriend."

"I can think of worse ways to go." Tanner grins at me.

I smile back. "Do you want some breakfast?"

"Sounds good," he says, coming to lean his elbows casually against the counter as he watches me grab eggs out of the fridge.

"I have to feed you if you're helping move the last things across to the new house today," I say over my shoulder to him as I fill a pan with water and put it on top of the cooker.

"Am I?" I can hear the amusement in his voice.

"Aren't you?" I say, getting out three mugs.

He chuckles, and just like that, the conversation flows easily again; no more talk of sharing beds, no more being reminded of just how messed up I am.

For now, at least.

FOURTEEN

TANNER

"This all looks good," I say to Drew as I finish looking over the contract papers. "Are you happy with Mike heading things up over there once I get everything finalized this week?"

Drew places his coffee cup down on my desk and sits back in his chair. "Yes, for the tenth time." He smiles at me easily. "Tan, mate. I know you're a control freak when it comes to working, but we've got this all covered. Mike is our best project manager in London, and it's only a three-month refurb. He's got the guys in the New York office helping him. They're happy to have him, what with Tina being off on maternity. Besides, I told him how beautiful the women in New York are."

"Uh-huh," I murmur, checking over the papers again. I don't have any doubts over Mike's ability to lead Tina's team while she's off. I just need to feel in control at work because I am sure as hell not outside of the office.

"What's got into you, anyway? You take a week off work with no notice and then call me in for a meeting on a Sunday afternoon, the day after I have a hot date. You're lucky I said yes." Drew drums his fingers around the side of his coffee cup.

"How did it go?" I ask, raising my eyes to his, glad for the distraction.

"Meh." He grunts.

I chuckle. "That good, eh?"

"No, man. I mean, phew, she's insanely hot." Drew puts his hands on the back of his head as he stretches.

"Why am I sensing there's a but? You took her out to dinner like you said you were going to, didn't you?"

Drew avoids my eyes. "Nah, slight change of plan."

"She turned you down, didn't she?"

"Of course not! She just needs a bit more persuading to sample the 'Drew Delights', that's all." He frowns.

I shake my head, smiling. "You drove for two hours to take a woman out for dinner, who hadn't even agreed to it, yet you're the one asking what's got into me?"

"Minor details, Tan, minor," Drew says, skirting the issue. "I'm not the one who's been cozying up with a rabbit and sleeping on the sofa." He laughs, slapping the table with his palm.

I scowl at him. "That's the last time I tell you

anything. Oh, and that bonus we were talking about? Forget it."

Drew laughs harder. "Tan, mate, loosen the fuck up. Seriously, what's this chick done to you, man? Have your balls shriveled up inside your body?"

"She's not done anything to me," I say as I lean back in my chair, blowing out a breath.

"Don't give me that. We've been mates for years," he says, finally having stopped laughing. "So? What's going on?"

"I don't know. One minute she's all over me, and then the next, she acts like it's nothing." I tap the heel of my foot on the floor as I look out the window at the street below.

"She sounds like a head-fuck," he says, his eyes on my face.

"She's complicated. I know she doesn't have any family, and she told me she doesn't have relationships, only 'friends'." I pick my pen up and slide my fingers down it, turning it once I get to the bottom and repeating the move while I think.

"Look, Tan. I get that she's hot. I dunno; maybe you feel like seeing her again out of the blue all these months after you got back from New York is a sign from the universe or something?"

I mull over his words. "It's more than that. I mean, yes, seeing her again at the auction was unexpected, but there's something about her. I can't even think straight." I throw my pen down on the desk.

"Maybe it's just a weird coincidence? When you

saw her at the airport, and she said that saying that made you think of your mom, it made you notice her." Drew shrugs. "You felt, I don't know? Connected to her or some shit?"

"Ugh." I let out a groan and lean my head into my hands on the desk. "There was just something about her, and yeah, it threw me when she used my mom's saying. I don't know. I just wanted to help. Look at the shit it's got me into now."

"Hang on? You said you were going to tell her?" Drew's eyes shoot up in surprise as I raise my eyes to his. One look at my face, and he's shaking his head in pity. "Fuck, man, you're in for it when she finds out. From what you've told me and what I've seen, she's going to have your balls on a spike."

"Thanks for the support," I snap.

"I can't believe you haven't told her yet. You've spent all week together, let alone the house viewing, and all the time you've had her number in your phone. What's been stopping you?"

"I know, I know," I groan. "But what was I meant to say? Hi, nice to meet you, Rachel, except I already know your name; I've been the one emailing you and sending you money for your worn panties for the past year and a half?" I shake my head. *This is so fucked up.*

"When you put it like that, it does sound weird," Drew says.

"Exactly." I look at him. "She'll think I'm a creep."

"Okay, look." Drew leans forward in his seat. "Women love all those honest, open conversations. Just tell her the truth. She already goes all weird on you after sex. What have you got to lose?"

Her. I could lose her.

Even if I don't get her fully, I still get a part of her when we're together.

"You're right; I know I've got to tell her, and I will. After New York. She's only fucking operating on the flight Penny booked me on tomorrow," I mutter as I gather up the contract papers, and we head to the door.

"No way! That's hilarious." Drew chuckles.

I glare at him. "You're not helping."

"Sorry, Tan. Hey, I'll come to your funeral, mate," Drew says, patting me on the back as we wait for the lift.

It's only a matter of days before I have to tell her who she was really talking to all these months. *Fuck.*

I can barely tear my eyes away from Rachel in her red uniform the entire flight out to New York. It's been over eighteen months since the airport coffee bar, and somehow, she looks even sexier in it than I remember. She's been looking after the section of upper class I'm seated in. I don't know if that was deliberate or just pure good fortune—well, *mine* anyway.

From the seat I'm in, I can just about see every time she bends over to get in the end trolley in the galley. Her perfect ass calls to me to hitch her red skirt up around her waist and slip my fingers inside her panties. *Oh, Fuck yeah.* Seeing her now, knowing that all those flights she was working just like this, then posting the panties underneath her uniform to me, has more of an effect on me than I expected. I feel my dick stir in my suit slacks.

"Would you like another drink, sir?" one of the other female flight attendants asks me. Her eyes roam down my shirt, down to my crotch, and back up slowly, a flirtatious smile on her lips.

"No, thank you. Rachel's got me covered," I say without smiling.

"Okay." She shrugs and walks off.

I watch her pass the galley and say something to Rachel, who then looks over at me. I smile at her, and she lifts her chin in acknowledgment before going back to what she was doing. I drop my gaze back to my laptop and the document I'm working on, but I can still see Rachel out of the corner of my eye. She finishes putting things away inside the trolley before she looks back over in my direction and stands with her arms crossed, leaning back against the galley side.

I love that she's watching me.

Oh, Snow, if only I could know what you are thinking.

"Hey, Mom," I say down the phone as I slide into the backseat of the town car the New York office has sent to collect me from the airport.

"Hi, Sweetheart, how was your flight?" Her warm voice expertly masks her relief. She's scared of flying. I always call her every time I land as I know she will worry otherwise and check all the news channels expecting to see a horrific crash headline.

"It was interesting. Rachel was working on it."

Mom's tone lightens immediately. "The girl you've been telling me about?"

"Yes, Mom." I smile at her sudden interest.

"How exciting! So, what are you going to do in New York together? I assume she doesn't just fly straight back again?"

"No, she gets two nights here, but, Mom, I'm here for work. I have no idea what she has planned."

"Nonsense, Tanner," she scolds. "You don't have to work the whole time you're there. I appreciate your call. Now, get off the phone with your old Mom and call Rachel! Ask to meet her later."

I shake my head and smile as Mom barks out her instructions. Some things never change.

"Fine," I say to placate her, rolling my eyes.

"Have fun." Mom giggles like a schoolgirl, obviously satisfied that I'm taking her advice.

"Love you, Mom."

"You too, Tan," she says as I end the call.

Before I can talk myself out of it, I fire off a text to Rachel.

Me: I know where to get the best caramel lattes in Manhattan if you fancy it tomorrow?

I stare out the window at the darkening sky as we drive over the Queensboro bridge. I always ask to drive this way from JFK airport rather than through the tunnel. Something about seeing the New York skyline on the way in and knowing we have an office there gets me every time. It reminds me just how far the company has come since I started it.

My phone buzzes in my hand.

Snow: I doubt your latte connections are as reliable as mine but sure.

Snarky. I smile. I guess she flies here most months.

Me: I should be done in the office by 2pm. I'll pick you up from your hotel.
Snow: No need, meet you at the corner of West 49th and 6th Avenue.

I shake my head at her text, typical. Heaven forbid she would listen to me for once and just agree to me picking her up. Growing up with a mom like mine, I've always had one strong-willed, independent woman in my life, and now I'm trying to add another. Surely this is a disaster waiting to happen.

What the fuck is wrong with me?

FIFTEEN

RACHEL

AFTER YESTERDAY'S FLIGHT, I COULDN'T WAIT TO GET TO this morning's kickboxing class in a studio near the crew's hotel. I needed to clear my head. I kept finding myself watching Tanner all flight. The way he held his pen, running his fingers up and down it when he was engrossed in his paperwork, his dark brows knitted together in concentration. It was like businessman porn to me. He was wearing the same suit as the morning he stole my coffee, only this time, the only thing he was stealing from me was any sense of control I thought I had.

"Argh, what the hell is wrong with me?" I say to my reflection in the bathroom mirror as I take in my sweaty, disheveled appearance. I really went for it in class, which would usually help me get my shit together, only today it didn't work. All I keep picturing in my head is Tanner. Tanner in his suit, Tanner painting the house, Tanner sleeping on the sofa,

Tanner's arms around me, Tanner's tongue against my skin. *Tanner, Tanner, Tanner!* I need to get a grip.

Then there's the small bombshell I discovered on the flight yesterday when I looked at the passenger manifest. His surname is only Grayson, isn't it? The owner of Grayson Designs. That hotel we went to in London for the whisky night, the construction posters in Vegas—he's only Tanner-loaded-fucker-Grayson. I don't understand why he didn't tell me. Is he lying about anything else?

I take my time in the shower, washing my hair before carefully blow-drying it into soft waves. I decide on a fitted cream jumper with a short black skirt, tights, and boots, and finally, I add a slash of red lipstick to draw attention to my lips. I look at myself in the mirror.

What am I doing?

I would never usually take this long to get ready, and as much as I tell myself, I'm not doing it for Tanner. I totally am, well, sort of. I'm doing it so I can watch the look on his face when he sees me. So I can feel that energy buzzing through my body as he runs his hand through his hair, his dark eyes drinking me in.

"Who the fuck are you?" I screw up my face at my reflection. The same face looks back at me. The eyes that have seen the expressions of pity when I tell people I grew up in foster care. The ears that heard all the whispers in the school corridors about the new "weird girl with a temper" when I was moved to another new school. The lips that shouted and screamed when I was told that I was moving families —again.

"We can't cope with her."

"She's too moody."

"Too unpredictable."

The same lips that quickly learned it did no good. It was better to save energy and just not say anything. I was never the one in control; it was never me making the choices. Yes, I look the same as I always have; yet, I don't even recognize myself anymore.

I'm looking forward to meeting Tanner, spending more time with him, and hell, dare I say it? I kind of want to wake up next to him tomorrow without freaking the fuck out. I *want* to trust him; I just do not know whether someone like me can even change.

I glance at the clock; I've still got a bit of time before I meet him, and being on the East Coast means the time in LA isn't so drastically different. It's a perfect time to call Holly. I grab my phone and hit video call on the screen. A moment later, her sun-kissed blond hair and bright green eyes appear on my screen.

"Rach!" she says excitedly.

"Hey, Holls." I beam back.

"You look nice. Where are you off to?" I hold my phone back so she can see even more of my outfit. "I always loved those boots!" She smiles. "Do I take it you are meeting this new guy Tanner you've been telling me about?"

"Mmm-hmm, that one," I say.

"Why do I sense there's more to that 'mmm-hmm'?" Holly probes.

"I don't know, Holly." I sigh, laying back against the bed pillows. "This is just so weird for me. I don't do dating. You know that." I glance up at her, and she's listening intently. "But Tanner... he... he's... well, he's Tanner." I shake my head.

"He's the guy who turned up at your house to paint with you for a week and then spent his weekend lugging your furniture about." Holly smiles. "Oh, and then, he's the guy that falls asleep with Nigel on the sofa after he's carried you to bed."

"Yeah, I know." I smile at her.

"Rachel, he sounds amazing!" She giggles. I look back at her. "Don't let your past hold you back from your future and finding happiness. Jay and I can tell you that letting the past hold you back is no way to live," she says seriously.

"I know, Holls. God, I know you two understand more than anyone how letting the past control you is self-destructive," I say, letting her words soak in.

"Jay says *hi,* by the way. He wants to know when you're next coming for a visit, as do I! He said he sees Matt's face all the time and needs you here to sort him out. He's on at Jay to build a guest house as he's here so much."

I laugh. "Maybe that's not such a bad idea. With the baby arriving, you're bound to have loads of visitors."

"True." Holly nods. "But they can stay in the house with us. Seriously, if we build a guest house, Matt will move in and never leave." She giggles. "As much as I love him, I don't think I could cope. Although it would be handy having an on-site babysitter."

"Show me the bump again. The photo you sent only shows one angle," I say enthusiastically.

Holly stands and props her phone up to turn side to side, her hands wrapping around her rounded belly, beautifully showcasing baby Anderson.

"You can really see him or her now!" I smile in wonder at Holly's perfectly emerging bump.

"I know." She smiles, picking the phone back up. "Please come and visit soon, though. I need you to have a word with Jay. Anyone would think I'm made of glass, not pregnant. He barely lets me do anything. Keeps making me sit down so he can rub my feet."

"Oh, God, how do you cope?" I roll my eyes. "Mr. Perfect sounds so hard to live with."

She grins back at me. "Yeah, yeah, I hear you. I'm a lucky woman. Now, go and meet *your* lucky man. Tanner's eyes are going to pop out of his head when he sees you."

"Okay, I'll give it to you. The coffee deserves nine out of ten," Tanner says as he takes another drink from his cup. He's wearing a dark blue suit and deep grey tie today.

God, how can he look so damn good?

"You're clearly jet-lagged or deluded. It's at least

nine and a half," I quip back at him, blowing steam off the top of my latte before taking a sip, "mmm, delicious."

This is easily my favorite place to get coffee in Manhattan. The small, independently run coffee house is tucked away, so only those who know it's even here visit. Although, business seems to be booming. Every time I come, people are sitting at the rustic wood tables, no matter the time of day. It's got a cool, boho vibe. Chunky wood tables with mismatched armchairs and sofas, trailing plants hanging down from shelves near the ceiling.

"They do a pretty great red-velvet cupcake here too," I say to Tanner.

His eyes drop to my lips around my cup as I take another sip. I knew the red lipstick would do the trick. When we met earlier, I saw his eyes rake over me from head to toe before he realized I'd spotted him. He may have thought he had gotten away with it, but there was certainly no hiding the obvious hair stroke his hand performed as I said hello.

"Really? Red-velvet, my favorite," he says absentmindedly as his eyes stay fixed to my lips.

I smirk as I continue, "although, nothing can top the cupcakes Holly and I used to get at the Magnolia Bakery."

"Holly's your friend who married the actor and moved to LA?" Tanner asks, his eyes coming back up to mine.

"Yes, how do you know that?"

"You told me when we were painting your bedroom together." He smiles.

He could have just said house—when we were painting your house. Why does he make everything sound so sexual?

"Do you get to see her much?" he asks, completely focused on my answer.

"Not as much as I'd like. I try to bid for a flight there each month, but it only gets granted half the time. Whenever I have a holiday, I go over. Until recently, anyway. I used my holiday to sort everything out with the move this time."

"You must miss her?"

I look back into Tan's dark chocolate eyes, and my mouth moves faster than my brain.

"I do, so, so, much. I love her. She's like a sister to me, and her family is amazing, such kind people. I still visit her parents when I can," I blurt.

"I'm sure she loves and misses you too." He reaches across the table and places his hand inside mine, interlacing his fingers with my own. I swallow down the sudden scratchiness in my throat.

"Yeah, I'm sure," I mumble, trying my hardest not to snatch my hand back. He's done so many things to my body with his hands, so why does this feel so intimate?

"Hey, do you mind if we head to a toy store later? I told my PA, Penny that I'd pick something up for her niece, Scarlett," Tanner says, stroking his thumb over my skin as he talks.

"Sure!" I cry, a little too enthusiastically, seeing my opportunity and pulling my hand back. "Why don't we go now?" I down the rest of my latte and grab my coat off the back of the chair. "You're done, right?"

"Yeah," Tanner says, a puzzled look crossing his face before he shakes it off and stands up. "Shall we?"

We walk for blocks and blocks, trying all the toy stores and department stores we come across, with no luck.

"What is this thing called again?" I ask, scanning the shelves of yet another store.

Tanner pulls his phone out of his pocket and leans close to me so I can see the screen. A hint of spicy aftershave teases my senses, and I'm momentarily back in the hotel room on that first night—his hot mouth on my neck as I dig my fingers into the skin on his back.

"Make me come to life, Kitty Meow," Tanner says seriously, enlarging the picture of a fluffy, interactive cat toy with rainbow fur.

I look up at his face, studying the picture, so intent on finding it for Penny's niece, and I feel a flicker of arousal. He's just said the words "Kitty Meow," and I'm about to soak through my panties.

What the hell has gotten into me?

"Come on." I pull on his arm. "Somewhere has to have it. You can't let Scarlett down. You said she's five years old, right?"

"Yeah." Tanner's eyes light up. "She's the sweetest little girl. Penny's been trying to get this toy for ages, but it's sold out in the UK. It's supposed to be a reward for being brave at school."

"What's she need to be brave about?" I ask, reading a box for a pooping mermaid toy.

Who buys this crap? And how does that even work?

"Oh, she's been nervous about making new friends. She's worried no one will talk to her."

My eyes fly to Tanner's face. "What? Why?"

"She's got Heterochromia." He looks at my blank face. "It's when each eye is a different color to the other."

"Oh, but that makes her unique!" The thought of a sweet, beautiful little girl worrying over being different makes me feel emotional suddenly.

Seriously, who has taken over my body?

"Did you have a toy flight attendant doll and airplane you used to play with when you were little?" Tanner teases.

"No," I fire back sharply. I look up at him and take a deep breath, "Sorry."

"You okay?" he asks, looking at me, concern etched in his eyes, unfazed by my bluntness towards him.

"I'm fine. I just didn't have the usual childhood... all the toys and that." I gesture at the shelves with one hand.

He rubs his lips together, his eyebrows pulling in. "Want to talk about it?"

"Nope."

"Okay." He nods, his eyes returning to the row upon row of toys. I watch as they light up suddenly.

"Yes!" he cries enthusiastically, reaching up to grab a box.

His coat is unfastened, so as he reaches up, his shirt pulls across his hard abs.

Fuck.

"Did you find it?" I ask as he lifts the box down.

He turns the box proudly to me, his cheeks flushed, a giant ear-to-ear grin on his face. I wish I could take a picture of his reaction while holding a bright pink box with a rainbow Kitty inside.

"What's so funny?" He raises a brow at me.

"Nothing, just you and your rainbow meow." I smirk.

"Hey!" He pretends to look offended. "What's wrong with a rainbow pussy?"

I throw my head back and laugh out loud.

I can't help it.

I don't know who I am anymore.

Tanner should look at me like I've grown an extra head, as this is just not me. I'm not the girl who laughs out loud with men in toy stores. I'm the girl who can throw back a whisky without wincing and hooks up with almost strangers for my fix. Yet, as my laugh dies down, I find him looking at me with a bright smile spread over his face, his eyes glittering like he's just seen a magician pull a rabbit out of a hat for the first time.

SIXTEEN

TANNER

"WHAT BUSINESS WAS SO IMPORTANT THAT YOU HAD TO fly over for a meeting then?" Rachel asks me as we take a stroll back toward her hotel.

"We've got a hotel refurb going on. It's only small. They want their function space re-done—ballroom, bar, restrooms, that sort of thing. It's only a three-month project."

"Pah! Could do it in one," she says.

I glance at her and see the hint of a smile. "Yes, of course, I should have known to expect that from the 'I'll paint the entire house by myself' superwoman." I chuckle.

She smiles properly, and I'm struck by how beautiful she looks right now. Her barriers are ever so slowly creeping down and giving me these breath-taking glimpses, teasers. Mom was right, it might take time, but God, will it be worth it.

169

"If only I'd known what I was letting myself in for, letting the guy who owns *Grayson Designs* into my house." She arches an eyebrow at me.

Shit.

I meant to tell her. I really had. But how do you casually bring up in conversation that you own a multi-million-pound hotel re-modeling business without sounding like a total dick?

"Why didn't you tell me who you are?" she asks calmly. Although, from what I've learned about her, this could be a smokescreen for the fire that could follow.

"I didn't think it mattered. You thought I was a smug wanker to start with, anyway." I glance at her. "Why add more ammo by telling you how successful my business is?"

"Yeah, then you'd have been a smug wanker show-off," she says. "Still, it would have been nice to know that about you before finding it out myself on the flight paperwork."

I look at her face, completely free of any emotion. I just can't tell how pissed about it she really is. *Hang on.* Why would she be pissed? She knew I had a successful business, just not to what extent. It's a minor detail surely, unless...

"You're upset that I didn't tell you, aren't you?" I say, grabbing her arm and pulling her up to the side of the building we are passing so that people can walk past. I'm standing straight in front of her now, and her eyes are burning into mine.

"No," she starts, annoyed.

"I'm sorry, Rachel. I'm sorry if you felt I wasn't honest with you." I hold her gaze. She cares; I can see it in her eyes. She wouldn't be bothered otherwise. I feel a small tug of triumph in my stomach and can't help a slight smile growing on my lips.

"In case you haven't already noticed, I don't care what you do or don't do!" she fires back harshly, glaring at me. "Am I amusing you?" she says, stepping closer and taking in my small smile.

"No, Rachel." My smile drops as I feel the briefest flash of anger threatening to spill out suddenly. Why does she keep pretending? Is the thought of caring about me really that repulsive to her? "Why would I be amused by you telling me you don't care? After all, I've heard it all before. You don't do relationships, you just have fuck buddies, you're incapable of having actual feelings, why should we be any different?" I hiss.

Her eyes widen, and her mouth falls open as she takes a step back from me.

Shit, what have I done?

"Rachel, I didn't mean—" I reach out for her, but the sight of her wild eyes makes me freeze.

"Fuck you, Tanner Grayson," she says, her voice thick with hurt. And with that, she turns and storms off down the street.

It's been hours, and she won't answer my calls. She's not at her hotel. I've sat here in the bar, watching the entrance for what feels like a lifetime. I've really fucked up. How could I say that to her? That she's incapable of having actual feelings? What kind of asshole am I? I don't even know what came over me. I just felt so angry when she said she didn't care what I did or didn't do. I know she's lying. I could see it in her eyes. She does care, and that my words hurt her so much proves it. Just when I thought we were getting somewhere, and she was starting to open up to me, I fucked it up big time.

"Hey, man, you want another?" The barman nods to my empty glass.

"Sure, why the hell not?"

"Woman trouble?" he asks as he places another whisky down in front of me.

"That obvious, huh?" I swirl the deep honey-colored liquid around in the glass before taking a large gulp. The burn feels good in my throat.

"By the look on your face, yeah, I'm afraid it is," he says kindly. "They're on the house." He gestures to my empty glass.

"Thanks." I give him a small smile as he goes to serve another customer.

I glance at my watch, six forty-five. This is ridiculous. I can't sit in the bar all night. If she doesn't want to speak to me, then I should know by now not to force it. If Rachel doesn't want to do something, Rachel sure as hell won't do it.

Fuck, what is it with strong-ass women and me? I get up from the bar and place a generous tip down for the barman. The drinks may be on the house, but he still had to look at my sour face for the last two hours.

As I walk into the lobby, I spot her coming in through the main revolving door. She looks up, and her eyes lock with mine. For a second, I expect her to keep revolving all the way back out onto the street to avoid me. She doesn't, though. Instead, she walks right over to me.

"Rachel—" I start, but she holds up a hand and cuts me off.

"Please, let me go first," she says.

I shut my mouth and wait.

"I would like to reimburse you for the time you spent at the house, painting," she says coolly.

She seems so in control, her voice steady. The only small sign that she's feeling uncomfortable is the subtle scratching of her wrist that she's doing without realizing.

"There's no need. I wanted to help you," I say carefully. *Where is she going with this?*

"That would imply that we are friends. And seeing as I am incapable of having *actual* feelings, then I don't see how that can be the case," she says flatly, her eyes trained on mine.

"I should never have said that." I search her eyes. "I am so sorry, Rachel," I whisper.

I can feel the hurt radiating from her towards me. I don't know all of her story, but I know that it's made it hard for her to trust and to be open. I've come along and thrown it in her face and basically called her fucked up. She was right to keep me at arm's length; I am a wanker.

"Maybe not, but it doesn't matter now. You said it, and you're probably right." Her gaze falters as she swallows.

"I'm not right. I'm an asshole," I say, inching closer to her, so we are almost touching. She doesn't move away. "I know you are very capable of feeling. I've seen it with Megan and Matt, and when you talk about Holly. I've seen it when you talk about that furry beast, Nigel." I take a gamble and reach forward, so the back of my hand brushes against hers. She sucks in a small breath as our skin meets. "You are more than capable of feeling, Rachel, and if you don't care about me, then that's because I don't deserve you to."

"There's a lot about me you don't know, Tan," she says, her voice quiet.

"Then tell me. When you're ready," I say, fighting back the urge to wrap her in my arms. I don't want to push my luck. I'm just grateful she's even talking to me right now.

She nods as though she's considering my words before looking away towards the lifts. I sense this conversation is over—for now.

"Will you have dinner with me tonight? Please?" I add, as she frowns. She stays quiet for a long time, still not looking at me, before finally she answers.

174

"Okay. Wait here while I change." She brings her eyes back to me.

I nod and watch her walk off and press the lift button. Knowing she doesn't want me to go up to her room with her stings. But I'm grateful she will even speak to me after my colossal fuck up.

Right now, I will take whatever I can get.

SEVENTEEN

RACHEL

I CLOSE THE DOOR TO MY HOTEL ROOM AND PULL MY coat off, throwing it onto the bed. I've spent the last two-and-a-half hours wandering aimlessly around the city. I spoke to Holly on the phone, who—like the incredible friend she is—listened to me go over and over Tanner's hurtful words. She didn't say "I told you so" or "serves you right." She just listened to me moan and whine and get lost in my anger and self-pity.

What the hell happened today? It started off so well. Then the next minute, we're arguing, and he's telling me I am incapable of having feelings. *God, that was low.* The only thing worse than hearing Tanner say that to me is the clawing worry inside me that it's true. What if I can't feel anything? Not properly, like a normal person?

I've never had a boyfriend before, just friends with benefits. I've never wanted to get close to anyone before. I've always thought I'm better on my own. No one else to rely on that will ultimately let me down. But recently, I've been wondering, what if I'm not a total lost cause? It must be real for some people; it must be possible. I mean, look at Holly and Jay. I've never seen a couple as in love as they are. Their path wasn't smooth, though either, not in the beginning. Although I doubt either is as fucked up as me when it comes to intimacy.

Holly said I should talk to Tanner. That a guy who's willing to do all he has for me wouldn't have meant what he said. She thinks he's as hurt by me pushing him away as I am by him basically calling me a cold-hearted bitch.

This is such a mess.

I walk across my room to my suitcase. Okay, what the hell do I wear to dinner? I've only packed casual clothes for the daytime.

I throw it open and pull the top layer of clothes out; I don't know what I'm hoping to find, although, *what the*? My eyes glimpse the silky material of one of my nicest dresses. It's a dark, smoky grey with thin straps and a gorgeous fabric that skims my hips and stops mid-thigh. Next to it are my black patent heels with a piece of paper tucked inside. I unfold it and see the words *You're welcome, Megan xxx* written in her fancy handwritten script. I'm going to have to have words with her when I get home, sneaking things into my case!

I feel a warm rush of happiness. I have great friends, one who will listen to me talk shit for hours on the phone and one who cares for me enough to know to put a dinner-worthy dress in my case. I wasn't intending to go to dinner with Tanner when he told me he was on my flight, but Megan is obviously more intuitive than me. It's more than the dress though, her doing this for me shows me I can have normal feelings.

Because right now, I want to hug her.

"I thought we could eat at the hotel I'm staying in," Tanner says as he holds open the door of the yellow cab for me.

"Sure." I pull my coat around me as I step out into the cool evening air.

He hands the driver some cash as I look up at the hotel and realize where we are. "You're staying at The Songbird?" I ask, taking in the hotel's exterior. It's magnificent and regal. It occupies one of the best spots in Manhattan, facing directly onto Central Park.

"Yeah, I'm friends with the owner."

"Griffin Parker," I say at the same time as Tanner.

He looks at my face carefully.

"Hang on, you—" I trail off as I look at Tanner, something niggling at me, deep inside. "I helped a guy get back a laptop bag once who was coming to meet Griffin Parker." I look at Tanner, who's smiling at me. "That was you?" I ask slowly, trying my best to remember more but drawing a blank.

"Yep. I'm not sure whether to be offended that you

never recognized me. I obviously made a great impression," he jokes.

"I was in such a rush I probably barely even looked at you," I say as I try my best to bring back any more detail of the day. All I remember was identifying a passenger to a security officer and hurrying off, so I wasn't late for my check-in time. I was on a warning for being late twice after getting stuck in traffic. The only reason I remember it at all is that he mentioned Griffin Parker, whom I had met on my previous flight. I remember Griffin because he was so charming and gave me some brilliant advice on web designing. *Of course, he didn't know what kind of website I was running.*

"I can't believe that was you." I study Tanner as though I might suddenly remember that day in vivid detail. "Why didn't you say something? And be careful how you answer that after earlier." I raise a brow at him.

"I was just another faceless passenger to you. I didn't expect you to remember me. Plus, schoolboy pride—why would I ask you if you remembered me when you clearly didn't at the auction? Especially when I was then admitting that I never forgot your face," he says, watching me with amusement dancing in his eyes.

"You never forgot my face?" I say, more to myself.

"Never." His eyes drop to my lips as he runs his hand through his hair.

Despite the cool evening air, heat fires through my body, heading straight between my legs. *Not this again.*

How can I lose all control over my body when he looks at me like that? It's almost as if my body surrenders control to him.

I can't believe we met before, albeit briefly. Then, a year and a half later, we were at the same auction. If I believed in higher powers at work, I might be tempted to wonder if this meant something. I know Matt would pee his pants in excitement, thinking it's some sort of magical sign when really, it's just a coincidence.

"You want to go inside?" Tanner's voice breaks into my thoughts.

"Yes, let's go," I say, as his hand goes gently to the base of my back as we walk. I pretend not to notice and let it stay there.

The restaurant itself is on a high floor set in a long, enclosed glass balcony with a glass roof. We are shown to a table with a spectacular view of Central Park and the Manhattan skyline.

"Wow, this is beautiful." I take in the regal décor. Beautiful creams and gold with dark pink velvet chairs and drapes. "Please tell me your company did this?" I say, looking around.

"We won that contract because of you." Tanner comes up behind me and slips my coat from my shoulders to hand to the server. His breath stalls, and when he lets it out, its warmth against my skin makes all the tiny hairs on the back of my neck stand up. "You look incredible," he says as his eyes roam my dress appreciatively.

"Thank you." I sit down as he pushes my chair in for me.

"You know, Griffin's a good friend now," Tanner says as he takes his seat. "We spent most of the meeting talking about his boat." He smiles over the table at me, and I smile back. "I went out on it with him quite a few times while I was living here for the year."

"Oh, I remember you saying you'd lived here for a year at the whisky night."

"You listen to me sometimes then?" He smirks, "When I'm not a total idiot, anyway." His face falls.

"Let's not talk about it anymore."

I don't know what happened this afternoon, but I don't need a replay; once was enough.

"Okay." He nods gratefully, running his hand around the back of his neck, his shoulders relaxing. "So, you like the design then?" He gestures around the restaurant.

"I do; I love it. It's regal and in keeping with the history of the building. Totally different to the place in London we went to with the *Grayson* bar." I smirk.

"Oh, don't," he groans. "I never wanted them to call it that. My friend, Drew, told them to go ahead. He thought he was a right comedian, heard about it around the office for weeks." Tanner shakes his head, smiling.

I settle back in my chair and listen as he talks about work, his face lighting up with enthusiasm and passion. I could watch and listen to him all night like this. Seeing him get so animated over something he has clearly worked so hard to achieve is wonderful. I swallow a niggle of unease down as something hits me—I am on a date, an actual date, and I'm enjoying myself.

"This isn't a guise to get you to my room, I promise," Tanner says smoothly as he opens the door to the penthouse suite. "I just wanted to show you more of the work we did when I was over here."

I can't stop the gasp from flying out of my mouth as I look around the room. It's the same regal theme as the rest of the hotel; creams and golds with dusky pink. A circular inner hallway greets us first, a giant vase of fresh flowers spilling out of it in an elaborate display. Sets of giant, ornate double doors lead off the hallway before opening into a magnificent open-plan kitchen, dining, and living area.

"Gym, office, meeting room." Tanner points at various doors off the hallway. "There are three en suite bedrooms down there, and the master is that way." He extends a hand across the open living area to another set of ornate doors.

"This is stunning," I say, running my hand over the cool marble of the kitchen island.

"Praise from you is praise indeed." Tanner smiles, his hands pushed deep in his suit pants pockets.

I shoot him a "watch it" look, and he shakes his

head as he laughs and looks down at the floor. "You're something else, Rachel."

Seeing him standing there, in his dark blue suit, my body's reaction to him betraying me is almost too much to handle. I can't take my eyes off his face—his dark eyes full of warmth when he smiles, the thick, dark waves of his hair. Some strands fall forward as he looks at the floor.

What the hell is going on here?

"Are you okay?" he asks, his eyes coming back up and resting on my face.

My heart races in my chest. *Am I okay?* I don't know what the hell is going on here. I just know that if he doesn't touch me soon, I feel like I might combust.

"Yeah, fine," I reply as he walks over to me.

Why does he have to have this effect on me? This isn't me. I'm always the one in control. His warm, spicy cologne dances into my senses as I look up at him. He's standing in front of me, close enough that if I just lean forward slightly, I could sink against his chest, into his arms.

"You don't sound fine," he says. "Where's snarky gone?"

I raise my eyebrows. "She's having a night off. It's exhausting being around you. You give her far too much material to work with." I look up at him from under my lashes.

Tanner gives me the most pantie-soaking devilish grin I've ever seen. "She's not so bad. I don't mind being called a wanker by you if it's under the right circumstances."

He lifts his hand and dusts his thumb over my bottom lip. I'm frozen to the spot, just watching him, my skin buzzing at his touch.

"Although, it might be nice to try something different while she's not here," he whispers as he puts his fingers under my chin and gently tilts it up, his lips coming to meet mine gently.

His kiss is soft, and he takes his time to caress my lips, his fingers still holding my chin delicately. "You're so beautiful," he murmurs against my lips, and his words act as a key, unlocking me so that my hands can wrap up around his face and draw him closer.

He brings his hands to cup my face, and we kiss deeply, savoring each other, our bodies pressed as tightly together as they can get. I could stay right here in this moment, forever.

Tanner's kisses pause, but his hands stay on my face, his thumbs stroking my cheeks as he looks at me with the depth of the universe in his eyes.

"Trust me," he whispers as he drops his hands to my bum and lifts me up with ease. My dress rides up around my waist as I wrap my legs around him, crossing my ankles around his back as I draw him back into another kiss, my hands never leaving his face. "I will never hurt you on purpose, Rachel," he murmurs, his deep voice sending shivers down over my skin as he carries me across the room. He holds me with one arm, his eyes never leaving mine, as he opens the door to the bedroom and takes us both inside.

We fall onto the bed together, Tanner's lips back on mine as he presses his entire body against me. This feels so different from the other times—his kisses, the slower pace, the way his hands caress my hair as he kisses me.

This feels tender. This feels loving.

"What's wrong?" He draws back, his dark eyes searching mine.

"Nothing," I answer quickly.

"You're all tense, Rachel." His eyes search mine.

Do I say it? God, this has never happened before.

"I'm nervous," I say quietly, avoiding his gaze as I blink furiously.

"Rachel." He turns my face back to him. His eyes are full of warmth, the amber flecks in them glowing, making me think of a log fire, the feeling of calm sitting in front of it with the heat radiating out on a frosty night. "I'm nervous too." He smiles. "You make me nervous every fucking day."

I stare back at him, feeling my body loosen slightly. "That is *not* true. How can being with me make you nervous?"

He rubs his thumb back and forth across my lips, his eyes watching their path as though he's contemplating his next words carefully. "It's not being with you that makes me nervous," he says, his eyes rising to meet mine again, "it's the thought of being without you that does."

My eyes widen as I look back at him. He's studying me carefully, waiting for my reaction. No one has ever said anything like that to me before, not even close. I can feel my heart beating in my chest, the sound of each pump strong in my ears, as Tanner continues to watch me.

I give him the tiniest nod. "Tan, let's be brave together," I whisper as I pull him back to me and kiss him with everything I have. His hand goes down to my leg, pulling it up around him as he sinks into the kiss, a low groan escaping his lips as I pull the back of his shirt from his pants and run my hands up the firm muscles of his back.

"God, Rachel," he moans, pressing into me so I can feel his erection against my inner thigh.

"Take it off, Tan," I murmur between kisses, "take it all off."

He sits back on his knees and smiles at me as he shrugs his jacket off, then yanks his tie loose, passing it over his head. I'm growing wetter just watching him, my pulse now taking up its own steady rhythm between my legs.

He's sultry, sexy, and wears a suit better than anyone I've ever seen. There's no way I could be anything less than soaking wet for him right now. My eyes rake over his hard, toned stomach as he discards his shirt and stands at the bottom of the bed. He kicks off his shoes, undoing his belt and removing every item of clothing until his cock hangs hard and thick between his legs.

"Your turn, Snow," he whispers.

I sit up and slide to the bottom of the bed, pulling my shoes off, before sinking my feet into the thick carpet as I stand up next to him. I watch his Adam's apple move in his throat as he swallows deeply. His eyes cast down to where my dress skims my legs. He clears his throat as I lift the hem and pull it off over my head, my hair tumbling back down to my shoulders as I drop the silk fabric onto the floor.

"Jesus." He lets out a breath at the sight of my white lace strapless bra and thong. I watch his jaw tense and his eyes darken as I reach around and unhook it, holding it out to the side and letting it drop on top of my dress. The air hits my nipples, and they tighten under his gaze. I've never felt so sexy, and all he's doing is watching me. Finally, I gently roll the thin lace down over my hips and let my thong drop to the floor before stepping out of it.

"I must have been a fucking saint in a previous life," Tanner says, reaching forward and gently pulling me against his body. The heat of his skin meeting mine makes me moan out loud. He smiles down at me. "Moaning already? I haven't even started yet," he says darkly as his lips take mine, and he moves us back onto the bed.

He lays over the top of me, one muscular thigh between my legs, teasing them apart. His lips continue their exploration of mine, and he gently pushes deeper, his tongue seeking mine, stroking and tasting me. I whimper against his lips; my body has been taken over by someone I don't even recognize.

"I love the sounds you make." His lips drop to my neck, trailing open-mouthed kisses from my ear to my collarbone and back as his fingers reach between my legs and swipe through my hot flesh. "You're so wet," he says in awe as he gently slides two fingers deep inside me and pumps them slowly, swirling them around, hitting my g-spot.

"Tan." I shudder, my back arching off the bed.

What he's doing feels so good, so intense. He's moving a lot slower than usual. We've always gone at it hard and heavy before, but this is different. He's taking his time, and it feels incredible.

I place my hands on either side of his face again, running my fingers along his jaw as I pull him back to kiss me. I want him closer, deeper; I need him; I need all of him.

"I need you inside me," I whisper, clenching down on his fingers to stress my point.

"Whatever you want, Rachel, I'll just get—" he tries to pull away to get a condom.

"I want you," I say, looking into his eyes. "I need all of you tonight."

He looks at me, his brow creasing as it dawns on him what I mean. "Are you sure?"

I nod. "I'm on the pill, and I've always used condoms... so if you have, too?" I search his eyes.

"I swear, every single time. I've never..." he trails off, "... it would be the first time."

"Mine too," I say, watching him.

He pauses before leaning forward and gently taking my lips in his again, our kisses deepening further while his skilled fingers continue their worshipping inside my body. The intensity of it has me bucking off the bed within minutes. I pull back and grab onto his wrist, my breath hitching in my throat. "If you keep doing that, I'm going to come."

A dark smile crosses Tan's face, "then what are you doing stopping me?" He tilts his chin forward, his eyes focused on my face as he continues stroking me in deep circles with two fingers, his thumb stroking my clit at the same time. I'm writhing underneath him, completely at his mercy, and he knows it.

"Tan," I moan.

"That's it, Snow. Come for me. You're so beautiful when you come." His command sends me over the edge, and his eyes never leave my face as the first burst of my orgasm pushes through to the surface, and I contract around his fingers.

"Tan," I moan again.

"I'm here, Snow, I'm here," he says, his lips finding mine again as his fingers delve deeper, harder. The next contraction hits me, and I'm unraveling beneath him, kissing him between each gasp and moan. My hands in his hair, his name keeps tumbling from my lips repeatedly as I shudder uncontrollably.

"Oh, God," I whisper as the last shudder leaves my body.

"You have no idea how long I've waited for you,

Rachel," he says as he slowly slides his fingers out of me, pausing to look at me as if silently checking one last time.

I give him a small nod and hold his gaze as he positions himself over me, holding himself up with his arms. He pauses for a second and then slowly pushes inside me, inch by thick inch.

"Rach," he hisses. His eyes look like they might roll back in his head. "God, you feel amazing," he forces out through gritted teeth.

My eyes see him, but I'm lost in my own intense pleasure, knowing that he's inside me, bare skin to bare skin. Nothing has ever felt so intense before.

So right.

A whole new wave of arousal spills from my body, surrounding him as he pumps into me slowly.

"God," he hisses again, his eyes coming to mine.

I lift one hand up to the side of his face, and he turns to kiss the inside of my wrist as I spread my legs wider beneath him. My other hand drops to his hip, and with each thrust, I pull him closer, brushing him against my clitoris. I want him as deep and close as I can possibly have him, wanting him and all of this to be mine.

All mine.

Even though it scares the shit out of me to admit it.

I want him more than I've ever wanted anything before.

His arms shake, and his chest expands with each breath he draws in as he slides in and out of me with increasing speed. I'm mesmerized by his face. His dark eyes haven't left mine, and his lips are murmuring my name as though he has to convince himself that I'm real and am actually here with him.

"Rachel," he groans loudly, lowering his arms, so they're on either side of my head, his hands reaching into my hair as he pushes into me again.

I grind against him. His eyes lock onto mine, and with one more thrust, he's coming hard inside me. The telling swell of his cock as he pumps out his hot orgasm is too much, and I feel my own release explode around him, wrapping him tighter, drinking him in.

I reach both hands around to his buttocks and pull them hard against me as I force my legs as wide as they will go, pulling his orgasm into me as mine continues to ravage through me. I want to feel every shudder, every tightening of his body inside me, and every response of mine around him.

His mouth finds mine, and he gives me a kiss that steals my breath. We ride our orgasms out together, sweat covering our bodies. Finally, we stop shaking, and our breathing returns to normal. Tanner's hands are still in my hair, gently stroking through it as our kisses grow softer and slower.

"You are fucking incredible, Rachel Jones," Tanner says quietly, a slow, sexy smile spreading over his lips as he rests his forehead against mine.

"And you're—" I begin.

"Don't say a wanker," he jokes, his eyes sparkling at me.

I smile back at him. "And you're not so bad yourself, Tanner Grayson," I say, pressing a kiss to his lips.

He grins back at me.

I don't stand a chance. I know now that I'm done fighting. I'm done pushing him away. As his dark eyes gaze into mine, I feel something I've never felt before.

I feel like I belong.

EIGHTEEN

TANNER

I HOLD RACHEL IN MY ARMS FOR A LONG TIME afterward, just stroking my hand up and down over her skin, her head resting against my chest. I'm the happiest I've ever been. This feeling—this fucking euphoria—is better than any multi-million-dollar business deal I've ever closed. We've turned a corner, she's finally letting me in. I've never made love like that with a woman before. All those previous fucks in my life mean nothing compared to what I feel when I'm with Rachel, and I have never had sex without a condom before—ever. Knowing she hasn't either but wanted to with me—I feel like I've won at the fucking game of life.

"As much as I could stay here forever, shall we take a shower?" I ask, pressing a kiss against the top of her head.

"No, a bath." She wraps her arm around my waist tighter. "I love taking a bath."

I smile; a bath it is.

Once she's filled it with more bubbles than I've ever seen in my life, Rachel announces the bath is ready, and I watch her petite frame slide in underneath the water, a small, contented sigh escaping her lips as the water comes up around her. Her nipples are covered by foam—much to my disappointment.

"It's a good job we designed this suite with giant bathtubs," I say as I step into the hot water and sink down behind her. She moves forward so that I can position my legs around her, and then she lowers herself back against my chest as I relax against the side.

I could get used to this.

"It's almost like you knew I'd be here one day," she jokes, sounding the most relaxed I've ever heard her.

"If I knew that, I would have spent every day since we met walking around with a permanent hard-on in anticipation," I reply dryly.

Her back moves against my chest as she laughs.

"So, why do you like baths so much?" I dip my head down to the side so I can press a kiss to her temple.

She blows out a long breath.

"You know I told you I didn't have any family?" she says after a long pause.

"Yeah." I stroke her arms under the water, marveling at how her skin is like silk against my palms.

"Well, I had a mom once, obviously. But she died when I was a baby, and because I never knew who my father was, I grew up in foster care."

I continue stroking her arms, not wanting to let the intense reaction go that's threatening to spill out of me.

My beautiful Snow.

"You didn't exactly get a minute to yourself to relax in the bath, there was always someone hammering on the door for their turn, and that's if you were lucky enough to have a lock on the door. I always knew that I wanted it to have a nice bathroom when I had my own house. Somewhere I could spend hours, soaking in peace if I wanted to."

"That's why you lit up when you saw the roll-top bath at Rich's—I mean *your* house now." I smile, a piece of the puzzle slotting in.

"Yeah," Rachel says thoughtfully, "I could see myself in there."

"I could see you too if there weren't so many bubbles." I cough, blowing one off my face.

"You make me laugh, Tan," she says warmly.

"Do I?" I beam, feeling rather pleased with myself.

"You do... when you're not being a smug, annoying wanker." She turns her head to the side so I can see her smirk.

"Can't be perfect all the time," I joke.

"No, I guess," she says, turning back around. "I'm certainly not."

"What are you talking about now, woman?" I mutter, keeping my voice light, hoping not to put her off sharing whatever it is she's about to let me into. Whatever it is, I'll take it. I want to know all about her, all her secrets, all her fears. I don't know what the fuck's got into me, but I know she is special, and I don't want to lose her.

"I push people away, Tan. I've always done it. I had some nice foster parents, but I would play up and get into trouble at school until they couldn't cope with me anymore. Then I'd get moved somewhere else, and the cycle would begin again. I just seem incapable of being normal."

Pain sears across my chest as her words sink in.

Everyone gave up on her. No one fought for her.

"If you want to let people in, then you need to be vulnerable sometimes," I say, holding her against me. "My mom was always fighting on her own when I was a kid—for years. She had plenty of friends, but it's only been since she met Peter that I've seen her look genuinely happy. She's got someone to lean on, share her worries and support her."

"I love the way you talk about your mom." Rachel sighs as she leans further into me. "It's obvious you're very close."

"We are. Although Drew calls it differently, he says I'm a momma's boy."

"Fire him." Rachel throws back without missing a beat, and I lean my head back and laugh in surprise. "He doesn't know what he's talking about. Plus, he called me feisty at the club."

"He was wrong, was he?" I tease.

"Hell, yeah. He should have called me a wild bitch!" She laughs. "Not just feisty, it's almost an insult.

I need to work on my confrontation technique if that's all that he took from it."

I laugh easily again. "I certainly got your wild streak that night. I thought you were going to rip my hand off when I held your wrist."

"I was," Rachel says, finding one of my hands underneath the water and pulling it up, holding it between her own. Hers looks so tiny and delicate in comparison. "I'm so glad I didn't, though, not now I know what they're capable of. It would have been a terrible waste."

"Are you suggesting I'm good with my hands?" I ask, raising my hips, so my erection rubs against her ass under the water.

"I'd say fair. Good is a little too generous," she teases, and my cock twitches in response.

"I see snarky bitch is back out of her cage."

"Yes, she is... why? Do you want to try to show her who the boss is? See where that gets you?" Rachel whispers over her shoulder at me.

"You bet I fucking do," I say as I spin her around in the water and wrap her in my arms.

One hard and fast fucking session later—that ended with the bathroom floor getting flooded by half of the bathwater—and we're curled up in bed together, under the duvet. Rachel's deep, rhythmic breathing tells me she's fallen asleep. I lift the duvet up gently to peek at her naked body, wrapped around me.

Yes, this shit is really happening. I'm the luckiest bastard alive.

I pull her closer with my arm that's wrapped under her, and she moans softly, her fingers moving lightly over my chest.

I'm going to get the best fucking night's sleep.

I can't get over that Rachel's still here and hasn't pulled a runner yet. She's still fast asleep on her side with me curled around behind her, holding her in my arms, a raging hard-on pressing into her ass cheeks. I can't help it; she's my ultimate fantasy—if only she'd wake up.

I nuzzle her neck, hoping to make her stir. Apart from a small murmur, it does nothing. I smirk; last night must have really worn her out. Okay, Plan B. This time, as well as kissing her neck, I snake a hand down between her legs and stroke gently. She shuffles slightly, her legs opening enough for me to slide two fingers down over her pussy and feel how wet she already is.

Fuck. My girl's even ready for me in her sleep.

I continue to stroke her in lazy, slow movements, grinding my cock against her ass, my balls tight from needing to fill her. Last night was fucking awesome. The memory of sliding into her bareback could make me blow right now. It was out of this world how well we fit together. She has to be mine now. She's ruined me.

It can only ever be her, always and forever.

I nip at her shoulder gently and hear another soft murmur. She's got to be waking up now. I move my fingers away from her dripping pussy and grip her underneath her thigh, lifting it enough so I can move my cock forward and rub it over her wet opening.

Come on, baby, wake up for me, give me a sign.

"Tan?" she sighs dreamily.

Bingo.

I push forwards and slide inside her, groaning as she gasps out loud. I hold still, deep inside her, the head of my cock throbbing as I fight to keep control. "Fuck, Rachel," I hiss out.

"What took you so long?" her delicate voice teases. "I've been awake ages."

"Why you... God, you'll be the death of me, woman," I groan as I let my control go and slam into her with hard, fast thrusts.

"I hope not," she pants, "who'll fuck me like this then?"

I grab a fistful of her hair as I plow into her, feeling her soaking my cock more with each deep thrust. "No one's ever going to fuck you again except me, do you understand?"

She cries out as she pushes back onto me, her greedy pussy sucking me in tight.

"Say it!" I growl as my balls slap against her ass.

"Tan," she moans as I feel her tightening around me.

"Don't you dare come until you say it." I pound into her, my hand in her hair, pulling her head back.

"No one ever fucked me right before," she cries. "It will only ever be you, Tan!" she screams as she convulses around my cock.

I feel every wave, every tightening of her as she rides it out on me.

It's fucking insane.

"That's it, Snow. That's it, baby," I growl as I dig my fingers into her skin and feel my balls explode. "Fuck!"

Her body sucks my release in, and I shudder from the force of it. As the last drop squeezes out, I let my head fall back against the pillows, panting, my heart racing wildly in my chest.

Rachel moves away, so my cock gently leaves her body before turning and laying her head next to mine on the pillow.

"If I knew that was how the morning would start, maybe I should have stayed the night a long time ago." She smirks.

"And if I knew you were awake, instead of pretending, I'd have fucked you hard a lot sooner." I smile, reaching out to run a hand over the naked curve of her hip.

"But where would the fun be in letting you get your own way all the time?" Her eyes gleam at me.

"With you, Rachel, I'm thinking getting my own

way any of the time would be an event worthy of making world headlines." I grin.

"Wanker." She smiles.

"Bitch," I throw back at her as she laughs.

I look at her, her dark hair tousled around her cheeks, her sweet, red lips parted as she looks back at me. Right here and now, she's so open and relaxed... *so fucking perfect.*

"So, what do you want to do today?" she asks, her fingers distracting me as they trace patterns across my chest.

"Stay in this room and fuck you on every surface?" I raise an eyebrow at her.

"Okay." She smiles.

"Really?" My eyes widen in delight.

"No!" She laughs. "I want to go out in the city. New York is beautiful at this time of year. The ice rink will be open at the Rockefeller Center now."

"I refer to my earlier comment—bitch," I say, sticking my bottom lip out and pretending to sulk.

"Come on, Tan," she says, trailing her fingertips up to my cheek.

"I'd rather come all over you," I say. Then I lean over and suck her bottom lip before pulling her in for a slow, deep kiss—the type of kiss that gets my previously spent cock feeling alert once again.

"If you play your cards right, then that can be arranged." She winks as she gets up out of bed and treats me to the incredible sight of her ass as she walks off into the bathroom.

I guess the conversation is over.

"I don't think I'm going to sit down for a week!" I moan as we walk.

"Don't be dramatic; you only fell twice," Rachel says, wrapping her hands around her takeaway latte and bringing it to her lips. There's a definite chill in the air today. Winter has come to New York.

"Five times! I fell five times. Did you not see that kid laughing at me? I swear, that little dude deserves coal in his stocking this year," I grumble, the muscles in my butt aching as I walk. Why did I agree to go ice-skating after taking Rachel back to her hotel to get changed? I've never been any good at it. Rach, on the other hand, glided around gracefully, like a fucking ice princess.

She looks up at the lights of the giant Christmas tree, stopping to admire it, a faraway look in her eyes.

"What are you so deep in thought about?" I ask, taking a drink of my coffee as I watch her.

"Just Christmas." She sighs. "Do you think Scarlett will like her present?"

"I hope so. It took long enough to find it," I grumble. Rachel turns to look at me. "Yes, I'm sure she will. She's a really sweet little girl," I say more gently. My lighter tone seems to please Rachel, and she turns back to the tree and smiles.

"Good, I hope so. Every little girl deserves to believe in magic, especially at Christmas time."

"What did little Rachel believe in?" I ask, hoping she trusts me enough to share but almost dreading hearing the answer more.

She shrugs her shoulders. "I wished every year to feel like I belonged, could be normal, like the other kids at school. Unfortunately, we don't always get what we wish for, Tan," she says, her eyes still focused on the tree.

"Maybe some magic just takes longer," I say gently, lacing my fingers between hers.

She wraps her fingers back around mine as she looks over at me. "Yeah, maybe."

Her eyebrows are knitted together, and I can tell she's overthinking again. I need to remember to be patient. She spent the night with me without freaking out, and now she's holding my hand in public. They're all victories worth celebrating, the best ones being the rare times I see her fully relaxed and smiling—*really* fucking smiling.

I swear I was made to live just for those moments.

"I need to head back. My check-out is in a couple of hours," Rachel says, walking again. I'm relieved that she hasn't let go of my hand.

"Sure, I'll walk you back."

"What are you going to do for the rest of your stay?" she asks.

"I'm having dinner with some of the team from the New York office tonight. We've got a site visit tomorrow, and I want to go over the plans and meet with the client again before work starts. Then I'm coming home and hopefully going to a housewarming party of a sexy woman I know."

"Sounds busy."

"It is. The best bit, though..." I lean toward her to whisper in her ear, her jasmine perfume evident on her skin, "is wondering whether she's going to be wearing any panties under the tight, red dress she'll be wearing."

I move back and look at her face. It gives nothing away.

"What makes you think she's going to wear a dress?" She stares straight ahead as we walk.

"Because then it's easier to slide my fingers up inside her tight pussy and rub that sweet spot she loves me touching so much."

"You sound rather sure of yourself. What makes you so certain she loves you touching it?" she asks as we walk, the people around us hurrying with their bags full of shopping, oblivious to our conversation.

"Well, it's either the way she moans my name like it's the only word that makes any sense, or how she comes in under three minutes every time I stroke it."

I glance over at the small smile pulling up the corner of her lips.

"Three minutes? I think you're exaggerating."

"Nope, I don't think so. I'm pretty certain." I smirk.

"We'll see." She smiles, throwing her empty cup in the bin, along with mine.

My enjoyment from our little chat is cut short as I recognize the tall blonde heading towards us.

Mandy.

God, this is all I need. She approaches us, dressed entirely in black, her makeup immaculate, her long, platinum hair shining under the winter sun. Like a black widow spider, ready to annihilate its prey.

"Tanner, what a lovely surprise," she says, leaning in to kiss me on both cheeks, a cloud of rich perfume tickling my throat.

"Hello, Mandy." I cough.

Her eyes scan over Rachel, her penciled eyebrows raising as she notices our hands held together.

"Rachel, this is Mandy. Mandy, Rachel," I say, my social etiquette taking charge when I'd rather just ignore her and keep walking.

"It's nice to meet you. I love your coat!" Rachel exclaims.

Mandy's brow furrows the tiniest bit—as much as her Botox allows, anyway—before she flashes a dazzling smile. "Why, thank you. It was a gift from Tanner," she says smoothly.

"That doesn't surprise me; Tan has great taste in clothes," Rachel replies easily, smiling politely.

My eyes flick between the two women. "Well, we've got to be going. Take care, Mandy," I say as I start walking, Rachel keeps in step beside me. I wait until the end of the block before my words tumble out.

"We dated for a few months when I was living here. I didn't exactly buy her that coat either. She forgot her purse when we were out together. She forgot her purse a lot when we were together," I say.

"You don't need to explain, Tanner," Rachel says lightly, brushing it off.

She stops in front of a building, and I realize we're already back at her hotel. "I'll walk you up to your room." I reach forward to push the giant revolving door.

"No." She stops me and pulls my arm back, wrapping it around her waist instead. "You won't. I need to get ready for my flight home, and you will just be a distraction."

"I thought you liked my distractions?" I grin, gripping her tightly.

"I never said I didn't," she whispers, leaning forward to kiss me, one hand still clasped in mine and the other reaching up to hold my face. Her lips are warm and sweet. If we weren't in the street, I would push her up against the wall right now and lose myself in them.

She breaks the kiss and steps away. "See you at the party." She gives me a smile that lights up her entire face, and then she turns and heads in through the revolving door without looking back.

NINETEEN

RACHEL

"Then what happened?" Megan asks, her eyes glued to me as I tell her and Holly about New York with Tan.

"Then we go ice-skating, and he falls on his ass."

"Aww no, bless him." Holly giggles.

I've got the laptop set up on the coffee table so we can all see each other. It's four in the afternoon here, eight in the morning for Holly in LA.

"He'll live." I snort, causing both Holly and Megan to laugh.

"Ever the concerned girlfriend, hey?" Megan jokes.

"Whoa, whoa," I say, stroking Nigel, who's spread himself out over my lap. "I'm not his girlfriend."

Megan folds her arms and smiles at Holly, both knowing me well enough to leave that point—for now, at least.

"We bumped into one of his ex-girlfriends, though."

"Did you use one of your kickboxing moves on her?" Megan's eyes light up.

"More like, killed her with kindness, I bet," Holly says.

"Exactly." I smile at Holly. "Although something she said has got me thinking. Well, something Tanner said, really."

"What was it?" Megan asks.

"She said Tanner had bought her this really expensive-looking designer coat she was wearing. It was really nice."

"What's wrong with that?" Holly asks. "If they were dating, I'm sure he gave her the odd gift?"

"Yeah, I know. Only, afterward, Tanner said that he didn't intend to buy it for her; she forgot her purse. He said she forgot her purse all the time."

"Gold-digging hussy!" someone calls out from behind Holly.

"Matt! Either get in the conversation properly or piss off," I fire back. "And don't get too comfortable there; you aren't getting a guest house built!"

Holly's camera is engulfed by Matt's up-close middle finger extended towards me as he walks by. "Stefan and I are off out for breakfast. You can fill me in on the rest at the house party when I get back," he calls.

"Finally, now we can talk about what the hell that is he's wearing!" I wink at Holly.

"Still here!" he yells back as we all laugh.

"Okay, so back to Tanner's ex. Why are you

bothered if she was using him for his money?" Megan asks, focusing us all again.

"Well, the way I see it, he was pretty unimpressed that she seemed all too happy to use him for his money when it suited her," I say.

"And?" Holly encourages.

"And... well, how am I meant to tell him I used to sell my worn panties for money now?" I groan, throwing my head back against the sofa. Nigel nudges his head into my hand, encouraging me to stroke him again. "I know, boy, I know you'd never judge me," I whisper to him as I rub his ears.

"That's totally different," Holly says.

"How is it?" I sigh.

"Holly's right," Megan says, glancing at the screen as Holly nods, "that was a business you set up to save for something really important—this house." She waves her arms around the room.

"Plus, you don't even do it anymore," Holly says. "You stopped as soon as you achieved your goal."

"Do you even need to tell him?" Megan asks.

"I don't know." I shrug. "Being honest goes with this whole 'new Rachel' I'm trying to embrace. The one who opens up to her feelings and stays after sex. It's a whole new world, I'm telling you."

"You like it, though?" Holly asks hopefully.

"It's... growing on me," I admit, with a small smile.

"Yes!" Megan grins. "I knew it. I said you'd meet someone that made you want the romance one day."

"Yeah, your soulmate of dating, remember?" Holly

smiles, referring to a conversation I had with her when she met Jay.

"Hang on, don't get carried away. I've only just learned his last name," I say seriously.

"Yeah, we know. He's Tanner-loaded-Grayson." Megan rolls her eyes.

"Exactly. He's Mr. Money-bags, who has an issue with an ex using him to get money spent on her. What if he thinks the panty business is the same thing?" I say.

"He won't," Holly says decidedly. "It's not the same thing at all, Rach. Loads of flight attendants do it, so it's hardly shocking. Plus, you weren't using men for their money. They were more than happy to pay, and besides, you only ever had one customer, anyway."

"When did you get so great at arguing a point?" I joke.

"Four words, Matt and guest house." She laughs.

"You're right. Maybe it makes it easier for a guy to handle, knowing there's only one potential weirdo out there sniffing on my things?" I joke.

"Totally." Megan nods. "There's just this one, unknown Mr. X, who doesn't even know who you really are and what you look like. He's not even a client anymore. He's probably forgotten all about you by now. Tanner has nothing to be bothered about."

"You're right, you're both right," I say. "He has nothing to be bothered about, and if he's going to be a dick about it, then that's his choice."

"So, you're going to tell him then?" Holly asks.

"Yeah, I'll tell him. What have I got to lose?"

Two days later and I'm applying my red lipstick when the doorbell rings. "I'll get it!" I call to Megan as I shake my hair in front of the mirror.

This will have to do. It's seven-thirty, and our friends will start arriving at eight for the housewarming. We've only invited a handful of people; some from the airline, a few of Megan's new colleagues from her office, our new neighbor Lucy, and Tanner and his friend Drew.

I walk down the stairs in my high black stilettos and open the front door.

"You can take instructions then?" Tanner says as his eyes roam over my figure-hugging red dress, an appreciative smile on his lips.

Wait for it. Yep, there's the hand in the hair too.

I give him a coy smile. "I don't know what you're talking about."

He puts the box of drinks and snacks down that he's holding and pulls me into his arms, his mouth flying to my neck as his hands roam over my ass.

"Just how well did you listen? That's the question," he growls into my neck, kissing it roughly as his hands try to slide up underneath my dress.

"Easy boy." I smirk, sliding his hand back down off my thigh. "If I think you deserve it, then I may give you the answer to your question later," I throw over my shoulder as I head into the kitchen.

I hear him groan to himself as he picks the box up and follows me. "I thought I may have gotten a warmer welcome than that. I haven't seen you since New York," he says to me, pretending to look hurt as he places the box down on the counter and starts taking out bottles of champagne and wine.

"Three days is nothing. Wait until I get rostered a Sydney flight again. You won't see me for at least a week," I say, peering into the box at all the fancy-looking cheese, crackers, and dips next to the bottles.

"That's not fucking happening," he blurts.

I look up and raise an eyebrow at his pouting face.

"I'd come with you. I can work remotely," he says, his expression already softening as he considers his solution.

"What? No!" I scoff, shaking my head at how ridiculous he sounds. "You're not following me around when I'm working."

He looks at me darkly. "We'll save this discussion for when it's more relevant. Tonight is your party, and it's about celebrating your new home and how hard you've worked."

I narrow my eyes at him. Why does he have to look so spectacularly sexy when he's all dark and brooding? He's got dark jeans and an olive-green shirt on, the sleeves rolled up his tanned forearms.

"So, what's all this?" I ask, happy to change topics.

"These..." he gestures to the Michelin star-worthy

items he's setting out, "are some things for your guests to enjoy."

"What did you do? Raid Harrods food court?" I pick up a bottle of Cristal champagne and quickly put it down as I mentally tally up how many bottles he's brought. "Tanner, there's at least two grand worth of champagne here, let alone all the wine and food."

His brow creases. "Oh! Almost forgot, there's one more thing in the car." He disappears out the front door, reappearing minutes later with another giant box in his arms.

"What the hell's that?" I cry as I move bottles aside so he can put the box down on the counter.

"This," he lifts the lid theatrically, "is your new home cake!"

I look in the box, and my hand flies to my mouth. "Is that...? Did you and Megan plan this?" I ask as I take in the picture on the cake.

"We sure did," a happy voice sings, and I turn to see Megan walk into the room. She's wearing a dark blue sparkly dress, her curls tumbling down her back. "Do you like it?"

"I love it," I whisper, staring at the printed illustration on the cake. There's the front of the house, looking all cool and sleek with its grey paint, large bay window, and black railings. Then stood in front of the door are Me and Megan, Nigel wrapped in my arms.

"I can't believe you two did this without me even knowing." I look up between the two of them.

"It was worth all the extra late-night sketching just

to see your face right now." Megan smiles, "Although I can't take all the credit. It was Tan's idea."

I look up at him, and he's watching my face carefully, an easy smile on his lips. "I'm glad you like it," he says, his voice warm and deep.

"I do, thank you." I reach over, squeeze Megan's hand, and then turn back to Tanner and wrap my fingers around his.

"Right, I'm just going to take Nigel next door to Lucy," Megan says.

Tanner looks at me.

"She's our next-door neighbor who's coming to the party. She's got older kids who are going to look after Nigel until the party's finished," I explain.

"We were worried he wouldn't like all the noise and people," Megan says as she goes to the dining room and picks up his cat-carrying crate. A moment later, she carries him in from the living room and encourages him into the crate with a treat. "See you guys in ten," she calls over her shoulder as she heads into the hallway with him.

As the door shuts, Tanner's eyes come to my face, glinting with mischief. "Ten whole minutes of you to myself. That's the most I will probably get this evening once your guests arrive."

I put my palms on his chest as I look up at him. "What are you going to do with your ten minutes?" I smile.

"Seven minutes, baby. I know exactly what I'm doing with my first three." And with that, he pulls my skirt up roughly around my waist. He leans me back against the kitchen counter as he expertly slides two fingers inside my pussy, where I'm already wet just from the desire of having him close by.

"Tan," I gasp.

"That's it," he growls as I part my legs wider, and his fingers find my g-spot while his thumb goes straight to my clit, rubbing in small circles with the perfect pressure. "I hoped you'd remember me saying I wanted no panties under this dress," he says as his lips crash against mine and his tongue claims my mouth.

I break our kiss, already panting from my growing orgasm. "And I remember you saying you didn't need three whole minutes," I say, watching his eyes light up at my challenge.

"Prepare to scream out my name, Snarky." He smirks as he leans in and bites my bottom lip.

I push back against him, kissing him hard, my hands braced on the kitchen counter behind me as his fingers continue their assault on my senses. He slides them out before slowly adding a third and finger fucking me roughly, hitting my g-spot and swollen clit with each thrust. My legs shake underneath me as I feel what's coming.

"Tan," I moan loudly as I roll my head back and come in deep, intense surges, my body hugging his fingers tightly.

"That's it, Snow. Cover my fingers with your juices. I'm going to enjoy sucking it off," Tanner growls as I look back into his eyes. His jaw is set hard as I writhe against his hand, whimpering at the intensity of the fast orgasm he just gave me. I take a couple of deep breaths and let out a contented sigh as relaxation sweeps through me.

Tanner's dark eyes hold mine as he slowly slides his fingers out and brings them to his lips, slowly sucking each one down to his knuckles. I could come again, just watching him do it. The intensity in his eyes looks hot enough to burn me. Once he's finished, he gently smooths my dress back down over my hips and thighs and plants a gentle kiss on my lips.

"That will have to be enough until I can have you again properly," he says, readjusting himself in his jeans. "And for the record, that was two minutes and fifty-three seconds." He smirks.

"Show-off." I smile at him, my senses completely heightened and every nerve ending on high alert in anticipation of when we can finish what we started.

This is going to be one long party.

"Then Tan says, 'leave it, mate, Drew can manage', and I'm left holding this fucking massive chandelier that costs sixty grand while balancing on the highest ladder. Scared shitless of letting go in case something didn't fix right, and it's about to smash all over the floor."

Matt titters in delight at another of Drew's stories about him and Tanner in the early days when less than ten people were working for him—before the business grew and started winning more and more lucrative contracts and expanding overseas. I look around at Megan, Matt, and a couple of guys from Megan's office who are completely engrossed in Drew's amusing stories.

"Want to escape to the kitchen for a refill?" Tanner whispers to me.

I lift my glass and down the remaining half glass of my champagne. "I do now." I smile.

As we head towards the kitchen, the doorbell rings.

"I'll get it, you go ahead," I say.

Tanner smiles at me, taking my glass, and heads into the kitchen. Lyndsey and Katie, two other flight attendants, clock him going in and make a beeline to talk to him. My eyes roll. He's been quite the star guest of the party. All my flying friends want to know who he is and how we met. And Megan's friends from her office want to pick his brains about business and talk about how he finds his inspiration for the designs. He's proving to be rather popular, and he's obviously used to it. He's answering everyone's questions with charm and humor, glancing across to me every few minutes when we're separated.

I head back through to the hallway and pull open the front door. The frosty night air whips me in the face, suddenly bringing things back into clearer focus after all the champagne I've been drinking.

"Hey, Rach." Chris leans forward and kisses me on

the lips before moving back and holding up a bottle of wine in front of my stunned face.

"What are you doing here?" I ask, unable to keep the agitation out of my voice.

"Matt mentioned you were having a party a while ago to celebrate your new house," he says, oblivious to my annoyance as he steps inside. "Looks good, Rach." He glances around. "You've done a great job." He leans a little closer, and I can smell his familiar, fresh aftershave. A scent I had become so used to after six months of *friendship*. Until recently, anyway. I haven't called or even text him once since the night before the house auction. The day that Tanner came into my life, turning it up like a hurricane.

"Thanks," I say out of politeness. "Glasses and food are in the kitchen. Actually..." I stall, remembering Tanner is in there. "Why don't you come and meet Lucy, our new next-door neighbor?" I say, steering him by the elbow into the living room and over towards the fireplace, where he can't be seen from the kitchen.

God, this is when I wish this house was bigger. Having only three rooms downstairs that all connect to each other is hardly helpful for keeping two people apart for long.

"Lucy!" I say brightly. "This is Chris; he's a pilot at Atlantic Airways. Lucy's son is interested in studying to be a pilot," I say with a wide smile as I nudge Chris forwards. I'm relieved when he extends a hand to Lucy, and her eyes light up in response as he talks.

Lucy is a total MILF, with long blonde hair and a

curvy body. I wouldn't put it past Chris to be asking for her number by the end of the night. Actually, that would really help me out. He's been texting, asking when I next want to meet up, and I've been ignoring him.

I head past Megan and her workmates, back into the kitchen where Drew has joined Tanner, Lyndsey, and Katie.

"So, tell me, is it true that some of you flight attendants sell your worn tights and panties online to make extra money?" Drew asks curiously.

I look over his shoulder accusingly to where Matt's getting himself another drink. His head snaps up, and his eyes meet mine. He shakes his head subtly.

Okay, he's usually the one with the big mouth, but he's implying it wasn't him. I groan inwardly. I hope this is just an unlucky coincidence.

"Where did you hear that?" Katie laughs.

"A friend," Drew says. "Aren't you all at it, then? Please, girls, don't disappoint me." He laughs.

I notice that Tanner's scowling, his jaw tense as he listens to Drew. Maybe confessing my old side business to him isn't the best idea, judging by his reaction.

"I don't think you should believe everything your friend tells you." Lyndsey giggles. "Sure, it happens, but it's not taught in ground training or anything. Some girls do it and do very well out of it. If they're lucky, they have a regular guy who they send things to."

"Is that so?" Drew sounds amused, his eyes sparkling while he looks like he's fighting back a grin.

I glance at Tanner again, and he looks like he's about to murder someone. His eyes are dark, his jaw is set, and his fists are clenched by his sides.

"Tan," I say gently, running a hand up his arm, "I need your help upstairs. I'm sure we've got a cake knife, but I think it's still packed in a box from the move. Will you help me look?"

He tears his eyes away from Drew. "Sure," he says with an edge to his voice as he follows me out through the dining room and into the living room. I sneak a look at Chris and am relieved to see he's still deep in conversation with Lucy.

"I think it's in a box in my room. I've got a special one Holly gave me for my eighteenth birthday," I say as I climb the stairs.

I open my bedroom door and head to my wardrobe, bending to root around in the box at the bottom. "I'm sure it's here somewhere," I mutter as I lift the photo albums and an old version of the flying uniform I still have. The one from before it was re-designed to the new one with patent red shoes.

"Did Megan draw this?" Tanner asks.

I look over to the picture on my wall he's staring at.

"Yeah, she did." I smile as I stand beside him.

"She looks like you, Rach," Tanner says, his voice faltering slightly as he continues to stare at the picture.

"She's my mom," I say, my shoulders drooping as I look at her beautiful, delicate face with fair skin, dark wavy hair, bright eyes, and red lips. "I don't have many photos of her, but this is one of my favorites. Megan drew it for me as a gift after she moved in."

"She's beautiful, Rachel," Tanner whispers, seemingly unable to take his eyes away from the drawing. "Why has she written this here?" He points to Megan's fancy script writing across the bottom of the picture.

"Oh, well, I think it was one of my mom's favorite sayings. She had it on a keyring. Again, one of the few things I have of hers. But it obviously meant something to her as she kept it," I say sadly as I reach for my purse and take the keyring out, holding it up.

Tanner reaches out and carefully takes the silver heart between his fingers, turning it over in his palm.

"Have you ever heard it before?" I ask, "It's quite unusual, isn't it?"

"Difficult roads lead to beautiful destinations," he murmurs quietly, totally absorbed as he looks from the picture of my mom to the keyring in his hand and back again. "I have heard it, yes. More than once."

"I've never heard it anywhere else before, but I think if I did, it would be Mom sending me a message." I smile, taking it from his hand and putting it back into my purse. "I'm too scared to use it on my keys in case it gets scratched," I explain when I see his puzzled face as I put it away.

I head back to the wardrobe and rifle around in the box some more. "Found it!" I smile, wielding the knife in the air like a trophy.

"Hey, watch it!" Tanner yells, "You almost had my balls off!"

"How do you know that's not what I was aiming for?" I smirk at him.

"Be careful, Snow, or I might have to fuck those pretty red lips of yours as punishment for your snarky attitude." He takes my hand and pulls me to my feet.

"You'd have to do it without your balls then," I tease.

He pulls me to him sharply, his teeth swooping down on my neck. "Don't fucking push me," he says through gritted teeth.

Something has definitely riled him tonight. Even though I've heard him talk like this before—and frankly, I love his dirty threats—tonight, his voice has a hard edge to it. He's pissed about something.

I curl my arms up around his neck and turn my head, inviting him to kiss me. His lips push against mine, all heat, control, and power.

As hot as it is, I'm merely a spectator, along for the ride.

"Rach! Tan! You better not be having sex up there! We want cake!" Matt's voice screeches up the stairs, breaking Tanner out of his emotionally fueled rampage of my lips.

His eyes are blazing as he looks at me. *What has got into him?*

"What's wrong?" I ask, searching his eyes.

"Nothing," he says, glancing away and back to the drawing of my mom, his grip on my waist loosening.

"Nothing." He blows out a breath. "Too much champagne, I think."

His fingers brush my hair away from my neck so he can look at where his teeth were. His face softens as he strokes my skin with his thumb. It obviously left a mark, but it can't be that bad as it didn't hurt. If anything, it was a fucking turn-on. "I'm sorry," he says softly.

"You don't need to be sorry. You just need to talk to me sometimes, like I'm trying to do with you. It works both ways, Tan," I say as I give him a small smile and hold my hand out to him to lead him downstairs. He nods silently as he wraps strong fingers around mine.

I can already feel the growing sense of dread in my stomach as we head downstairs. I did not think this through properly. There are less than twenty people here. There's no way Tanner and Chris will not see each other. Does it matter, though? It's not like Tanner will even know who he is.

God, this is one downside to having someone who is more than just a friend with benefits. This sick feeling, wondering what their reaction will be when they meet someone else you've had sex with. I would never have been in this situation before. What have I got myself into?

I look back at Tanner. His deep brown eyes widen in response to my attention on them. He's dark, brooding, and irritating. I look at his thick, wavy hair and perfect, kissable mouth. He's also sexy as fuck and funny. Maybe this is why people put themselves in awkward situations like this because against the odds, they meet someone who makes them wonder if it might be worth the risk.

I shake my head. I've had too much champagne; I sound all sloppy, like Matt, for fuck's sake. I should have stuck to the whisky, stayed with what I knew I could handle. It must be the champagne's tiny bubbles —tiny globules of mass destruction, turning your head and emotions to shit.

"What took you two so long?" Matt asks as we walk into the living room, and he quickly bustles us through the dining room towards the kitchen, where most people are squeezed in. I glance around quickly but can't see Chris. He must have been in the dining room.

"Speech!" Megan smiles as she moves aside to make space next to the cake. Tanner lets go of my hand, and I squeeze in next to her, giving her a subtle elbow in the ribs for throwing me under the bus.

"Thanks, Megan." I smile at her in mock sweetness as people laugh.

"Okay, I'll keep it short. Thank you all for coming and for helping to celebrate the new house with us. I hope you'll all visit whenever you like; you're welcome anytime." I look up and straight into Chris' eyes as he leans on the kitchen door frame, listening to me. "Well, most of you," I continue as people laugh again, thinking I'm joking. "It's been a long time coming, but here's to new starts!" I smile.

There are some cheers and whoops, and Tanner

passes me a glass of champagne, clinking his own against it as I take it from him.

"To new starts," he says, smiling. His strange mood from earlier is either momentarily forgotten or at least well disguised.

I take a sip and then place the glass down and pick the cake knife up. It seems such a shame to cut into Megan's incredible picture.

"Don't worry, I've got the original," she says to me as if sensing my hesitation.

"Well, in that case—" I laugh as I push the knife in, chopping the image in half and carving out slices, handing them to Matt, who plates them and passes them around.

"It's like being at work all over again," he jokes, "tea or coffee, anyone?" He laughs.

Lyndsey laughs and then draws him into a conversation about his next roster. I hear him say he's back in LA for most of the month. Now, why doesn't that surprise me? Megan talks to Drew and her work colleagues, telling them about the traffic cone incident. From the sounds of her work mates' comments, they think her boss is a dick too. I can't see Tanner, so I head off to find him, but I don't get far when Lucy stops me.

"Rachel, thank you for inviting me," she says warmly.

"You're welcome, Lucy. Thank you for coming."

"I love what you've done with the place. You must have worked day and night to get this all done," she says kindly. "I really love the blue in the living room. You'll have to let me know the name of the color."

"Midnight lover, wasn't it, Rach?" Tanner appears and wraps an arm around my waist, pulling me into his side.

Lucy's eyes light up as she looks at him.

"Lucy, this is Tanner. He's who helped me get the house ready so fast," I say, as his hand slides down to cup my ass out of view.

"Yeah, she had me hard at it in the living room especially," he says smoothly as he squeezes. "Isn't that right, Rach?" He flashes a dazzling smile at Lucy, who beams back at us both.

"Well, looks like you chose a good helper," she says to me. "Nice to meet you, Tanner." She turns to leave.

"You too, Lucy," he says as I flash him a "behave" look.

"I'll see you to the door," I say, following her out.

"If I had him helping me, I'd make sure he was hard at something too." Lucy laughs as she steps out the front door. "I'll see you when you're ready to pick Nigel up. No rush, though. My son will keep him company, and he will be up for hours—teenagers," she tuts as she walks down the path and back to next door.

I close the door and turn straight into Chris's chest.

"God, Chris! You're lucky I didn't hand you your ass, sneaking up on me like that." I scowl, stepping back.

"Who's the guy that had his hand on your ass?" He cuts straight to it.

"Is that any of your business?"

"No." He shrugs, his playful eyes assessing me. "Just wanted to know who the guy is that's caused you to stop returning my texts."

"His name's Tanner," I whisper, glancing over Chris' shoulder towards the living room.

"Are you worried he's going to hear us talking?" Chris says, following my eyes.

"Yes. I mean, no." I fold my arms across my chest.

"Relax, Rachel. I'm just messing with you. I'm pleased for you, really. Even if this means the end to our mutual agreement." He looks at me questioningly as I nod my head.

"Yes, Chris. It does." I roll my eyes at his audacity. He would have happily kept it up if I'd been willing.

"I never thought I'd see the day that someone tamed Rachel Jones." He smiles.

"I'm not a wild animal, Chris." I give him a small smile.

"Could have fooled me... plenty of times." He winks.

That's when I see Tanner over his shoulder. Chris follows my gaze and turns.

"Chris, you're a friend of Rachel's?" Tanner says, smiling and offering his hand.

"Yes, nice to meet you," Chris says, shaking it.

Tanner's a couple of inches taller than Chris and his complete polar opposite. Dark and tanned, sexy, and authoritative, compared with Chris, who's more of a pretty boy with his blonde hair and playful eyes and smile.

I stand rooted to the spot, watching their exchange with interest.

"You're a very lucky man," Chris says as he takes his hand back.

Tanner says nothing, just nods his head, effectively bringing the conversation to an end.

Chris turns back to me. "It was nice to see you, Rachel. Congratulations on the house." For a second, it looks like he may lean in and give me a kiss on the cheek, but he seems to think better of it. *Thank fuck*.

I open the door and happily close it behind him as he leaves.

"That was Chris?" Tanner asks, as though I've mentioned Chris by name before when I clearly haven't.

"Yes, that was Chris." I move to walk past him.

He takes a step to the side, blocking me.

"He's one of your 'friends,' I take it?" His voice is deep, his expression unreadable.

"He *was* my friend, yes. Not anymore." I look at him, waiting for the shit show to erupt. He's too calm, too in control. Not what I expected when he just shook hands with the guy I used to meet for casual sex. But then, did I get jealous when we bumped into Mandy? Well yeah, I did, but I didn't show it. Tanner has no clue that I wanted to stuff that expensive coat down her whiny throat at the mere idea of her having shared private moments with him.

"Not anymore?" he repeats my words in question as his hand reaches up to cup my chin.

"That's what I said." I stare at him, waiting.

"Good, that's settled then," he says as he brings his lips down onto mine and kisses me like he owns me.

If I had any doubts over just how intense his feelings are for me, then this kiss has just wiped them into oblivion.

TWENTY

TANNER

I PULL BACK HARD ON THE ROWING MACHINE IN MY GYM, sweat already soaking my t-shirt.

Fuck, I need to sort my head out.

At the party at Rachel's house, I nearly lost my shit in front of her and all her friends. First, there was Drew, bringing up the panties with those other flight attendants—I've already ripped him a new one for pulling a stunt like that. Then there was Chris, her ex-fuck buddy. God, I could have strangled him knowing that he's had his hands on her. But then Rachel didn't react badly at all when we bumped into Mandy, so how would it have looked if I had fired off? Of course, I can't expect her not to have a past; mine's probably worse. There've been women—a lot of women—but it's always been short-lived. And the relationships I had, well, they turned to shit once it became apparent they liked my name and money more than anything else.

The thing that's bothering me most, though, is

Megan's drawing of Rachel's mom with that quote on it. It's what made me listen more intently to their conversation at the airport all that time ago; it's what started all this. My mom used to say it to me all the time, and my nana to her too. I've never heard anyone else say it before.

This is a head fuck. It's got to be a coincidence. What else could it be? I don't think I believe in all that shit about signs. Although, I do like to think that Nana hears us talk to her, wherever she is. It's just a weird, head-fucking coincidence, that's all.

It has made me wonder how the hell I'm going to tell Rachel, though. Seeing that drawing, spending these past few weeks with her—I'm worried. I don't want to lose her. But surely telling her the truth will undoubtedly mean that I do. She's going to think I'm a weird creep. How can I explain that isn't what it's like at all?

I quit rowing and pick up my towel to wipe my face. I only saw Rachel last night, but I need her again, especially if our remaining time could be cut short soon. I grab my phone to send her a text.

Me: Now you know my surname, it's only right you should see my house.

It's crazy that she hasn't been here already. A part of me was probably holding back after all the relationships I've had where money just confuses things. I should have asked her sooner. I know she's not like that; I've always known. I have to force my help on her, and she kicks and screams in protest. I chuckle at the thought—my wild firecracker.

Snow: Okay, I accept your invitation to view your smug wanker pad.

I laugh, shaking my head as I take a swig of my water bottle before replying.

Me: I'll pick you up at six. Bring an overnight bag and don't wear any panties.
Snow: Your request will be given consideration.

She's a cheeky bitch. We both know full well I will have her naked and fucking soon after she gets in the door.

And I know she wouldn't want it any other way.

"So, how was New York? And the party?" Mom asks as she sits down next to me at my kitchen island.

"It was great. Rachel wanted to go ice-skating."

"Tanner!" Mom laughs. "I can't imagine you doing that. She must be special."

I smile into my coffee. "I don't think I will make a habit of it; I've only just stopped aching."

"Oh, Tan!" Mom smiles, looking over at me, her brow creasing. "Is there something else going on, Tan?"

I focus my eyes down on the counter. "What do you mean?"

"You seem like you've got a lot on your mind," she says kindly. "A mom always notices these things." She sits and waits patiently while I have another drink and delay answering.

"I have to tell her something, Mom, and I'm worried that when I do, she won't want to know me anymore." I put my mug down and rest my arms against the counter.

Mom places her hand gently on my arm. "It can't be that bad, Tan."

"Can't it?" I stare down at my hands.

"You're a grown man. I know you don't tell your old mom everything, and that's how it should be, but I know you, Tan. You've got a good heart, and you would never cause hurt on purpose." She squeezes my arm gently before continuing. "Whatever it is, you need to tell her. I'm sure she will understand once you explain."

"You don't know her, Mom." I smile sadly.

"No, I don't. We need to change that. Why don't you bring her over tomorrow if you're both free? I can make us all lunch?" she says brightly.

"That sounds nice, Mom, thanks." I smile back at her.

If only a homemade lunch would solve all my problems.

"Rach! Tan's here," Megan calls up the stairs after she lets me in.

"I'll be down in a minute." I hear her shout back.

Megan tells me about her latest work dramas as I follow her into the lounge and take a seat on the sofa. Almost immediately, Nigel hops over, looking up expectantly at me.

"I think he wants you to pick him up." Megan giggles.

God, a few spinach leaves, and he's anyone's pet. He needs to work on his negotiation skills.

"Come on then, big fella," I say as I hoist him up into my arms. He immediately rolls to the side, so I'm effectively cradling him like a baby.

Megan looks at him in delight and shakes her head. "He's smitten with you."

I look down at him. He's quite cute, really, and he gives Rachel a lot of happiness, so I guess he's not so bad—biting aside.

"Apparently, they're going to announce something big at the meeting this week." Megan goes back to telling me about her job.

"You'll have to let me know how that goes. It could mean you'll get a new boss," I say with interest. I know her current one is a bit of a dickhead, from what she and Rachel have told me.

The door creaks open, and I look up as Rachel

pokes her head around the door, her face lighting up when she sees Nigel in my arms.

"I'm ready for the grand tour," she jokes. "Although, it looks like Nigel may have something to say about you getting up right now."

"I think he must have found his BFF for life." Megan laughs.

I look down at him, stretched out, and smile. "You're much better to look at than Drew. I'll give you that. We can work on the conversation," I joke as I ease my arms apart. Nigel reluctantly relocates to the sofa next to Megan.

"See you tomorrow," Rachel calls as we leave.

"See you," she calls back.

The drive to my house takes less than half an hour, and before I know it, we are pulling through the two metal gates and into the private crescent-shaped road of just a few spaced-out houses. Their timber and black glass fronts are modern but also blend into the established trees surrounding them.

"I knew it! I knew you'd live somewhere like this. I bet you've got a home gym and a giant home office." Rachel smirks and shakes her head as she looks out the window.

"Don't forget the hot tub," I joke good-naturedly. "I'm not sure whether to be disappointed that I'm so predictable or impressed at your powers of deduction." I laugh.

"Impressed will do," she says as she climbs out onto the driveway and looks up at the house.

"Come on then, show me inside." She grins, walking up to the front door.

I open it and catch the impressed look on her face. The double-height entryway is flooded with light from the glass wall at the front of the house. I designed an indoor garden of plants by the bottom of the staircase and put in a clear glass banister. It's very white and minimalist.

She leans down and takes her boots off as I step out of my shoes. Her toenails are bright red, her legs long and tanned.

I can't wait to have them wrapped around me later.

I put her bag by the bottom of the stairs and lead her down a hallway, passing the lounge with its giant entertainment system, my home office, and the laundry room.

"What's in there?" She points to a closed door.

"The basement. There's a gym and games room down there," I say, leading her into the kitchen, my favorite room of the house. The bright walls and glass back wall overlooking the Japanese-inspired garden make it the perfect spot to have a coffee in the morning while I catch up on work emails.

"You have a kitchen bigger than the entire downstairs of my house, and yet you've spent more time at my place than your own this last couple of weeks." She shakes her head as she looks at the ten-seater dining table and a large sectional sofa horseshoed around the other end of the room. "You really are loaded."

"You say that like it's a bad thing." I walk over to her, effectively trapping her between me and the marble kitchen island.

She smirks as she realizes what I'm doing. "Are we talking about you being loaded or hanging around my house so much?"

"You've got such a smart mouth." I take another step towards her, so she's forced to tilt her head back to look up at me. She blinks slowly before dropping her eyes towards my groin and licking her lips.

I don't wait for an invitation. I put a hand into her hair and pull her against me sharply, so we are pressed against one another, our lips almost touching. She sucks her breath in as her eyes light up.

"Don't tease me, Rachel," I growl against her mouth as I lean in and claim it as mine, my kiss pushing into her deeply and pulling pleasure back with each dance of my tongue against hers. She kisses me back with force, and I feel her snake her arms around my neck, inviting me in further.

I pull back, panting, and hold her around her neck with one hand. "You are so fucking beautiful. I want to bend you over this counter right now," I murmur. "Did you leave your panties at home like I asked you to?"

"You have a one-track mind, Tanner Grayson. Finish showing me around, and I might let you find out," Rachel says, her eyes challenging mine. *Fuck.* She knows what she does to me, and yet she's holding back, making me wait even longer. I run my fingers through my hair and let out a deep groan.

"Fine." I sulk. "After you." I gesture with my arm. At least I can check out her ass and legs as she goes up the stairs first. Surely, she can give me that pleasure for now.

Her eyes glitter at me as she holds out her hand. "No, it's your house, I insist. Besides, how will I know where to go?" she says sweetly.

I swallow down my annoyance. She knows just how to push my buttons. She'll regret being a tease later once I have her begging me to let her come. The thought pleases me as I head back to the hallway and stride up the stairs, wanting to make this part of the tour as quick as possible.

"Bedrooms, bathrooms, you've seen plenty of those before," I say as we get to the top, and I turn to go towards the master bedroom.

"Hang on," Rachel says slowly, walking off in the wrong direction.

For fuck's sake.

She insists on looking in every room and asking me multiple questions about the décor before looking out of each window and commenting on the individual views.

Finally, we get to my bedroom door.

"I'm starting to wish I lived in a tent," I grumble. "We would have been done ages ago."

"Where's the fun in that?" She winks at me as she slides past me into my room, and I smell her jasmine perfume. She takes her time looking around at the giant bed with deep, white bedding piled high on it, the dark frames with black and white architectural style prints on the walls.

She wanders inside the en suite with a giant walk-in shower and twin sinks. I hear her gasp—it sounds like she's just noticed the giant freestanding bath with the floor-to-ceiling window next to it. You can soak in it and stare right out at the garden.

She comes back out and walks over to me. I'm leaning against the doorframe, failing to disguise the bulge of my cock as it stands to rock-hard attention in my jeans.

"I think you've been very patient," Rachel says as she looks up at me from under her lashes, her hands going to my jeans and slowly undoing them.

I suck in my breath. Fuck, she's so arousing. The way she smells, the way she looks at me, her pretty little mouth that pours out such horny filth. "I have... so patient," I agree, reaching up to brush a loose strand of hair from her face.

"I think you deserve something for being such a good boy." She smirks as she drops to her knees and pulls my jeans and boxers to my ankles with her. I step out of them and rip my socks off.

"Fuck, yes I do!" I say, standing back up and grabbing the base of my cock, pumping it slowly. Rachel parts her sweet red lips and leans forward so I can rub the dripping end of it over them. My pre-come makes them glisten before she darts her tongue out and licks it off hungrily. "Fuuuuucck," I hiss, tapping the head against her open mouth as her eyes look back up at me.

"Tan?" she murmurs before swirling her tongue around the tip. I tilt my head back and let out a low groan as she sinks down, drawing my length into her mouth and sucking.

"Yes, Snow," I barely hiss out.

She sucks down onto me again, one of her hands gently tugging my loaded balls at the same time. I shudder as my cock throbs.

She pulls back, her warm breath against the tip of me as she talks. "I want you to fuck my mouth."

I look up, silently thanking God for bringing this woman into my life.

"If that's what you want, baby," I say, looking down at her darkly as I place a hand on the back of her head and cradle it.

"It is. I want to taste your hot come pour down my throat," she purrs, her baby doll eyes regarding my face carefully as she bites her lip to hide her smile. She's a fucking vixen disguised in a sweet Snow-White package.

Fuck, I'll be lucky to last two minutes.

"You'll tell me if I'm too rough?" I ask as my knuckles stroke over her cheek.

She fixes her eyes on mine. "I can handle it."

God, this woman.

I push forwards and slide between her parted lips; she lets out a small moan, and my cock drips into her fiery mouth in response.

Jesus, she feels fucking fantastic.

I pull back and slide in again, further this time, my hand gently guiding the back of her head forward to meet me. She still has one hand cupping my balls, and the other, she's resting on my inner thigh.

She never takes her eyes off mine as I build up pace and start fucking her mouth, my hand pressing harder against the back of her head. Her eyes are full of desire, which just spurs me on even more. I thrust even deeper and hear her gag, making me pause for a moment, but she sucks back onto me greedily and gives me a look that tells me not to dare stop. It's almost too fucking much.

I bring my other hand to the back of her head and thrust my hips up and forward as I push her down. She's taking my entire length now, my balls hitting her chin as I make her gag a couple more times. I'm ready to fucking explode when she reaches around behind me and slides her thumb up inside my ass.

"Fuck! Rachel!" I yell as I come suddenly, the sensation so unbelievably strong. She swirls her thumb around, and I jerk violently in her throat as my cock pumps it out. The vibration of her giggle in her throat rubs the head of my cock, and I jerk again as the last hot spurts come out, emptying me completely.

"What the fuck?" I look down at her as she sits back onto her heels, removing my cock from her throat at the same time her thumb vacates my back passage.

She smiles at me and licks her lips. "Turns out smug wanker pads are a bit of a turn-on."

I can't help but laugh as I pull her up quickly, lifting her, so she has to wrap her legs around my waist. I'm pleased to feel her wet, naked pussy against my skin—no panties—just like I asked. I turn and rest her up against the wall.

"Where have you been all my life, Rachel Jones?" I ask against her lips before I kiss her, my tongue delving between her lips and tasting the salty remnants of my come in her mouth. She moans against me and brings her hands up to my hair as she kisses me back passionately. God, this woman, what she does to me—it's fucking insane!

We keep kissing each other hard until we're both panting. I pull back to look at Rachel, and her cheeks are flushed with arousal. I should really make her wait and draw it out, like she did to me—delayed gratification. Only I'm not sure my willpower is as strong where she's concerned. She only has to look at me, and I'm like a pubescent boy, ready to go again with an almost permanent raging hard-on.

I carry her over to the bed and throw her down onto it, climbing up over her as she lands.

"Someone's eager." She smirks.

"You fucking bet I am," I say as I reach down and unfasten her belt. My hands go to her dress next. *What is this?* It's got like a thousand buttons down the front, and I'm tempted just to rip the stupid thing off.

"Don't go throwing a tantrum." Rachel laughs, seeing my irritated face as I work on the buttons. She

245

grabs the bottom of the fabric and pulls the whole thing up and over her head.

Thank fuck for that.

I reach a hand around underneath her and unhook her bra, tossing it to the side.

Bras I can handle.

I pause for a moment to take in her incredible tits, their deep pink nipples already hard and straining towards me, begging me to suck them.

"I love your tits," I say, kneading them in my hands as I bring my mouth down and suck on her perfect nipples. Rachel moans in response and arches up into my mouth. I swirl my tongue around one and then the other, stretching it back between my lips as I suck hard.

"Ah! Tan," Rachel cries out. Judging by the way she's grinding her soaking pussy against me, I'd say she likes it.

"You like it rough, don't you, baby?" I say, rising onto my knees and straddling her ribs. She knows just what I want to do and brings her hands to her tits, pushing them together as I rest my cock between them. I grip onto the headboard and slide forward. She looks so incredible, lying there like this for me, her eyes wild with passion. I slide back and forth slowly a few more times, my cock straining to pump fast. I'm being greedy, though, and I think I've made her wait long enough.

"I think your sweet pussy is feeling left out," I say as I climb off her and move to stand at the bottom of the bed. She looks up at me in amusement.

"Your cock may be big, Tanner, but it's not going to reach from over there." She laughs.

"Cheeky bitch, who said anything about my cock?" I grin wickedly at her as I kneel on the floor and grab her ankles, pulling her in one swift movement, so her ass is right at the edge of the mattress. She moans out my name as I lift her feet over my shoulders and lean forward, inhaling deeply.

"You smell delicious. I can't wait to have you come all over my face."

"You're a bad boy, Tanner Grayson," she says, her hands moving to my head and fisting in my hair.

I respond by leaning forward and sliding my tongue between her soaking lips, finding her swollen clit and tracing circles over it. Rachel's hips writhe on the bed, and she pulls on my hair. "Your pussy is a hungry little thing, begging me to give her an orgasm," I say before sinking my tongue deep inside Rachel's body and licking in large, deep circles. Fuck, I can't get enough of tasting her like this. She's so warm and wet, so sweet. I slide my tongue out and back onto her clit, groaning as she grinds against me.

"You taste incredible." I suck her clit hard.

"Tan," she moans.

God, I love hearing her say my name like this.

She pulls my hair, forcing me onto her harder, and my cock weeps in response. I love it when she can't get enough of what I'm doing to her.

I move one hand up to pull her nipple sharply at the same as I slide three fingers deep inside her.

"Tan!" she hisses, but I know she can take it. Her wetness is all over me.

"Make sure you scream my name loudly when I'm sucking your orgasm out of you," I growl.

"Fuck you!" Rachel pants.

I smirk as I suck on her clit extra hard, and she bucks off the bed.

"Have I told you that you're a wanker?" she forces out between her gasps as my fingers pump into her harder, the sound of her wetness echoing around the room.

"Not often enough when you're like this." I smirk at her before really going for it with my mouth, sucking and swirling my tongue over her in fast circles while my fingers continue to fuck her hard.

I can sense she's getting close, so I push her feet back up onto the bed, so she's spread wide for me. Then I push my fingers back inside her, changing the angle, so they rub up against her front wall, finding that magical, sweet spot. Her hands pull my hair even harder, and she lets out a loud scream as she bucks up off the bed and her legs shudder. I use my free hand to hold her opposite leg down, pinning the other to the bed with my elbow as she comes hard against my face.

"Oh fuck, Tan!" she screams as I keep tracing hard, fast circles against her with my tongue. I can feel her contracting around my fingers as I keep plunging them into her in quick, smooth strokes. I will never tire of this—her riding an orgasm out that I've given her.

It's what dreams are made of.

I let out a low, deep growl of contentment as I feel her orgasm slow, her fingers releasing their vise-like grip on my hair. I kiss her gently all over her lips and inner thighs, gently sliding my soaking fingers out of her and sucking them clean.

"I'll never get enough of tasting you like this," I say, more to myself, as I savor her taste on my last finger.

"I'll have to make you do it more then." She pulls me up to lie next to her.

"You won't hear me complaining." I smile and lean in to kiss her as my erection presses against her thigh.

"And you said I was greedy?" Rachel tuts.

"No, I said your pussy was hungry," I correct her, which earns me a slap across the chest.

I laugh as I roll over and pull her on top of me. She looks down at me playfully as I reach my hands up to cup her tits.

"Now ride my cock like a good girl, and I'll run you a bath after."

TWENTY-ONE

RACHEL

"I think I'm in heaven." I sigh as I lean back against Tanner's solid chest and look out at the night sky through the window. He's run the bath right to the top for me and filled it with bubbles.

"Does that mean I'm your God then?" he says, wrapping his arms around me and leaning to kiss the side of my face.

"Where do you get these lines?" I scoff. "Surely, they've never worked."

"Drew," he answers quickly, trying to shift the blame before laughing.

"Figures." I laugh before hesitating for a moment... It's now or never. I fight to keep my voice casual. "What was all that about at the party with Drew?"

"What do you mean?" Tanner asks as he tries to move the bubbles away from my breasts.

I smile and move his hands back to the sides of the

bath, where I link my fingers through his. "Stop. Haven't you seen enough for one night?"

"I will never have enough of you, Rachel." He nips my ear with his teeth. "Now, why are you thinking about Drew when you're naked in my bath, trapped between my thighs?" he asks, flexing his thighs around me to prove his point.

"It was just that thing he was asking Lyndsey and Katie about. You know, the selling panties thing?" I say, my mouth dry.

Tanner clears his throat and shifts behind me as though he's uncomfortable. "Oh, that? That was just Drew being Drew. Why do you ask?"

I pause. *How do I play this?*

"He just seemed quite interested, that's all. I wondered what you thought about it?" I turn my face to the side to look up at him, but I can't see his eyes properly from this angle.

"What do I think about it?" Tanner murmurs as if deep in thought. "I think people invest in all types of businesses, sometimes for very personal reasons."

"But what do you think of that type of business? Say, if I had done it, for example?" I turn my face back away from him and screw it up, so glad that he can't see me.

He clears his throat again. "Why are you asking, Rachel?"

"Well, you made that comment about Mandy forgetting her purse sometimes."

"All the fucking time." Tanner laughs a humorless laugh.

"I was just wondering whether you thought of that as the same thing?" I ask, removing my hand from his to scratch at my wrist.

"It's not the same thing," he says without a thought. "Mandy was out for what she could get without considering what I wanted. It's nothing like a business agreement two parties invest into with mutual benefits."

I relax back into his chest a bit more. "I see."

"Why are you asking all these questions, Rach?" He leans round to kiss the side of my face. "Are you trying to tell me you do it?"

"Do what?"

"Sell your panties," he says, his voice deep.

It really is now or never.

"What if I used to? But not anymore?" I add quickly, leaning forward to turn the top half of my body around and look at his face.

Tanner's brow furrows as he looks at me. "You used to sell your worn panties?"

I hold my breath and nod.

"When was this?" His face is blank, unreadable. He's using his business negotiator's face on me. I'm screwed at guessing what he's really thinking.

"It started over eighteen months ago until I bought the house." I swallow.

He continues staring at me.

"And how *many* men did you send your panties to?" He emphasizes the "many."

"Does it matter?"

"It does to me." He glares at me.

Fuck, he's pissed.

Damn this new relationship—whatever the fuck it's called—thing we have going on. I never had to tell Chris any of this. I just feel like I should be honest with Tanner. I have this urge to want to be honest with him.

"One," I say.

"Only one?" Tanner's eyes bore into mine.

"Well, I'm obviously not as good at running my own business as you, because yes, I only had one client," I say sarcastically.

If he's going to be a dick, then I can handle it.

"Why just one?" He pushes.

"He said he'd pay extra if I promised to only sell to him, and I always keep my promises," I say, feeling my temper rising.

"So, there was only ever one?"

"For fuck's sake, Tanner. Yes! There was only ever one," I snap.

He reaches forward and brushes his thumb over my lips, his face softening. "What happened to him?"

"I told him I wanted to stop as I'd saved enough to buy my house," I say underneath his thumb, not sure whether it's safe to relax yet. "That was my goal all along, and I reached it." I study his eyes, which are now staring at me.

He sits forward suddenly and brings his warm lips to mine, kissing me slowly, sensually.

Okay, I'm confused. Is he pissed off or not?

"Doesn't it bother you?" I ask, breaking away from him.

"Are you asking me whether the thought of another man having pairs of your panties with the scent of you on them bothers me?" His eyes on my lips as though he's going to kiss them again any second.

God, this is weird.

"Yes, that. Does it bother you?"

"Yes, it does fucking bother me, Rachel," he whispers, leaning his forehead against mine. "I don't want to think about another man having anything of yours ever again."

"You're not going to be a wanker about it?" I ask, not quite believing it. I expected him to hit the roof.

"No." He shakes his head as one hand reaches up to cup my cheek. "I'm not going to be a wanker about it."

Then he kisses me again, and all thoughts of panties and Mr. X vanish.

"I'm so over this pregnancy insomnia thing already," Holly moans, her tired eyes looking through the screen at me.

"I didn't think it started yet?" I say, leaning back against the pillows on Tan's bed.

"I know, lucky me!" She gives me a fake smile. "I'm

255

only just coming up to my third trimester. I hope it eases off soon," she says through a yawn.

"So, where's Jay? Please tell me he's snoring like a pig in bed. Mr. Perfect has to have some flaws," I joke and watch her eyes light up.

"Rach! He does not snore like a pig." Holly giggles. "He is in bed, though. He's been insisting on getting up with me every night, and I've had enough. I told him he needs his sleep, what with all the filming he's doing for the TV show. Plus, he needs to get it while he can because once the baby is here, I have a feeling things are going to be quite different."

"I can't believe you're going to be a mommy soon." I smile at my best friend.

"I know." Her eyes widen. "Scary, huh?"

"You'll be amazing, Holls. I can't think of better parents for this baby. He or she is going to be so loved."

I smile sadly. I can't help thinking of my mom and wondering how different life could have been if she hadn't died when I was a baby. I'm not even entirely sure what happened, as the story has changed so much depending on who tells me. I'm not sure my old caseworker knew for definite. I've heard everything, from a fall to a car accident to a brain hemorrhage.

"He or she definitely is." Holly looks down at her stomach. "So, what are you doing for the rest of the day? I take it you have plans with Tanner as I don't recognize those pillows behind you?" Holly raises her brows with a smile as she looks back up at me.

"Yeah, okay, busted." I laugh. "I spent the night at his place for the first time last night."

"And?" she probes.

"And what?" I ask, looking at her.

"Oh, come on, Rach! This is me you're talking to, remember? You can't pretend this isn't a huge deal for you?" she says excitedly. "What's his house like?"

"Fancy and rather huge. It's ridiculous, really." I smile. "He must rattle around here by himself."

"Not now that you're there to keep him company all night long," Holly sings mischievously.

"Stop." I shoot her a look before rolling my eyes and smiling. "Okay, I'll admit, I kind of enjoy spending the nights together. For some weird reason that I haven't worked out yet."

Holly smiles as she listens to me. "I think I may have an idea why you like it."

I look at her eyes, which are now bright and eager, all signs of her previous sleep-deprived state gone. "No, no, no." I shake my head. "Don't go getting ahead of yourself. I like him, and we have fun—when he isn't annoying the hell out of me." I glance to the doorway to make sure Tanner hasn't returned from downstairs.

"Whatever you say, Rach." She smiles, now taking her turn to roll her eyes at me.

"No, really, Holls. It's not that serious. We haven't put a label or anything on it. It's not like I'm calling him my boyfriend," I say quickly, not sure who I'm trying to convince more—her or me.

"Rach, relax. So, what if you like him more than

anyone else you've met before? I'm so happy for you. You've found someone you want to stay all night with. Someone you obviously feel quite comfortable and want to share things with."

I run over her words in my head. *Someone I feel comfortable with? Share things with? Is that who Tanner is to me?*

"You know, Holls, I did share something else with him last night." I cast my mind back to our bath.

"Oh, yeah?"

"I told him about the panty business." I lower my voice, even though I know he won't be coming back yet. He said he had some business calls to make in his office.

"You did?" Holly's eyes widen. "What did he say?"

"That's the thing." I shrug. "I thought he would be all pissed off about it. He's such a hothead about some other things."

"Says you?" Holly giggles.

"Yeah, yeah, anyway," I carry on, "he didn't even seem that surprised. He was more bothered about how many clients I had rather than the fact I had done it."

"Hmm," Holly muses. "Maybe he just thinks that since it's in the past that it doesn't matter now?"

"Yeah, maybe. I would have just expected him to be more bothered, you know. The first time we spoke on the phone and I mentioned Matt, he almost bit my head off, wanting to know who Matt was." The corners of my lips turn up at the memory.

"So, he's jealous when it comes to other guys then?" Holly asks.

"Well, I thought so. But then he kept his cool when he met Chris at the house party, so who knows?" I sigh. "This is why I don't do relationships. All this second-guessing shit. Casual sex is much simpler."

"Maybe, but nowhere near as good, Rach. Admit it; it feels good to have Tanner on your side. Building up that trust in each other." Holly smiles at me encouragingly.

"Yeah, it has some merits, I suppose. Although, guess what he wants to do today?" I moan.

"Do I want to know?" Holly giggles.

"Oh God, he wants to do that all the time!" I laugh. "But I'm talking about the fact he's told his mom we will both go to her house for lunch!" I hiss.

"He wants you to meet his mom? Rachel, that sounds lovely. Doesn't it?" Holly asks, looking at my face.

"I don't know," I groan, looking up at the ceiling. "I've never met anyone's parents before. Plus, he's really close to his mom. Like *super* close."

"What's wrong with that?" Holly pauses for a moment. "Wait, Rach, are you worried his mom won't like you?"

"No! Of course not," I say quickly, chewing on my lip.

"It's okay if you are, you know? I was worried about meeting Jay's family for the first time," she confesses.

"Yeah, but come on, Holly. This is you we're talking

about. You're every parent's dream. Me, on the other hand, not so much." I frown.

"And why not?" Holly says, screwing her nose up. She's such a gentle soul, but when it comes to her family or friends, well, "look out," is all I can say.

"I'm hardly the ideal lunch guest, am I? No family of my own, a fucked-up past with no actual normal relationships, just a string of fuck buddies I've lost count of."

"You have a family! You have me. And Matt and Megan," Holly says.

I know she's right. She's like a sister to me. And Matt, well, he's the annoying brother, I guess, and Megan has become such a close friend since living together.

"Thanks, but you know what I mean."

"They'll be lucky to have you there. Will you tell me how it goes?" she says, a yawn creeping back over her pretty face.

"Yes, I will provide a detailed debrief later." I smile. "Now go back to bed. It looks like you might be in with some luck if you try to sleep again now."

"Thanks." She smiles at me. "Love you, Rach."

"Love you too." I hit the end call button and sink further into the pillows.

When Tanner told me his mom was expecting us for lunch today, I was pissed he had made plans without even asking me. But the more I think about it, the more I'm kind of pleased about it. What I told him last night in the bath certainly didn't have him running a mile. And judging by the extra energy he had afterward—and again this morning—I would say it hasn't altered his attraction to me at all. If anything, he seems even more intense than usual. I've never had this with anyone before. It's both exhilarating and terrifying.

I look up as the door opens. Speak of the sexy devil. He's wearing a pair of grey sweatpants and nothing else. His chiseled abs and strong 'V' running down into the low waistband are on full display. He is hot, steamy, and erotic sex in sweatpants. His eyes are dark, and his brow is furrowed as he looks up at me.

"How was Holly?" he asks.

"She's good. I think our chat may help her get some sleep now. It's the middle of the night over there." I look at Tanner, who's nodding as though he's listening, but I can tell he's distracted, his mind elsewhere.

"What's wrong?" I ask as he comes and sits on the edge of the bed next to me. The warm, slightly spicy smell of his skin makes my nipples harden underneath his t-shirt I'm wearing. I watch the muscles in his back ripple as he leans his elbows onto his knees and lowers his head into his hands.

He lets out a low groan. "We've just been let down by an artist at work. Fucking creative types," he hisses through gritted teeth. "He was supposed to be doing a giant commission for us to go in the foyer of this new hotel in London we've got the re-modeling contract for. It's the official re-opening in two weeks, and he told us this morning that he can't do it. We hired him months ago. There's no way we can get someone else at such brief notice."

"Shit. I'm sorry, Tan. He's a real dick for letting you down at the last minute," I mutter, sitting up. I instinctively wrap my arms around Tanner's back from behind and hold on to his chest. I press gentle kisses between his shoulder blades, wishing I could kiss away all the tension built up there.

"It will not look good for the company," he says, pulling my hand up from his chest and kissing my fingers.

An idea hits me. "Megan could do it!" I say suddenly, sitting up straight.

Tanner turns his upper body around to look at me. "No, Rach. It's an enormous job. It would take her hours, and she already has work."

"She does this week. But she's off on leave next week," I say, my voice gaining speed as I plan it all out. "She's talented too, Tan. You know she'd do something incredible!" I look at him, excitement growing in my eyes.

"You really think she'd want to take this on? It's a huge ask." He looks at me, and I can see hope forming in his eyes.

"There's one way to know." I pick my phone up off the bedside table and hand it to him. "Call her."

I sit and listen as Tanner calls Megan. I hear her excited squeal down the phone as he tells her about the brief and which hotel it will be showcased in. Then

I hear him tell her how much his company is offering as payment, and I have to hold my cough in.

Fuck, maybe I should have gone to art school.

He hangs up and throws my phone down onto the bed, then turns and pulls me across his lap, his eyes glittering. "You, my sexy little Snowball, are a genius." He smiles as he brings his warm lips to mine and kisses me hard, his skilled tongue parting my lips and probing my mouth with deep, devilish confidence. He pulls back and looks deep into my eyes. "I owe you big-time."

"Big-time?" I tease, wriggling against his erection, which is pressed into the back of my thigh.

His eyes darken. "There's still plenty of time to start thanking you before we go out. If you have something in mind?"

"What do I have in mind?" I murmur, looking down at his lips. "You know, I'm feeling quite tired this morning. Some horny fucker kept me up late." I smirk as he leans forward and nips my bottom lip between his teeth. I feel a rush of moisture between my legs and instinctively moan against his lips as I run my fingers along his jaw.

"Sounds like a lucky, horny fucker to me." He grins, slipping a hand up my t-shirt and straight to my breast, where he rolls my nipple between his thumb and forefinger.

I tip my head back, and Tanner's lips graze along my neck, his warm breath dancing over my skin between his kisses as he works his way up to my ear.

"You know, if you're feeling tired, maybe it's a good idea if I use something that will stop you from being tempted to exert yourself too much," he whispers.

I move my head, so my eyes meet his. "Sounds intriguing."

He gives me a sexy grin before laying me back onto the bed and pulling the t-shirt up over my head. I watch him stand back up, his eyes running down my body and back up again. It's another great opportunity for me to eye fuck him as well, while he's topless and in sweatpants that can't hide his enormous erection. He reaches down into his bedside drawer and pulls out a thin piece of black lace.

"Are those?"

"Yes, they are indeed." He grins, bringing the lace panties I wore to the whisky tasting up to his nose and inhaling deeply, his eyes fluttering closed as he groans gently. "I told you, they were my consolation for you being gone in the morning."

"I can't believe you've kept them in your bedside drawer." I look up at him as he leans over me and brings my wrists together above my head.

"They've kept me good company on the nights we're apart." He smiles as he wraps the delicate fabric around my wrists, binding it, so my hands are held together.

"Have you got yourself off while holding them?" I ask, the panties I'm wearing now soaked with arousal at the idea of him touching himself and thinking of me.

His eyes stare at me intently as he speaks slowly. "Yes, Rachel. I've stroked my cock until I've come. I've done it while holding them, smelling them, and remembering you wearing them while I fucked you that night with my tongue." His voice comes out deep and gravelly, like he's trying to restrain himself. His eyes stay glued to my face as he slides his sweatpants down and releases his cock. I can see the wet beads of arousal on its tip. He climbs onto the bed and slowly slides my panties down my legs before leaning over and dropping them into his bedside drawer, pushing it closed.

"Oh, God," I moan quietly, unable to do much with my hands tied except drop my legs wide on the mattress, hoping Tanner will soon give me some relief to the pulsating in my pussy.

"Tell me how you want it, Rachel," he says, coming to kneel between my legs.

I arch my back off the bed. "I want it now, Tanner. Fast, hard, and dirty. Stop fucking around and give me your cock," I groan.

He laughs as he lifts me and places a pillow underneath my bum. "You're very impatient, you know that?" He trails a finger from my chin, down over one nipple, and to my pussy. I buck off the bed, willing him to sink his finger deep inside me or touch my clitoris. Instead, he removes it and tuts. "What's the magic word?"

"Wanker," I fire back, fuming that he's teasing me.

He laughs, a deep, sexy laugh. "That's my girl," he

says as he lifts my ankles together, placing them over one of his shoulders, and slides his cock deep inside me in one slow push. I moan at the sensation of complete fullness—the incredible stretch and slight burn at the size of him inside me.

"Fuck yeah." He lets out a ragged breath as he draws back slowly before sliding back in again. His eyes are cast down, watching where our bodies meet. I arch off the bed, my wrists still held tight together over my head. I'm completely under his control, unable to move anywhere. I have to trust him completely, and it's a fucking turn-on.

"Harder," I moan.

Tanner speeds up in response, sliding in and out of my body with increasing speed, his moans growing louder. All I can do is throw my head back and enjoy the sensations his cock is creating. So good, it feels so, so good.

All too soon, he takes his cock out and pulls the pillow from under me, flipping me in one quick, powerful move so that I'm lying on my front on the bed. "Let me see that gorgeous ass," he growls, pulling me up to my knees in front of him. I rest on my elbows and part my legs for him. "That's it, baby," he says darkly, sucking in a breath. "Show me your pussy, soaking wet for me." He rubs the tip of his cock over me, sliding it through my wetness.

"Fuck me, Tan," I groan impatiently. He chuckles and slides into me until his balls are kissing my skin. "You feel so good," I moan, pushing back against him, wanting him even deeper. He picks up the pace, slamming into me with hard, punishing hits. The headboard bangs against the wall as he clasps my hips tightly and fucks me how I asked.

"Such a tight little pussy," he murmurs in awe, pounding into me, his breathing growing ragged.

It feels so good, so deep. I can feel my orgasm building, and it's going to be intense. I just know it. I can feel tingles spreading over my entire body. I clench around him.

"Fuck, Rachel," Tanner hisses.

I moan his name loudly; I'm so nearly there. He moves one hand, and I feel an extra fullness as he slides what I think must be his thumb inside my ass.

God, it feels good.

I feel like I've got even more of him inside me, totally at his mercy as he uses my body to pleasure himself.

"Tan," I moan as his cock rubs against my G-spot. He pumps his thumb in time with his cock, and I feel any control I had, leave my body, the sudden urge to pee coming over me. "Tan!" I scream as I come hard and release a sudden gush of wetness all over him.

"God, Fuck!" he hisses, sounding taken aback but delighted. As my orgasm rips through me, making my legs shake, he groans deeply, and I know that he's coming too. I murmur his name as I shudder and convulse around him, one of his hands firmly clutching my hip, the other still on and inside my ass.

He keeps thrusting into me as we both moan and ride down together.

"Rachel." He lets out a big breath as our bodies slow. "That was fucking incredible. I didn't know you could—"

"Neither did I," I pant back, just as surprised by my squirting as he is. I've heard about it and almost come close with my vibrator before, but never actually done it.

He slides his thumb and cock out of me, and I feel an aching emptiness from where we were joined.

"Stay there, baby." The mattress moves as Tanner gets off the bed and goes into the en suite, appearing a moment later with a warm washcloth. He tenderly cleans me before pulling me down onto the bed with him and wrapping me in his arms.

"I don't want you to ever leave me," he whispers as he carefully unties my wrists, drawing each to his lips so he can kiss them in turn.

"I'm not going anywhere, not until my next flight, anyway." I smile.

"I mean it, Rachel." He gazes at me. "You're everything I want."

I swallow as I look back at him.

I want to open my mouth and speak, but I can't.

All I can do is stare at him as I say the words silently in my head.

You're everything I always said I never wanted, Tanner Grayson.

Only, do I still mean it?

TWENTY-TWO

TANNER

"TELL ME, RACHEL, WHAT'S IT REALLY LIKE BEING A long-haul stewardess? Is that what you call it? I bet you get some awkward passengers?" Mom asks across the table.

We've just finished a lunch of Mom's specialty, salmon en croûte with salad. She and Rachel have barely stopped talking since we arrived. I smile, listening to them. I was sure they'd get on, but I couldn't have even dreamed it would be so well—so effortless.

Rachel's eyes catch mine mischievously, "yes, some more hard work than others."

Mom laughs, catching on that Rachel's talking about New York. Rachel turns her focus back to Mom before continuing. "We tend to say, cabin crew. Although every time I fly to the States, they call us flight attendants. It's a great job. I would never have dreamed of being able to visit all the places I have with work."

"Where's your favorite?" Mom's eyes light up.

Peter catches my eye and motions to the sink. I help him clear the table and take the plates over.

"Sit down, you two," Mom calls. "I can do that later."

"No, Mom. You made lunch; the least we can do is help tidy up."

"It was lovely, thank you, Nell," Rachel says as Mom beams at her.

I watch the two of them chat as I load the dishwasher with Peter. "They seem to get on well," he says to me quietly.

I look at Peter, his eyes full of love as he looks back at Mom. He's a good man, and he makes her happy. The image of Rachel and I doing this with our kids hits me suddenly, and I clear my throat. I shouldn't feel surprised. If I'm honest with myself, I've found myself thinking of a long-term future together for a while. I just hope she can understand when I tell her what I've been keeping back. I can't keep putting it off, not when she's been so honest with me. Secrets have a way of coming out. I need to be the one who lifts the lid.

"What are you two giggling about?" Peter asks as we go back to the table and sit down. He puts his arm around the back of Mom's chair, and she smiles back at him.

"That's girl talk, for us to know, isn't that right,

Rachel?" She winks across the table, and Rachel grins back at her.

Looking at the two most important women in my life, getting on like a house on fire is the best thing I could have hoped for. I slide my hand underneath the table and rest it on Rachel's knee. God, I love it when she wears skirts or dresses, and I can stroke her smooth skin.

"I used to love collecting coins from other countries when I was a boy," Peter says, directing his attention to Rachel. "There are some very unusual ones."

Figures, I can just imagine little Peter in his corduroys and braces poring over his coin collection. He's steady and dependable, exactly the kind of man my mom needs.

"There are, indeed. I think I've got some, actually." Rachel reaches down to her bag on the floor and pulls out her purse. She unzips it and tips the coins out into her hand. As she does, something else falls out, catching the light as it drops onto the table between her and Mom. Rachel goes to pick it up between her red nails to put it away.

"Rachel. May I see that?" Mom's voice sounds odd. The way I remember it sounding as a child when she told me Nana had passed away. I look at her face, and it's pale, her smile gone.

"Are you okay, Mom?" I ask, growing concerned. She doesn't answer me, just continues to stare at the object in Rachel's hand.

"Oh, um, sure." Rachel smiles politely, seeming to

sense something is off as she places it in Mom's palm. She turns to glance at me, her eyes questioning. I shrug and squeeze her knee. I don't know what's got into Mom, either.

"It can't be," Mom says, turning the item over in her hand and studying it closely. I lean forward to see what's got her acting so weird and see the heart shape. I don't need to read the words inscribed on it to know what they say—*Difficult roads lead to beautiful destinations.*

"That's lovely," Peter says to Rachel as he leans over Mom's shoulder and reads.

"Thank you. It belonged to my mom," Rachel says. I watch as Mom's eyes snap up and her other hand flies to her mouth.

"This was your mother's?" Mom asks Rachel, her voice barely a whisper.

"Yes," Rachel replies carefully as she places her hand over mine on her leg. I know Mom won't make her feel uncomfortable on purpose, but judging by how little Rachel talks about her past, I'm worried she's more affected than her calm face suggests.

"Was your mom called Helen?" Mom says gently, completely focused on Rachel.

"How do you know that?" Rachel asks suspiciously, looking over at me in confusion. I turn my hand underneath hers so that I can wrap her delicate fingers in mine. I don't know how the hell Mom would know that. Rachel's never even told me her mom's name.

"This is going to sound strange," Mom says as she

places the silver heart keyring down on the table. "I think I knew your mother, Rachel. I think I knew her a long time ago."

What the hell?

"What are you talking about?" Rachel's voice shakes as she looks between us all.

"Mom?" I screw up my face, bewildered.

She takes a deep breath and blows it out slowly as she looks at the keyring. "Not that long after I moved back to England with Tanner, a new lady moved in next door. Her name was Helen." Rachel's hand tightens its grip on mine as Mom looks up at her. "She was pregnant. She didn't have any family, and I don't know what happened to the baby's father, but she barely talked about him, so I learned not to ask."

"You think this Helen was Rachel's mom?" I ask in disbelief.

"Are you sure, love?" Peter asks gently, glancing uneasily at Rachel, who's sat up straight, frozen in place.

Mom's gaze doesn't leave Rachel's face as she talks. "It sounds crazy, I know. But we became good friends, supported each other. We both knew what it was like to be single mothers. She had her baby six months later—a girl." Mom smiles sadly. "She called her Rachel."

The back of my hand stings where Rachel's nails are gripping it tightly, pressing into my skin. I swear I can hear her heart beating from here.

"I don't understand." Rachel clears her throat, and

her voice wavers. "What makes you think that was my mom?"

"This," Mom says, her finger gently stroking over the silver heart. "I gave this to Helen as a gift when she was about to move away. She told me she had found a new job, a good one that would give you both a better life." Mom stares at the heart, lost in her own memory. "It's a favorite saying of mine, isn't it, Tan?" She smiles at me. Rachel's eyes whip to my face questioningly. I nod at her, her haunted eyes holding mine.

"That's why you asked about the saying on the picture Megan did for me?" she asks slowly, searching my face. She drops her voice. "Why didn't you say anything?"

"I just thought it was a weird coincidence. I never thought..." I trail off as I look at Mom.

Mom reaches across the table and grasps Rachel's free hand between hers. "We used to write to each other when she first moved away. She would send me photos, and then they just stopped coming. I tried to call the house phone at her address, but a new couple said they bought it from a landlord. They told me the lady who lived there before had died saving a child who had fallen in the local river. They thought a relative was caring for her baby." Mom's voice is loaded with emotion as she looks at Rachel, who's sitting deathly still next to me.

"There was no relative," Rachel says, but despite her voice being steady, her hand is hot and clammy in mine.

"I'm so sorry, love," Mom says genuinely, her voice full of compassion. "She was a lovely woman and a brilliant mother. She loved you dearly. You could hear it in her voice when she spoke about you."

Rachel nods mutely next to me. I want to wrap her in my arms and soak up the pain radiating from her.

"I've got some photos somewhere if you'd like to see?" Mom asks gently.

I look at Rachel and see her neck contract as she swallows. It seems to take her a great deal of effort. "Rach?" I ask.

"Yes, please," she replies, her voice barely a whisper.

"I'll be right back." Mom smiles kindly at her. "Peter, could you help me please?" she says as she gets up and leaves the room, and he follows behind.

I move my chair right up next to Rachel's, so my thigh is pressed up against hers. "Rach?" She doesn't answer, just stares at the keyring on the table before reaching forward and wrapping it tightly in her fist. I take my hand from hers and wrap my arms around her. She stiffens immediately. I press a kiss to her temple. "It's just you and me here now." She blows out a long breath and relaxes slightly, dropping her head against my chest.

"What the actual fuck, Tanner? I've spent my entire life knowing hardly anything about my mom, and then I come here and find out your mom was friends with her? We lived next door!" she cries. "This can't be happening."

I can't believe it either. Our moms were neighbors? Friends? The words on the keyring... this is the freakiest fucking coincidence I've ever heard of.

My blood runs cold—the words. The first time I heard Rachel say them at the airport—they were what made me pay attention to her conversation with her friend, who I now realize must have been Holly. Fuck me. This is crazy. Either the world has gone mad, or I have. Things like this don't really happen, do they?

"It's a fucking weird coincidence," I say as Rachel looks up at me.

"There's no way, Tan. Your mom must be wrong," Rachel whispers, the unshed tears in her eyes betraying her attempts at calm, logical reasoning. Her eyes dart over to the door as Mom comes back in holding a patterned shoe box.

"Sorry, that took a while. I've left Peter putting things back together upstairs. Here they are." She sits back down opposite Rachel and places the box in front of her. She lifts the lid off carefully, and I tighten my arm around Rachel as she leans forward and watches.

"I took this one when she brought you home from the hospital." Mom smiles as she passes the old photograph over.

"Oh my God." Rachel takes the photo in both hands and studies the smiling woman, who's holding a small bundle wrapped in a blanket. There's no mistaking the same dark hair, big, bright eyes, and red lips that I saw in the drawing at Rachel's house.

"You look like her," Mom says kindly.

"You're both beautiful." I smile, kissing her hair as she keeps staring at the picture. Mom catches my eye and gives me a worried look. I give her a small nod to continue.

She shows Rachel picture after picture of her mom with her as a baby. Her first bath, first steps, first birthday, complete with cake all over her face. The pictures stop before Rachel gets to two years old.

"There's plenty more in here. Why don't you take it home, Rachel?" Mom says kindly, placing the lid on and sliding the box across the table.

"Are you sure?" Rachel says.

"Yes, love. They're yours. I've got stories I can tell you too when you're ready to hear them."

"I would love that." Rachel runs her hands over the top of the box. Her face is strangely emotionless.

"Come over anytime. Just you and me, we can have a good chat. Your mom was a bit of a live-wire," Mom chuckles.

"Why doesn't that surprise me? Must be where you got it from," I say, giving Rachel a playful squeeze.

The lack of smack to my chest or "wanker" comment tossed my way tells me her head's really spinning trying to take all this in.

My beautiful, beautiful girl, how I wish I could make this easier for you.

TWENTY-THREE

RACHEL

"Are you sure you don't want me to stay?" Tan's eyes gaze into mine as he leans his forearms on the side of the bathtub.

I sink a little lower into the deep bubbles and let out a sigh. He insisted on running the bath for me and practically stripped me and put me in it himself.

"I'm fine, Tan, honestly. I just need some time alone. It's been a headfuck of a day." I tip my head back against the cool side of the bath and close my eyes, letting the steam and hot water ease the pounding in my head.

Strong fingers stroke my neck, easing out the tension in my muscles. "You know I'll stay, Rach. I'll even crash on the sofa with hairy-beast-Nigel, if you like? I just don't like you being alone to deal with this."

I moan as his fingers continue their caress, moving down to my shoulders. "I'm not alone. Megan's home."

"You know what I mean."

279

I open my eyes and look straight into his. Vibrant amber flecks shine back at me, and I'm hit with the urge to pull him into the bath with me—clothes and all—and kiss him until I can't think straight. Kiss him until my mind is filled with nothing but chasing physical pleasure together.

"Fine." He blows out a breath when I say nothing. "But I want you to call me before you go to sleep, okay? And again in the morning. I need to know you're alright."

"I'm not made of glass, Tan," I snap. Immediately regretting the harshness in my tone.

He doesn't flinch, just gives me a small smile. "I know. You're made of diamond. The strongest thing on earth."

I tip my head, and the corners of my mouth twitch as I look at him. "Hmm, you're learning."

He lets out a low chuckle. "With you, Rach. Every day is a fucking school day."

"Teacher's pet." I eye him sideways, and he drops his head to his chest, his shoulders shaking.

"Do I get extra credit?" He laughs.

"You'll get detention if you don't do as you're told and piss off," I say, smiling at him.

"Ooh, sexy. Will you—?"

"Goodbye, Tanner," I say as I arch an eyebrow at him.

He brushes a thumb over my lips. "I'm just at the end of the phone, Rach. Call me. I can be back here in no time at all."

"Do you want me to drown you in this bath?"

He smiles, and his eyes soften. "Okay, I'm going. Deal with this how you need to in your own way. But just so you know; that way can include me if you want it to."

"I'll suffocate you with the soap first."

He laughs as I smile at him, then gets to his feet and heads to the door. I swallow down the lump in my throat as he opens it. I need to be alone to figure this all out. I know I do. It's how I work. It's how I've always done things.

Alone.

Yet, seeing him about to leave has a strange voice screaming inside me to tell him to stop. To ask him to stay. A strange voice that sounds a lot like my own.

He turns back and leans his shoulder against the doorframe. "Call me before—"

"Yes!" I roll my eyes. "I'll call you before I go to bed to tell you the same as I'm telling you now. *I'm fine.*"

"Okay, make sure you—"

I throw a wet washcloth at him, and it hits the door as he closes it just in time to avoid being soaked.

"Bye, Tanner!" I call toward the closed door.

"Bye, Rach," he replies, the amusement in his voice almost hiding the underlying concern that I know is there.

I listen to muffled voices as he talks to Megan. No doubt giving her strict instructions to keep an eye on me and call him if I look like I'm about to stick my head in the oven or something similarly tragic. I blow out a breath and look up at the ceiling. Today has been a crazy as fuck day. But I will get through it. I know I will. I get through everything that's thrown at me. What choice do I have?

I look back over at the closed bathroom door as I hear the front door open and close.

Tanner is gone.

I sink a little lower into the water. I should feel relieved. He's left me alone, like I asked. But instead, all I feel is... numb.

Numb and alone.

And wishing more than ever that my mom was here right now. That I knew her. Really knew her. Not just from a handful of photographs and stories from other people.

"What. A. Day," I groan, allowing myself to soak in the water.

I lay back and think until the water goes cold and goosebumps appear on my arms.

Only then do I finally move again.

"Call me in the morning, okay?" Tanner says.

"Uh-huh," I mutter, cradling my phone between my ear and shoulder.

"Rach?"

"Yes! Okay? I will call you in the morning."

"Okay, good." His voice is warm, and I can imagine

the self-satisfied smile on his face at getting me to agree to something he's asked.

We say goodbye, and I throw the phone down on my bed next to me. He sounded happy to hear from me, and I almost asked him to come back.

Almost.

But I know I need to do this alone. Once that lid comes off, I don't know how I'm going to feel or react. What emotions it might stir up. What weaknesses it might unveil. I can't allow anyone to bear witness to it. I have to do it by myself.

I pull the duvet up to my chin and stare at the box Nell gave me. I put it on top of my drawers and haven't been able to look inside it again yet. I'm scared to look. What if once I let those emotions in, I can't handle it? Seeing those photos of my mom just brought so much anger and hurt back to the surface. Emotions I thought I had dealt with years ago but now feel heart-wrenchingly raw once again. I feel cheated, fucking *cheated* out of the happy childhood I could have had with a mom who loved me. Everyone thinks I'm this strong, takes-no-shit girl, but I'm not. I didn't lose my mom and grow up without a proper home because I was strong and could handle it. I handled it because I had no choice. I don't know who I am right now, apart from a girl who's afraid to face her grief all over again.

Nigel shifts on top of the duvet to move closer to me. "Hey boy," I coo, reaching an arm out from under the covers and stroking him. He rarely comes upstairs, but it's like he sensed something was wrong when I arrived home. He sat at the bottom of the stairs until I carried him up. He's been keeping me company on my bed ever since I got out of the bath after Tanner left. "You should have been a therapy pet," I say softly, watching his eyes close as I run my fingers over his head. He's the only company I can handle right now. I know Tanner, Megan, Matt, Holly —they're all there for me. But this is something I need to work through on my own tonight, at least until it sinks in.

"Be brave with me, Nigel," I whisper as I slide out of bed, fetching the box and bringing it back with me. This box holds more of my mom in it than I've ever seen before. I had given up hoping there were any more pictures of her. Knowing that this has been in Nell's house for almost thirty years is simply crazy. It defies logic. That she would have kept them, that I would meet her, by dating her son? I mean, what the hell? It's overwhelming. I feel like I'm in a dream or a parallel universe. This can't be real.

Taking a deep breath, I slide the lid off the box. Nigel sits up, his nose twitching as he sniffs at it. "Sorry, Nigel. No treats. Do you want to see my mom?" I ask, my voice shaking as I hold up the photo of her with me as a newborn so he can see. He looks at me expectantly. "I look like her, don't I?" I sniff. The thought makes me feel better. I may not remember her, but it's a small connection.

I look at the other photos Nell showed me at her house before pulling one out I haven't seen yet. It's of a toddler girl—me, I assume—and a boy, a couple of years older. I'm sitting in the bath grinning, and he's standing up, completely naked, except for a superman cape, looking proud as punch. There's only one person it can be.

Tanner.

I don't know why that's the photo that finally bursts the dam, but it is. My eyes sting, and my breath catches as my chest erupts into heaving sobs, tears streaming down my face.

I cuddle Nigel closer and let myself cry.

I'm flying in the air, the force of the wind lifting me up under my arms. Below me, the coastline stretches as far as I can see. I get the impression it's early morning in the summer because my skin feels warm under the sun's rays, and there's no one on the beach. A tinkling sound makes me turn my head. Next to me is Mom. A bright light radiates around her as she laughs, and the sound of tiny bells fills my ears again. I beam back at her as calmness washes over me.

A buzzing breaks through the air.

No, not yet. I'm not ready to say goodbye, not yet. I need more time—please!

I jerk awake, my eyes falling onto my bedroom door, which is ajar. Nigel is gone. Megan must have come in to get him so she could feed him. I pick up my phone and see Tanner's name on the new text.

Tan: Hey Sleeping Beauty. I came to see you but figured you needed the lie-in. I've got some meetings at work this morning but will come by later. I want to see you before your flight tonight. Call me when you wake up.

That's right, I've got a flight to Johannesburg tonight. Ugh, it's the last thing I feel like doing today. But saying that, it could be a good distraction. My head feels all over the place. It took me ages to get to sleep last night, and when I did... *God, that dream.* I can still see her face so clearly. Smiling at me, like she was telling me it will be okay.

It will all be okay.

"I must be losing my mind," I groan, throwing the covers back and sitting up to text Tanner back.

Me: Thank you. I appreciate you giving me some space last night. See you later.

My phone rings almost immediately.

I answer it and hold it to my ear. Tanner's smooth voice is already speaking.

"Whatever you need, Rach, just say it. Anything at all, it's yours."

I smile at his words. He's a good guy. I thought he was such a materialistic wanker when we first met. But he's proving time and time again what a good heart he has. What I did to deserve such treatment, I've no idea.

"A ticket out of the twilight zone?" I smirk.

"Do they sell those on Amazon? If so, consider it done."

"Idiot," I snort.

I hear him chuckle, then blow out a breath. "How did you sleep?"

"Next question."

"That good, huh?"

"Something like that." I stretch my arms above my head and swing my legs out of bed. "Listen, I was just calling to tell you I haven't gone nuts or anything, so you don't need to keep calling me."

"Point taken. I shall leave you in peace. See you later, yeah?"

A sudden image of him in a superman cape as a child pops into my head, and I squeeze my eyes shut. "Yeah," I answer. "See you later."

I head downstairs and can hear muffled voices coming from the dining room. I head in through the lounge and see Matt and Megan sitting at the dining table, where a small feast of luxurious-looking pastries, granola, yogurts, and juices is set out.

"Tanner," Matt says by explanation as he rises to wrap an arm around my shoulders, guiding me into a chair.

"He brought it all around while you were still asleep," Megan says, reaching her hand over the table to give mine a squeeze.

I look at all the food; there's enough to last both Megan and me a week here.

"Sounds like you had a shock yesterday. Megan and

Tanner called me," Matt says kindly, getting straight to the point. "I've already texted Holly. She's going to call later, before your flight. If you're still going, that is?"

"Of course, I am. Why wouldn't I?" I mutter, picking up a croissant and tearing a strip off.

He glances at Megan, who chooses her words carefully as she speaks. "Well, it's perfectly understandable. What you've just found out, you need time to process it."

"It's not going to change anything, though, is it?" I sigh, rubbing at my puffy eyes. "I mean, it was a complete shock to find out that Tanner's mom knew her."

"Totally, it's like a soap opera," Matt says, shutting his mouth quickly as I look up. "Sorry, I didn't mean it like that, Rach."

"No, Matt, you're right. It's like some weird, messed-up fictional story. I mean, what are the chances?"

"Maybe it means something?" Megan says. We both look at her. "I mean, maybe it's a sign? You met Tanner, and he's made you open to the possibility of having a *conventional* relationship. Now you find out his mom knew yours. That you and he knew each other as babies?"

"It's just a fucking weird coincidence, Meg," I say, reaching for another croissant, even though I haven't eaten the one I've torn apart.

"I'm just saying. If you'd never met him, if things had never got serious enough for him to take you to meet his mom?" She looks from me to Matt.

"Maybe we should phone one of those psychic phone lines!" Matt says. "Get them to read the cards or something."

I laugh a humorless laugh. "You couldn't make this shit up."

"What are you going to do?" Megan asks.

I lean back in my chair. *What can I do? Do I need to do anything?* It's not like it changes much. My mom is still gone. Those years we never had together will always be lost.

"I guess just get on with things. I'm going to visit Tan's mom, Nell, when I get back from my flight. She said I could go and talk to her. She's got stories about Mom she said she would tell me."

"That sounds lovely," Matt says.

"It does," Megan agrees, nodding her head.

We sit and eat breakfast together as the conversation turns to Megan's commission for Tan's company and Matt's upcoming time off in a couple of months. He's going to Hawaii with Stefan. I do a good job of nodding and making the odd comment, but really my mind is miles away.

It's upstairs in my bedroom, at the bottom of a shoe box.

Tanner came to see me as he promised before my flight, the worry in his eyes clear. I assured him I'm fine; I just need some time for it to sink in. He begrudgingly left at the same time I had to leave for Heathrow Airport to check-in for my flight. Before he went, he kissed me with so much tenderness that I almost called in sick so that I could stay with him. The temptation shocked me; I really am a whole different person recently.

Me: Hey. I'm at your mom's. I'll give you a call later when I'm leaving.

I tap my fingers against my bottom lip as I wait for him to reply. I know he will. He always texts me straight back. Truthfully, he's been incredible. He's been there whenever I've needed him. And given me space whenever I've asked for it. I haven't even always had to ask. He just seems to know. Sometimes I think he knows me better than I know myself. Finding out all of this stuff about Mom. It's felt so surreal and overwhelming at times. It would have been a million times harder if Tanner weren't around.

It's been two weeks since Nell gave me the shoebox of my mom's photographs, and I wish I could say it's gotten easier. But I would be lying. The shock may have worn off, but I still feel... I don't know.

Numb.

Tan: I bet she'll have made a cake again. I swear if she has, then it's official... she likes you more than me!

I smile as I picture what his face must have looked like as he typed out that message. I've been to see Nell a few times over the last two weeks. All without Tanner. Another prime example of when he's sensed to give me space. The first time was strange. I didn't take my jacket off for the first half an hour. I sat on the edge of my seat, feeling like my legs would work of their own accord, and I would bolt for the door—find it all too much and escape.

But Nell soon made me feel at ease. Maybe it's a Mom thing. Or maybe it's just a Nell thing. But I've found myself relaxing more and more in her company each time I visit. Now I look forward to our time together. We don't even talk about my mom the entire time. She asks about places I've flown to and tells me about the holiday to Australia she and Peter are planning.

She's made me feel safe in her home.

Safe enough to explore years of hidden memories.

Safe enough to wonder. Wonder about my future.

Because the more I learn about Mom and my past, the more I can't help feeling like it means something. Like it's telling me that it's okay to dream about a different future for once.

One where I don't have to do it all alone.

I take a deep breath and slide my phone into my pocket as I head to the front door and ring the bell. It really feels like I've spent more time here in the last two weeks than at my own house.

"Rachel!" Nell beams as though this is the greatest surprise, even though she knew I was coming.

"Hi, Nell." I smile, stepping into her welcoming hug. She smells of cocoa butter and vanilla—sweet and comforting.

"You're looking well, love. Did you sleep better last night?" she asks, studying my face.

I'll admit, I have been sleeping better now that the shock of her revelation has sunk in. Either that or the new eye cream Holly sent me from LA is working wonders, and I look more awake. Nell fusses around me as we head inside, handing me some treats she's picked up for Nigel, and then putting on the kettle and grabbing two mugs.

She doesn't even ask what I want anymore; she just knows.

"How was Saint Lucia?" she asks over her shoulder as she cuts two large slices of cake and puts them onto plates. "You remembered to cream your back, didn't you?"

I smile. "Yes, Nell, I remembered."

"Good, good. These things are important." She hands me the plates to take to the table. "It's coffee and walnut, one of Tanner's favorites. I've got half wrapped up for you to take."

"Thank you." I smile as I sit down, warmth spreading in my chest as I think about his text and cake comment.

I can take it to his house later. I'm spending the night there tonight as it's the hotel re-opening night, and I want to go to support Megan. She showed me her artwork this morning. It's amazing. The hotel is in a prime position for business travelers, so it has been re-designed with a vintage travel theme. Megan's picture is an incredible collection of men and women in both modern and vintage uniforms, all merged into a large circular canvas, made to look like an aircraft engine. It's going to look incredible in the foyer as the central piece. I'm going to get ready with her at home so we can share a taxi there. Tanner said he would pick us up, but I know he will be tight on time after work, and besides, I wanted it to be just Megan and me as I know she will be nervous. Maybe I can get a whisky into her before we leave. That will help her nerves.

Tanner and I have fallen into a routine these last two weeks of spending every night together—except when I was in Johannesburg and Saint Lucia with work. We alternate between his house and mine. I've noticed he's even started leaving things at my house. First a toothbrush, then a razor. Then this morning, I saw that he left a pair of sweatpants. I swear he thinks he's a genius, and I haven't noticed yet. But I knew the second the toothbrush arrived. I just didn't tell him. Seeing it there in the bathroom bothered me a lot less than I expected. But I'm more than happy to let him continue thinking he's gotten away with it. He's probably feeling smug as shit, knowing him. Marveling at his perceived stealth-like abilities and powers of deception.

"You, and his cake. He'll think it's his birthday."

Nell laughs, pulling my attention back to her as she sits down opposite me and hands me a steaming mug of caramel latte. I wrap my hands around it and smile at her. She catches my eye, hers twinkling. "You're incredibly special to him, Rachel. You're the only girlfriend he's ever brought for lunch," she says, taking a sip of her tea. I must look surprised as she laughs again. "You didn't know?"

"No, I never thought about it, I guess."

Thinking about it now, I know Tanner's had lots of women in his life before, but the only girlfriend I've ever really heard about by name is Mandy. From what he's said, all his relationships have been short-lived. But then, we haven't been seeing each other that long, and he still brought me to meet his mom.

"Maybe that's a good job, after how our first meeting went," I joke.

Nell reaches across the table and pats my hand. "You've had a lot to take in. I think you're doing a grand job," she says kindly.

"I think it's sunk in now. Seeing all the photos has been incredible. I'm so grateful you hung on to them. I feel like I at least know a bit more about her now."

Nell looks thoughtful for a moment. "Did I tell you about the time Helen and I caught Tanner drawing on you with my lipstick?"

"What? No!" I laugh.

She leans back in her chair, her eyes bright. "You were barely old enough to sit up, but he was always trying to include you in his games. He was obsessed with Superman." She rolls her eyes, chuckling. "Wore this little cape everywhere."

I smile as the bath photograph comes to mind.

"Anyway, we had only left you together in the living room while we got lunch ready. We could hear you giggling away and just thought he was amusing you as he always did."

Really? Tanner always made baby me laugh?

"Then, we go back in the room and can see he's drawn all over your face with red lipstick. Said it was your superhero disguise." Nell's face creases up with laughter. "It took your mom fifteen minutes to wash it all off. Probably wouldn't have been so long if she weren't laughing so hard. You looked like a tomato!" Nell sighs, wiping her eyes with a tissue as she tries to control her giggles.

"Really? Tanner did that?" I'm still mulling over the idea of him knowing me as a baby. We were both too young to remember, yet we had this whole little friendship going on by the sounds of it.

"Yes. He always included you in his games. He loved you back then, too," she says before her eyes widen and she tries to backtrack. "You know what I mean. You were sweet together," she says before biting into her cake.

I look at her as a thought forms in my head. Just what has Tanner said to her? He's told me they're close. Does he tell her everything? *Is he in love with me?* I swallow down the lump in my throat, unsure what to make of the idea, as Nell glances up at me.

"Do you want to hear about the time your mom gave the postman an earful?"

I smile back at her. "Yes, yes, I do."

Just like that, hours pass in Nell's company again, talking about my mom and me and Tanner as a baby and toddler. With each story she tells me, I feel a stronger connection to who my mom was and how my life started. With each hour I spend in her company, I feel like something shifts inside me. I imagine this is what the connection feels like when you have a sense of belonging somewhere.

A feeling which has been so alien to me.

Until now.

TWENTY-FOUR

TANNER

I THROW MY KEYS DOWN ON THE KITCHEN SIDE, PULLING my tie loose as I read the note Rachel left on the side.

Cake from your mom. See you later.

I laugh. I knew Mom would make one. I peel back the foil. Coffee and walnut. Hopefully, that won't be the only sweet thing I'll be tasting tonight. I can't wait to see Rachel at the hotel re-opening. I would have much rather she got ready here and went with me, but she wanted to go with Megan to support her. Probably a good job, really, considering work at the office ran later today, and I have less than an hour to take a shower, get dressed into black-tie, and get myself to the hotel twenty minutes away.

I take the stairs two at a time, stripping my suit off and laying it over the chair in my dressing room. Rachel's overnight bag is here. The sight of it brings me more pleasure than I can describe. That I got her to accept a key to my house under the initial pretense it

297

was for "emergencies only" has been a tremendous step for her. She wasn't keen at all, but the fact that she's used it happily today to drop her things around just goes to show that we're making progress.

I can't fuck this up. Mom knows just how serious this has all become. She and Rachel have grown close since the revelation about Helen, and us knowing each other as babies. And Rachel has taken it in her stride. She's been so strong. Some days I wonder if it's even affected her at all. Those are the days a sliver of worry creeps in. She's so adamant about being in control all the time. I just hope she knows she can count on me. Mom thinks Rachel is amazing too. Not as amazing as I do, though. Apparently, it's "written all over my face".

I'm in deep.

Hell, I'm in fucking love.

I make it to the hotel in record time and arrive as the drink reception is starting. It's already busy. The large foyer is almost filled with a mix of business guests who have been invited to spend the first night in the newly re-designed rooms, local business owners checking out the facilities and offering their support, and members of the press. I take my time greeting people I know and introducing myself and the company to those I don't, before grabbing a moment alone to take in the large foyer.

I can't help but feel a sense of pride at what an

outstanding job the team has done. It's elegant and modern, without losing a sense of comfort. All around are subtle nods to vintage transportation, from the train-carriage-style velvet booth seating areas to the large sails artistically suspended high overhead. Megan's artwork has pride of place on the wall behind the long reception desk where every guest will see it. She has done an incredible job; she really has. I didn't doubt that she would; I knew she was talented. I was just worried about the scale of such a short-notice commission and how she would cope. She's always seemed quite timid. Lovely, but shy. Her art is obviously where she lets loose and expresses herself. The passion that pours out of the piece is undeniable. This is going to open doors for her. There's no way artwork like hers will go unnoticed now.

"Another job well done," a familiar female voice says.

I turn as my assistant Penny comes to stand next to me and admires the design. I'm pleased she could make it tonight. She doesn't come to a lot of work functions as her two boys are eight and ten, and she's usually needed at home with them in the evenings. Her husband is there tonight, holding down the fort. She's worked with me for years and puts so much into her work, but she never usually gets to see the end result. It's nice that tonight she gets the opportunity.

"It's a team effort." I smile at her. Her short blonde hair catches the light as she smiles back.

"Never one to take all the glory, are you?" She

smiles. "Although, you have to with Scarlett's Christmas present. She's going to adore that kitty you bought her in New York. Thank you so much. My sister says she will love you forever." Penny laughs.

"I'm happy to hear that, but I can't take sole responsibility for that one either." I chuckle, plucking two glasses of champagne from a passing server and handing one to Penny.

"Ah." She smiles knowingly. "So, is Rachel coming tonight?"

I raise an eyebrow at her over the top of my glass.

"I actually pay attention, you know." She smiles. "Unlike some others, I could mention," she says playfully as Drew comes to join us.

"Hey, Penny. You look stunning," Drew says, his eyes sweeping up and down her black evening dress. "Remember where I am if you ever divorce John."

"His name is Jake, as you well know," Penny scolds light-heartedly. She's used to Drew's open flirtation after years of working with him. "Oh, I've just seen Melanie from Design. Catch you both later." She smiles as she heads off across the room.

"Married women are hot," Drew says, watching her go. "What do you think it is? The off-limits element that does it?"

"I couldn't tell you." I shake my head.

He turns his attention to me fully, his eyes widening.

"Tan?"

"What?" I clear my throat, avoiding his gaze as I take another drink.

"You've fallen in fucking love with her, haven't you?" he says quietly as some guests pass us.

I nod politely at them.

"What if I have?" I reply, annoyed.

Drew blows out a long breath. "Nothing, man. Congratulations, I guess." He turns to me and clinks his glass against mine. "Have you told her?"

I scan the room. Rachel and Megan aren't here yet. They're late. They should have been here by now.

"No. Not yet."

"But you've told her about the other thing now, though, haven't you?" Drew says, studying my face. "Fuck, Tan." He throws his head back in disbelief as one glance at my face tells him all he needs to know.

"I'm going to. Tonight," I say, my jaw set, tension spreading through my body.

"Rather you than me. Fuck, man. Why have you left it so long?"

"I was going to, and then all that stuff with her mom happened, and it just didn't seem right. One shock seemed enough," I mutter as I cast my eyes back to the entrance. Still no sign of them.

"Maybe she's already found out and blown you off," Drew says, following my gaze.

"Real helpful, Drew." I shake my head.

"Hey Tan, I'm just joking. I'm sure she'll be here any minute."

I glance at my watch. She better be.

"So, what's happening with the woman from Bath?" I ask Drew, happy to move the conversation in a new direction.

He shrugs and tilts his head to one side. "Nothing yet. It's only a matter of time, though. She's been texting me."

"She has? What, asking you to leave her alone, or she'll file for a restraining order?" I joke, but Drew isn't listening; his eyes are staring over at the main doors.

"Looks like Cinderella has made it to the ball." He grins.

I lift my chin, whipping my eyes around to find a break in the crowd. When I do, I see Rachel and Megan walking in. I fight the urge to let my mouth hang wide open at the sight of her. She is literally the most radiant, beautiful woman I have ever seen. She's wearing a long, strappy silver dress. The satiny material touches all the right places, showcasing her sensational body underneath while still being classy and elegant. Her dark waves skim her shoulders, one side swept off her face with a crystal hair clip. Her lips are pin-up red. She looks like a fifty's starlet. I run a hand through my hair as my eyes meet hers. They're smoky and dark, but there's no hiding the way they light up as she looks at me watching her.

Fuck, Snow, no wonder I'm a lost cause when you look at me like that.

I place my glass down on a sideboard and make my way over to her, closing the distance between us as quickly as is possible in such a full space. I finally reach her, stopping inches from her face as my eyes burn into hers. She says nothing, just looks at me, a slight trace of amusement dancing in her eyes.

"Good evening, Mr. Grayson," she says slowly as I slide one hand around the back of her neck and the other around her waist, pulling her hot lips against mine and pressing a kiss to them. I can feel her pulse underneath my thumb.

"You look stunning," I whisper into the jasmine-scented skin by her ear before moving back, keeping one hand firmly on her waist. The silky fabric of her dress slips beneath my fingers as she leans into my side.

"And we are both still here," Drew jokes, clearing his throat and making Megan giggle.

"I'm so sorry." I cough awkwardly and smile as I lean over to kiss Megan on both cheeks. She looks amazing too, in a long deep blue dress with a side split. Her curls are piled up on top of her head, loose strands falling and making her look young and innocent.

"No, you're not," Drew pipes up. "Who can blame you, though?" He smiles as he kisses first Megan and then Rachel on the back of the hand. Megan smiles at his easy-going, flirty nature, and Rachel raises a brow at him, a small curve at the corner of her mouth.

"Practicing your chat up lines on us already, are you Drew?" she says as he releases her hand.

"And why not? You two are beautiful women, and I am a very willing student. I must say, I especially excel at lessons of a practical nature. The more hands-on, the better," he says shamelessly.

"I love your enthusiasm, Drew." Megan giggles, rolling her eyes.

"Why, thank you." He grins, smug as the Cheshire fucking cat.

"Yeah, it's a shame he can't always muster up the same enthusiasm about the weekly Monday morning meeting," I joke, watching as he pretends to look outraged.

He turns to address Rachel and Megan. "I do a superb job of looking interested while my uptight boss drones on about figures and boring shit. I've perfected the face. Look." He sets his face into an expression of interest, turning down the corners of his mouth and nodding as though in agreement.

"That's incredible," Megan says, playing along.

"Yeah, amazing," Rachel snorts.

"I'm sure you've had to perfect your interested face when Tanner's going on," Drew says to Rachel.

"Tanner knows exactly what my face looks like when he's *going on* at me. Don't you, darling?" Rachel lays a hand on my chest and gives me the best come fuck me look. If I didn't have to make a speech shortly, then I would pull her out of here right now and back to my car.

"That is not what I meant." Drew groans as an unwanted mental image likely pops into his mind. "Come on, Megan. Let's leave these two alone before they eat each other's faces in front of us." Megan happily takes his arm and smiles at us as they walk off together.

"Smart move," I say quietly to Rachel. "Drew couldn't wait to get out of here."

She smiles back at me, looking up at me from under her lashes. "Not just that, but now Drew will introduce Megan to all the people who admire her artwork and want to meet her. Something I know you would have been doing otherwise. This way, I get to keep you closer until the speeches start."

I stare back into her eyes, mesmerized by the way they're looking back at me tonight. Something's changed in her. I can sense a shift, as though the last barrier has finally lifted.

"You want to keep me closer?" I drop my eyes to her lips as she smiles and nods at me.

"Uh-huh," she says playfully. "I enjoy being really close to my boyfriend."

Fuck. Did she just call me her boyfriend? For real? I mean, I know that's what we are. We spend so much time together. She sleeps at my house now and me at hers—in the same bed after all her hang-ups over it. She's got my mom on speed dial. I've given her a key to my house. I know that's what she is to me. But to hear her say that I'm her boyfriend. This is a fucking huge milestone.

I'm sure I'm grinning back at her like an idiot. "Way to give me a fucking hard-on in a room full of people, Rach," I murmur into her ear as I move her to stand in front of me, concealing the evidence. She inclines her head over her shoulder to talk to me.

"I'll take care of that later for you." She smirks.

I grab onto her hips and hold her in place as I see the hotel manager across the room. He catches my eye and gives me a smile and wave. His signal that it's almost time to do the official opening speeches and raffle an all-expenses-paid stay in the new penthouse suite tonight.

"I'm going to have to go in a minute," I say into Rachel's ear, flexing my hands on her hipbones, fighting the blood back out of my cock. Think about something unsexy. Painting... no, fuck! Hot sex on Rachel's living room floor. Okay, plumbing... no— mind-blowing sex in the bath with Rachel. *Shit*, I need something fast. I glance over and see Drew has separated from Megan and is chatting to one of the hotel receptionists. *Bingo!* There's nothing sexy about watching Drew flirt shamelessly. I loosen my grip on Rachel as my shoulders relax, along with my cock.

Rachel's looking around the room. "Who's that Megan's talking to?"

I look over to where Megan is deep in conversation with an older man. His dark, exotic features have only made him more handsome with age—lucky fucker.

"That's Jaxon King. He owns a publishing company in London. I see him at a lot of events like this. He's always looking for new locations to host book signings and literary events."

"Whatever he's saying must be funny," Rachel

says as, across the room, Megan throws her head back and laughs. Funny, I don't remember him being much of a talker whenever I've met him. He's pleasant, sure, but usually keeps himself to himself. He's extremely well-educated and went to Oxford to study. I just figured he was a quiet, academic type, but the way he has Megan captivated, I'm beginning to think I'm way off the mark as far as impressions go.

I lead Rachel over to the reception desk, where a temporary raised platform has been set up. She turns to talk to someone next to her, and I'm relieved to see it's Penny. She will look after her while I'm busy. Not that Rachel needs babysitting. I know full well she can hold her own. Still, I don't like the idea of leaving her alone in a room where at least half the guests are businessmen who would think nothing of slipping their wedding rings off when they're away on a work trip. She glances at me with a smile before continuing her conversation with Penny. I hear the words 'New York' and 'Scarlett' mentioned.

"Tanner." The hotel manager, Edward, approaches me, holding out his hand. He's a friendly-looking man with impeccably high standards. It took twice as long as usual to get him on board with the design team's vision, and he isn't even the owner. Rumor has it the wealthy lady heiress who owns this hotel and a few others around the capital has a soft spot for her younger, male hotel managers.

"Edward, you're looking great." I smile, business

mode fully entered as I shake his hand. "This is such a brilliant turnout."

"It is, and it's thanks to you and the team. The re-opening caused quite a buzz. I've seen three big papers and a couple of style magazine journalists here already," he says excitedly.

I smile; his enthusiasm is infectious. This is why I love my job, my company. Seeing the client's face when it's all revealed and knowing what a difference it will make to their business as a result—bringing them in new clients, getting them noticed. It's all worth it. If I'm honest, though, my absolute favorite part is the college apprenticeship programs we help fund. Drew always says we should ditch them as they don't make us money, but I can't. I started with nothing, and I love that I can give back and give opportunities to those just starting out on their journey. The head for this project, Imogen, started studying to be an electrician at college on one of the company-funded programs. Then after working her ass off on sites for us, she showed an interest in design. Now she's one of the company's top-paid project managers. I love that my company did that —opened that door up for her.

I smile and greet Imogen as she comes to stand next to Edward and me on the podium. For the next twenty minutes, we each take turns to welcome the guests and tell them about the hotel, the inspiration behind its new design, and the scale of the re-modeling. There's a general hum of excitement in the air and a collective sound of appreciation as I talk about Megan's focal artwork and how it draws the entire design together.

"Now, ladies and gentlemen, before we finish, we must draw the winning raffle ticket for the first stay in our newly refurbished penthouse suite," Edward announces dramatically, enticing some "oohs" and "ahs" from the audience. "First, let me choose a willing assistant to pull the ticket."

He steps down and into the front of the crowd, holding out the large glass bowl full of folded paper slips to a lady in a purple dress. She blushes at being put on the spot before twirling her hand around inside the bowl and making her selection.

"Madam, if you would please read the winning ticket number," Edward instructs as a hush falls across the room. Everyone eagerly waits to see who will win the four-figures-a-night stay in luxury.

"Number three hundred and thirteen!" she calls out clearly as chatter breaks out around the room, along with the sound of people pulling paper tickets out of purses and pockets to check their numbers.

"Looks like that's me," a deep voice calls out.

I look to where the call came from and see Jaxon King holding a ticket up in his hand. Edward makes his way over and checks the ticket before shaking Jaxon's hand and handing him a golden envelope, which I assume contains the penthouse keycard. Camera clicks can be heard, along with a rumble of applause as the official opening presentation ends.

"Nice speech, Mr. Grayson." Rachel smiles, sliding

her arm into mine as I find her and Megan in the crowd again.

"Thanks." I smile, tearing my eyes away from the sultry look she's giving me, aware that Megan is with us. I don't want to seem rude again, even though Megan doesn't seem in the least bit bothered that I can barely think straight when Rachel is nearby. I guess she's used to the two of us by now.

"How's your evening been, Megan? Every time I've seen you, it looks like someone else has grabbed you to tell you how much they love your art," I say to her.

"It's been incredible. Thank you. This would never have happened if you hadn't given me the opportunity." She beams with undisguised excitement.

"You know it was actually Rachel's idea, and you did me a favor, not the other way around."

"Yeah, Meg," Rachel adds. "You deserve this! You worked so hard." I see her eyes subtly glance over Megan's shoulder before she lowers her voice. "Who's the older fox you were talking to?"

I clear my throat and move my arm down, encircling Rachel's waist tightly. She looks back at me, her eyes narrowing before turning back to Megan.

"Oh, his name's Jaxon," Megan says innocently. "He said my picture reminded him of his favorite illustrator's work. He said he works in publishing."

Playing it down, huh, Jaxon? I know for a fact he's the biggest guy in publishing this side of the Atlantic. Not just traditional either. His company also owns one of the most successful eBook sites there is.

Megan's eyes look from Rachel and then to me as she keeps talking. "Actually, I really wanted to talk to him again. He said he was going to write down some illustrator's names from old books he thought I might like to look at."

I bet he did. I chuckle internally. I've not heard that one before, but I've got to admit, it sounds way better than anything I've heard Drew use as a chat-up line. Judging by how Jaxon keeps looking over here towards Megan, I would say I'm bang on the money that he hopes she will return to finish their conversation.

"You don't need a ride home then?" Rachel asks.

"No, thanks, though. I'll see you tomorrow," Megan says, giving Rachel a quick hug and then leaning over to give me one too, before heading off back towards a delighted-looking Jaxon King.

"What was all that about?" Rachel says playfully, her attention fully back on me as she moves in front of me and reaches her arms up around my neck. Public displays of affection—I must be in her good books.

I slide my hands low on her back to where the curve of her ass starts. "What was what about?" I ask, pulling her against me tightly, so there's no denying what it does to me when she looks up at me like this.

"Don't give me that. The way you practically growled when I called Jaxon King a fox." She arches an eyebrow at me as her eyes sparkle.

A flash of jealousy surges through me. "I did not growl. I cleared my throat," I say, keeping my expression solemn. "I can't say that hearing my girl call

311

another man a fox is something I wish a repeat of, though," I add sulkily.

"I'm your girl, am I?" she teases.

I look at her darkly. "Don't fucking forget it."

She smirks, running her fingers around the collar of my dress shirt. "Did I tell you how sexy you look in a dinner jacket?"

"You can't get off that easily," I mutter as I drop my eyes to her lips.

She rises on her tiptoes, and the smell of her skin mixed with jasmine renders me momentarily speechless as her warm breath dusts against my ear. "I get off really easy when you're involved, Tan," she whispers, causing blood to race to my already twitching cock.

I slide my hands lower, squeezing her ass underneath my fingers.

"I think it's time we went home now, don't you?"

TWENTY-FIVE

RACHEL

"Harder, Tan!" I moan, throwing my head back as Tanner thrusts into me again. I'm on my back on his bed, my legs around his ears, and my hands gripping his biceps underneath my thighs with white-knuckle force.

"God, Rach, you saying my name like that will not help this last longer," he pants, keeping a relentless rhythm going.

I bring my chin back down and stare into his eyes. They light up as I smile and clench around him tightly.

"Argh, fuck! Okay, you asked for it." He laughs, pushing my legs even wider apart as he slams into me so hard his balls slap my skin.

I moan loudly at how good it feels before letting out a giggle.

"Not helping, Rach." His voice wavers as he bites his lip.

I look at him, the concentration on his face clear as he fights to hold his orgasm back. I've already had two; I don't know why he thinks I need to have another before he's allowed. But then this is Tanner, and as I've come to learn, he's extremely generous when it comes to dishing out the big O's.

I bring one hand to his lips, and knowing what I want him to do, he draws two of my fingers into his mouth and sucks, wetting them for me.

He drags in a breath through clenched teeth. "You know I love watching you touch yourself," he groans as I slide my hand down to my throbbing clit and rub in circles.

"And you know I love that you love watching me." I smile as I stroke myself faster.

His eyes drop to my hand and then back up to my face as I feel the tingling building in my toes and up my legs.

"Come for me, baby," he growls, pressing his cock into me hard and deep, over and over.

There's no way I could disobey him when he talks to me like that, even if I wanted to. His voice is deep, sexy, and in control—*in control of me.*

"Fuck, Tan!" I cry as I tip over the edge of my release, spiraling out of control as my back arches off the bed, and I shudder underneath him.

"That's it, baby. I love feeling you come on my cock." His eyes look stormy as he drives into me, drawing my orgasm out for longer.

Holy shit, I love the way he looks at me.

His cock swells against my walls, and a rush of heat ignites inside me as he groans loudly, coming deep inside my body.

"God, Rach, I..." He struggles with his words as his orgasm takes his breath.

"You what?" I pant back, bringing my hands to either side of his face as he looks at me and draws in deep breaths.

"I..." his eyes search mine.

Fuck, is he going to say...?

"I can't get enough of you," he says quickly, leaning down to kiss me.

I welcome his warm lips to mine, but I swear he's only kissing me now so that he can avoid eye contact. I would bet anything that Tanner was on the verge of saying he loves me.

Only he didn't.

I shift in his muscular arms, trying to ease the burning discomfort in my chest. I'm disappointed. No, it's more than that. My lungs deflate like someone has sucked all the air out, and everything falls quiet around me, except the sound of my heart racing in my ears.

That sudden lurch in my stomach when he didn't say what I hoped he was going to can only mean one thing—I am totally in love with Tanner Grayson.

Shit.

"Morning, beautiful." Tanner grins as he walks around the bed in his boxers and places a steaming mug of caramel latte on the bedside table next to me. He's made it with the new machine he bought, specifically because it makes lattes exactly how I like them—smooth, creamy, and hot.

"Did I tell you how much you've grown on me?" I smile, stretching my arms over my head before pulling myself up to a sitting position against the headboard, bringing the sheets with me to cover my breasts.

"Nowhere near enough. Tell me again." Tanner grins as he climbs over me on the bed, pausing halfway to straddle me, and pulls the covers down so he can suck on both of my nipples. "Don't cover yourself up, Rach. I love your tits," he growls playfully as he swings his second leg over and leans back against the headboard next to me.

I turn towards him, so I can study him. He starts scrolling through emails on his phone, one arm slung behind his head. His eyes scan side to side as he reads, deep in thought. He looks a lot younger than thirty-one right now, with his messy bed hair and pouty lips, which move slightly as he reads. A sudden image of him naked except for a superman cape suddenly comes to me, and my heart squeezes.

"You love them?" I ask slowly.

"I love all of your body, Rachel," he answers easily, his eyes staying on his phone as he continues reading.

I watch him for a few more moments, and when

I'm sure he's not about to drop any bombs of the "I love you" variety on me, I pick up my latte and take a sip, blowing out a long sigh as its heat spreads through me.

"This is so good. You didn't have to get a whole new coffee machine just for the odd night I'm here, though."

"Of course, I did," Tanner says, still studying his phone, a small frown on his face. "It's more than the odd night, and I like my girl sufficiently caffeinated." He throws his phone down on the bed and looks up at me, the amber flecks in his eyes glistening. "She can be a bit of a snarky bitch if you get in her bad books."

I narrow my eyes at him. "She sounds like a nightmare. Why do you put up with her?"

Tanner shrugs a shoulder and pushes out his bottom lip. "Well, we've sort of known each other since she was born. I must have imprinted on her or some shit as I can't stop thinking about her."

I snort. "I thought you were superman, not a werewolf."

"Rach, if it turns you on, I'm happy to dress up as any kinky shit you like." He grins as I shove his shoulder.

"Wanker," I mutter, not able to hold back my smile as Tanner turns his head and kisses my temple. I look down at his phone on the bed. "Work emails?"

"Yeah," he groans, dragging a hand down over his face. "We've won a contract with a client in Vegas to redesign their entire casino. It's a three-month project, which was supposed to start in the spring. Only now they've decided they want to bring it forward."

"Can't you tell them no?"

Tanner rubs his lips as he thinks. "Yes, we can. They've signed the contract; we don't have to be flexible at all. But it would benefit us if I can sort out the logistics as spring will be busy for us, especially in London. Tying this one up early would actually make sense." He drums the fingers of his other hand against his thighs as he speaks.

"So, what's the problem?"

He pauses for a moment. "Nothing really." He turns to smile at me. "Just need to juggle some people around a bit to make it possible."

"I bet being the boss makes you really unpopular sometimes, especially messing with people's work schedules so close to Christmas. More unpopular than you already are, I mean," I tease, glancing at him.

"Hey, my staff love me!" Tanner cries, his eyes rounding on me. His face softens as he sees my smirk.

"Not what Penny said last night," I joke.

"Oh, really?" He lifts his chin, daring me with his eyes to continue.

I widen my eyes and lower my voice. "Did you know your staff used to call you 'Grumpy Grayson?' I think they were being quite kind, actually." I giggle as I see the outraged look on Tan's face.

"I am not grumpy. I buy the snacks every week for the Monday meeting." He shakes his head, tutting to himself before looking back at me. "You said used to? What do they call me now? Or don't I want to know?"

"Actually, Penny says you've been delightful the last three months. Not a grump in sight. Said you even smile."

"The last three months, you say?" Tanner looks thoughtful.

"Yeah, now what's happened in the last three months that could have put a smile on Mr. Grumpy's face?" I tease. I watch as the corners of Tanner's mouth twitch.

"No idea," he says, avoiding my gaze.

"None?" I smile, placing my mug back down on the bedside table.

"Nope." He blows out a breath, putting his hands behind his head and pretending to sound bored.

"Maybe I can help you remember just what's been happening the last three months that could be considered as life-changing." I smile as I run my hands over the stubble on his jaw and turn his face to me so I can lean in and kiss his lips.

"Maybe I need a memory jog," he murmurs against my mouth, cupping the back of my head with one hand as he kisses me back deeply.

I break the kiss and slide a hand down into his boxers, where his cock is already hard. I wrap my fingers around him.

"Let's get jogging."

"Is Drew okay?" I ask absentmindedly as Tanner comes back into the bedroom. I'm finishing packing my bag. I've spent the day here but need to head home. I've got an early flight tomorrow and need a good night's sleep. I know I would be too tempted to stay up late, 'jogging' Tan's memory some more if I stay here.

"Yeah, yeah. He's good," Tanner says, sounding distracted.

"You weren't on the phone long?" I look up at him. His brow is furrowed, and his jaw is set. He looks tense about something. "Everything okay?"

"Yeah. You're going to Miami tomorrow, aren't you?" he asks, obviously not wanting to talk about whatever Drew said.

"Yep. Just for one night. I'll see you when I get back, though. You can come and stay at mine. I think Nigel misses you," I joke, glancing up at Tan's face as I pull the zip around my bag. He's staring into space still —*what is up with him?*

I finish zipping my bag shut and stand up, moving over to him so I can slide my palms up onto his broad chest, the cotton of his t-shirt soft beneath my fingers.

"There's no need to sulk. I know you're going to miss me," I say sweetly, reaching up to kiss him. He looks back at me with an expression I've never seen on him before. His brows are drawn together, his eyes intense, something clouding over them.

He looks tormented.

"Tan, what is it?" I say, my voice sounding serious, even to my own ears.

He brings a hand up and holds my bottom lip with his thumb, his eyes staring into mine, anguish now clear in them. "Since meeting you, Rach..." he starts and then stops, his eyes looking upwards as though he's trying to find the right words. "I've never felt like this about anyone before." He rests his forehead against mine.

I move my head, so he has to look at me again. I know what he's trying to say, so why does he look so pained to say it? Maybe being in love with me feels like torture to him? The look on his face would certainly make anyone think so.

"Tan," I whisper, looking into his eyes and smiling. "You can say it. It's okay. I'm a big girl and meeting you has changed me. These last three months, they've been incredible. I can handle what you're going to say without running out on you." I kiss his lips, wanting to reassure him I'm not the girl he first met—who couldn't allow herself to be loved. But he just stands frozen and doesn't kiss me back.

His voice is so quiet I have to strain to hear him. "Rachel, there's nothing I want more than to tell you exactly how I feel about you. But there's something you need to see first."

He must see the confusion on my face. "Come with me," he says, taking my hand in his and leading me down the hall into one of the spare bedrooms.

"Are you secretly hiding a dead body in here or something?" I joke, watching as he goes to the cupboard and lifts out a large cardboard box, setting it on the bed.

His eyes look up to my face. His mouth is set in a grim line, as though he's waiting for a prison sentence to be read out to him.

"I'm a fucking idiot, Rachel. I should have told you so much sooner. I just didn't know how."

"What are you talking about?"

I look at his face, searching it for answers, but Tanner just rips the tape off the top of the box and opens it. I take a step closer, peering inside. It's full of brown and white packets. I don't know why the hell he's showing me these. I lean in so that I can see more clearly. What are—?

Oh, Hell no!

Nausea grabs my stomach, twisting it as the blood in my veins turns to ice. I reach out to touch a packet, pulling my hand back as though it's burnt me. I don't need to lift it up to see my handwriting on the address label or know what it says. I wrote it so many times over those eighteen months that I lost count.

To Mr. X.

"What the hell!" I cry, stumbling backward as my hand flies to my mouth.

He can't be.

"Rachel, I can explain. It's not what you think!" Tanner's frantic voice cuts through the fog that's descended over me.

I trusted him.

"You don't know what the hell I'm thinking," I hiss.

He takes a step towards me.

"Don't you fucking dare!" I spit, pointing a finger at him.

My heart's pounding in my ears. *Why does he have these?* But it's obvious. There's only one reason he has every single packet I ever posted in a box in his spare room.

Tanner is Mr. X.

The generous, funny, caring man I've spent the last three months with cannot be the same man who was sending me money—a lot of money—for my worn panties.

He can't be. He just can't be!

I shudder, remembering the special embroidered ones I had made in Shanghai, back when Mr. X was just some stranger I would never actually meet. Back when it was anonymous. When I couldn't be identified.

Back when I couldn't get hurt.

I've opened myself up to a man for the first time in my life, and this is what I get?

Way to fucking go, Rach.

"Are you some weird stalker? Is that what this is? You thought you'd seek out the girl who provided help with your fetish and try to date her?" I stare at him, and he stands rooted to the spot, probably unsure whether to risk moving any closer to me again.

"Of course not!" he fires back angrily.

"I even told you I used to do this in the bath that night. You never said a word! It was you the whole time! All you went on about was how many clients I had. Is that why you were so bothered? You wanted to know you were the only one?" I glare at him, wishing this is all some kind of sick joke and Matt is going to jump out filming and shout, "Gotcha!"

Tanner drags both hands back through his hair, but not in the way he does when he's turned on. He looks frantic. "Yes! I mean, no. Fuck, Rachel, this isn't how it is. Please, just let me explain," he pleads.

I shake my head. "A dead body would have been better than this." I look at him in disgust. "I have no idea who you are, not really. Is your name even Tanner?" I say, my voice threatening to break.

These last three months have been a lie, a complete lie. I opened up to him. I let him into my heart. I'm a fucking idiot. The first man I really let myself be vulnerable with, he doesn't even exist. All this time, he was just pretending. I don't even know him.

How could I have missed that he was lying to me every damn day?

How could I have been so stupid?

My heart constricts in my chest, and it feels like the air has been sucked from the room.

How could I have fallen in love?

"I need to leave. I don't want to be anywhere near you—whoever the fuck you are!" I shout as I turn to leave the room. "Don't you dare follow me!" I add over my shoulder as I race back to Tanner's bedroom and grab my bag.

Thank fuck I'd finished packing.

I run down the stairs, pulling my boots on quickly as I hear Tanner calling after me. He drove me here in his car, so I'm going to have to call a taxi and wait down the road somewhere. Anywhere as long as it's nowhere near his lying face. My throat burns, and my eyes sting as I wrench open the front door. All this time, I've never needed anyone. And then I finally met someone I thought I could trust, someone I was imagining a future with.

And it all turns out to be one giant fucking con.

I should have known better.

Never again.

I slam the door behind me and tear down the driveway to the gates. Luck must be on my side for once today, as one of Tanner's neighbors is just driving in as I get there. The gates swing open automatically, and I slip through, glimpsing Tanner running down the driveway behind me, shouting my name. He has to slow down, so he doesn't end up under the neighbor's tires, and the gates close again before he makes it through them.

I take a deep breath and stride off down the street, never looking back.

"I just don't believe it!" Matt says, looking at Megan and then at Holly on the laptop screen. They both nod in agreement.

Luckily, Matt was on a day off today, and Megan

and Holly were free when I texted them all for an immediate group crisis meeting.

"The entire time?" Holly asks, her eyes wide.

"The entire eighteen months," I confirm, holding Nigel against my chest. He's been extra cuddly recently. After all the stuff with my mom and now this, he seems to know that I need it. I sink my nose into his soft grey fur as I let out a small sigh.

"How did he know it was you, though, Rach? You only had photos of your legs and feet on your website," Megan says.

"I don't know, it's so weird—" I'm struck by a sudden realization and struggle to swallow the bile in my throat. "Wait. When we were in New York, he told me we met briefly at Heathrow. He left his laptop behind, and I helped return it. I was in such a rush, though, since I was on a late warning, that I barely looked at him. I certainly didn't remember him."

"But he never forgot you," Matt says, leaning forward on the sofa so he can rest his elbows on his legs as he thinks. "Still, it's got to be a weird coincidence that you met, and then he contacted you through your website, surely? There's no way he could have known that was your site."

"I've had enough of weird coincidences, thanks," I mutter.

"I still can't believe your moms were friends," Holly says, her voice gentle, worry oozing from it. I can tell she probably wishes more than anything she was here right now and not an eleven-hour flight away. I wish she were too.

"I know. Just too many coincidences, don't you think?" I snort.

"Do you really think he's got a screw loose? That he somehow stalked you?" Matt asks, sounding worried and not making a joke about something for once.

"He seemed so nice," Megan murmurs into her mug of tea, disbelief still showing all over her face.

"I just don't know. I thought I could tell a bullshitter from a mile away, but he's been lying to me for months. I don't know why he bought all the underwear I sold or whether he sought me out on purpose. I don't know anything." I chew my lip as I lean my head back on the sofa and stare at the living room wall. 'Midnight lover' blue paint stares back at me, taunting me. God, we even had sex on the floor in here. What was he thinking then? How clever he was that I had no idea who he really was?

"Did he, you know, have any weird requests when you two were together?" Matt asks.

I look at Matt, unimpressed.

"What?" He shrugs. "I'm just wondering since he paid thousands to buy your lingerie. Most men don't go to that extreme. He's a hot guy too. Surely he can get plenty of women to give him their panties for free happily."

"Not helping," I warn, before blowing out a breath, all my fight gone. "Besides, I don't care if he's into it. I'm hardly a saint."

It only looked like there were packets in my handwriting in that box, but what if there were more? Others that I hadn't seen from other women? I shake the thought from my head. What the hell is wrong with me? I can't be jealous of the thought I wasn't the only one. Yet, I want to know if there were others. Not that it matters now: He isn't the Tanner I thought he was.

It was a lie.

He was one big lie.

"So, if him being Mr. X isn't the actual issue, then what is?" Holly asks gently.

I look at her open, encouraging eyes. Their emerald, green glittering through the screen. "It's that he lied to me every single day. He wasn't honest. Everything we had was a lie. Everything…" I trail off.

She nods as she listens.

I don't know how to explain it. I feel stupid. So stupid for believing that he was different. But I'm angry too. I'm so fucking angry and disappointed in myself. I've never needed anyone before. I've been fine by myself. Being single suited me. But Tanner, he made me want new things. I let my guard down with him.

A mistake I will never make again.

My phone buzzes on the coffee table. No need to guess who's calling me—again. "You can fuck off!" I shout at my phone, letting it go to voicemail.

Megan looks up at me. "Don't you want to know what he's got to say?"

"Nope," I say without missing a beat.

"Maybe there's an explanation," Matt says, although even he doesn't look convinced.

"You've had a shock, Rach. Take some time to process it. Let it sink in," Holly suggests.

"That's a good idea. I've got the Miami flight tomorrow. I checked the loads, and it's full, so that will keep me occupied. There'll be no time to think. Then I can go for a drink down-route with the crew and get shit-faced, forget the wanker ever existed," I say as I plan out my next few days.

Matt and Megan glance at one another and then at Holly.

"Keep us updated, Rach. We are all here if you need a chat, anytime, day or night," Holly says, giving me a lopsided smile. "I wish I was there so I could hug you."

"I'd like to see you try with that bump," I joke weakly as I look at her growing belly, most of it hidden below the camera.

"I'd find a way, trust me." She smiles.

My phone beeps with a text, and I groan as Megan passes it to me.

Tan: Please talk to me, Rachel.

There's no way I want to hear anything he has to say, but there's a strong chance the stubborn wanker will drive around here and camp outside if I don't answer him.

**Me: Everything out of your mouth is a lie. I've
heard enough. Don't even think about
turning up here. It's over.**

I press down the off button on my phone and watch
the screen go black, just like the walls that are building
back up around my heart.

TWENTY-SIX

TANNER

I'M A TOTAL IDIOT. THIS LAST WEEK HAS BEEN HELL. Rachel won't answer my calls or texts. She's completely shut me out. She warned me about turning up at her house, and I promised her I won't do that. I know how much her home means to her. The thought of making her uncomfortable in it makes me sick. I would never intentionally hurt her or cause her distress.

But that's exactly what I've done.

I've hurt her more than she will admit, even to herself. I know her better than she gives me credit for. I know this will have hit her hard. I betrayed her, lied to her. I've become another addition to the long list of people who've let her down. I'm a total and utter shit. If she never speaks to me again—Hell, I deserve it.

I climb out of the car, wincing as my muscles scream out in protest. I grab my gym bag, heading into the studio where the kickboxing class is due to start in ten minutes. She may not want me at her house, but she said nothing about her classes. I've been coming to all three classes a day for the last four days; in the hope, I will see her. She has to turn up for one eventually, and when she does, I'm going to hope she agrees to talk to me. It's a bit of a shit card to play, but she's left me little choice. I won't let her go this easily. Not until I explain, and she's heard me out. Then, if she doesn't want to see me again, I will leave her alone.

I'm already sweating with nerves as I head out of the changing rooms and into the bright and airy, modern studio. There are another eight people already here waiting, partnering up and collecting gloves and pads from a large bag to the side of the room.

"Hey, Tanner." The instructor, Mike, raises a hand in greeting as he sees me. "Back for more, eh?"

"Something like that," I say as he walks over and pats me on the shoulder.

"Uneven numbers, so it looks like you're the unlucky one that gets me as a partner." Mike grins.

"I'll take it easy on you," I joke, casting my eyes over his giant frame. I'm a tall guy, but he towers over me, and he's built like a truck. He chuckles as he digs in the large equipment bag and pulls out some pads.

"Ah, looks like you won't need to." He lifts his chin as he looks over my shoulder.

"Hiya Rach, how are you doing?" he calls out.

"Fine, thanks, Mike," a sweet voice answers.

I know too well not to be fooled. She sounds like she couldn't hurt a fly, but I know she could decimate an entire species if she puts her mind to it.

I turn to look at her and hold my breath as her eyes clock me. Her step falters, but she recovers quickly, striding over to me, her face drawn before she glares at me like I'm something she trod in.

"Looks like you've met your match," Mike says as he passes some gloves to Rachel and pads to me. "Rachel's tough; you might find you'll be screaming for mercy." He laughs as he heads back to the front of the group.

If only he knew how much I've ached to see her and talk to her this last week.

My heart is already screaming for mercy.

Mike takes us through a group warm-up. Rachel is next to me, and I can feel her disdain for me reaching over, trying to inch down my throat and suffocate me. She doesn't look at me once, not even a quick glance. It's all I can do to keep my eyes forward and not stare at her the entire time. She's even more beautiful when she's mad. I just hope all that fire inside her that's licking at her skin, waiting to burst free, can be redirected back into the passion I know she felt for me.

Either that or I'll be incinerated.

"Okay, guys, time to partner up." Mike claps his hands together as though he enjoys this part of the class the most.

Everyone straps their gloves and pads onto their hands. The sound of ripping Velcro echoes around the studio. Maybe it'll muffle the sound of Rachel tearing my balls off if the look she's giving me now is anything to go by. I strap the pads onto my hands as I turn to face her head-on.

Mike fiddles with his phone at the front of the class. I know what's coming after the last four days I've been here. Loud high-energy workout music pumps through the studios' speakers, and Mike has to raise his voice to be heard over it. "Okay, everyone, I want you to just start with some jabs with your partner and then work in some cross jabs and uppercuts. Let's go!"

The sound of thick leather gloves hitting pads with force erupts as the others start with enthusiasm, the odd grunt arising with their efforts. I raise the pads in front of my chest as I look at Rachel. She's sweating lightly along her hairline, her dark hair pulled back off her face in a high ponytail. If she didn't look like she was about to kill me, then I would happily drop my eyes to fully take in the cropped workout top and black leggings she's wearing.

Fuck, if she were a trained killer, I don't think any man would put up much of a fight if she turned up looking like this. He'd be too busy picking his jaw up off the floor.

Bang! The first jab she throws catches me off-guard, and I take a step back to gain my balance.

I look at her in surprise. "Thanks for the warn—" I'm cut short as her glove connects with the other pad, throwing my shoulder back sharply. I grit my teeth, sucking in a breath through my nose.

"I don't know what you're doing, Tanner," Rachel says, keeping her eyes on the pads as she fires jab after jab at me. Only now, I'm ready for each one and stand firm. She hits again, harder, frowning as I don't even flinch.

"You won't talk to me. What did you expect me to do?" I say, keeping my voice down, although there's probably no need. The guy next to us is grunting like a bad porn movie, droplets of his sweat flying over. I glance down as one narrowly misses my trainer.

"I expect you to fuck off back to the lying little hole you came from," Rachel hisses as she throws a jab-cross in quick succession.

"I'm sorry I lied to you, Rachel. I'm an idiot, a fucking loser," I say, willing her to look up and into my eyes, but she keeps her eyes on the pads as Mike calls out to switch to uppercuts. I raise my hands up with the pads facing the floor, so Rachel must hit upwards. As she bends, I get a direct view of her cleavage down her top, glistening in sweat.

"At least you're telling the truth about that," she pants as she takes another hit at the pad. "So, what was it? You found my website and somehow worked out my identity, then engineered our paths to cross?"

"No, of course not," I hiss, glancing back to sweaty porn man to make sure he doesn't look like he's going to stop with the loud grunting anytime soon. He looks like he might have a heart attack, but he's not showing any signs of slowing down. Good for him.

"I heard you and Holly talking at the airport before

you returned my laptop to me." I take a deep breath. Rachel's punches have lost some force, so I know she's listening. "You wouldn't let me thank you, and I had this stupid, impulsive idea that I would find another way to re-pay you."

She screws her face up as if she doesn't believe a word. Why should she? I've already proved I'm a good liar.

"Okay, so you're not a crazed stalker, but why the hell would you choose to do that? I told you it was nothing."

"And I already told you that me losing that laptop would have jeopardized a multi-million-pound deal," I fire back.

God, she's so stubborn.

She smirks. "So, it was just a lucky coincidence then that you could *thank me* at the same time as feeding your kink?"

"No, it wasn't a happy—Fuck! You're infuriating," I whisper to her, lowering my hands so I can lean closer.

"I'd get those pads back up if I were you," Rachel snaps, her eyes glinting darkly at me.

I grit my teeth and raise the pads again so she can continue her anger-fueled attack. She's got stamina; I'll give her that.

"I haven't even opened the packets, Rachel," I confess.

She finally looks up into my eyes, lost for words. "You haven't opened them?"

"No." I chance a small smile at her after delivering this piece of information.

Whoosh! The air whizzes past my ear as Rachel knocks the pad up past my head.

"I can't believe you didn't fucking open them!" she seethes. "I even had special ones designed in Shanghai for you!" She hits out again.

Okay, I was not expecting that reaction.

"You spent *thousands* on parcels you never fucking opened!" she cries loud enough that sweaty porn man glances over. I scowl at him, and he looks away, getting the message to mind his own business.

I turn my attention back to Rachel. "It was never about the lingerie."

"Yeah, I know. You just wanted to *thank* me." Rachel glares at me, sweat running down her face. "The fact you didn't even open them, Tanner... It makes me feel like a charity case. I had a business. Okay, an unusual one. But I was going to make money, my own way," she says, her voice growing quiet.

I stare at Rachel as her words sink in. This is more than me lying to her. This is about her pride, wanting to be in control of her own future. I've taken away that sense of achievement she had in herself.

Mike calls out for us to change over, and Rachel hands me the gloves, taking the pads from me and strapping them to her hands.

"You have never been a charity case, Rach," I say gently.

"You expect me to believe that you helped me—a

stranger—just to say thanks? You never heard me mention my past when you were eavesdropping?" she says, shaking her head at me.

I finish strapping the gloves to my hands. "I... yes, I heard you mention your past."

Rachel rolls her eyes.

"But hardly anything about it. I swear, Rach. It wasn't talking about your past that gave me that extra push to do it."

She raises the pads up in front of her face, and I jab lightly at them.

"Don't insult me further by treating me like glass," she snaps, referring to my pathetic jabs.

I strike the pad on her hand with more force, but still nowhere near as hard as I'm capable of. She wobbles before straightening herself.

"What was it then? What did I say that was so *unforgettable* to you?" she mocks, looking at me.

I clear my throat. This is going to sound weird, but fuck it, I'm here, and she needs to know the truth. I force my words out. "It was the saying: difficult roads lead to beautiful destinations. I heard you say it, and it just made me think of my mom and my nan. I felt... I don't know... a connection?" I blow out a breath, sweat running down my back as I try to talk and punch. "I just felt like I had to stay in touch with you somehow. It's stupid, I know."

Rachel's gone deathly quiet, her face pale. "Rach? Are you okay?"

She looks at me dead in the eye. Her earlier fire

338

replaced by a look of utter hopelessness. "No, Tanner. I'm not okay. And it's all because of you." Her voice wavers as though she's trying to hold back tears.

"Rach..." I tear off a glove and reach out to her, but she's already pulled her pads off and is heading over to the equipment bag. She says something to Mike, and then she's gone.

Out of the studio.

Out of my life.

For good.

TWENTY-SEVEN

RACHEL

No matter how bad I've felt over this last week and a half, today is a million times worse. The dull ache in my chest won't ease, and every time I think I've exhausted all my tears, a fresh new bucket-load falls.

"Are you ready to do this?" Megan asks, her voice barely a whisper.

I place my arm on hers and squeeze as I nod. "Are you?"

"No." She looks at me with bloodshot eyes. "But we have to, don't we?"

I swallow the lump in my throat. "Yeah, we do."

Megan pauses as the doorbell rings, glancing at me.

"I'll see who it is, and tell them now isn't a good time," I say as I head to the door.

I open it and see Tanner standing there—looking like a lost sheep—and the urge to slam it shut again is overwhelming.

"Please, Rach," he says.

His voice sounds flat, and I look at him. Despite being dressed for work, he hasn't shaved for a day or two, and his hair looks like it hasn't seen a comb this morning. Irritatingly, the rugged look would suit him if it weren't for the dullness in his usually bright eyes.

"What are you doing here?" I sigh, crossing my arms, hoping my face isn't showing how hard the last ten days have hit me.

"I'm sorry for showing up like this, but I wanted to give you this." He holds out an envelope to me.

I stare at it but make no effort to reach out and take it. "What is it?"

"It's an envelope, Rach."

"I can see that. Why would I want it?"

He lets out a deep breath as his shoulders sag. "Please, just take it. I hope you'll at least read it before you shred it and use it for Nigel's litter tray or something."

I let out a small gasp, a fresh wave of tears burning my eyes as they threaten to fall.

"Rach?" Tanner looks stricken. "I'm so sorry. I never should have shown up here. I should have just posted it. I just wanted to see you. I'm a selfish jerk."

"It's not you. For once," I say as my shoulders shake.

Tanner steps forward and pauses as though waiting for me to stop him. When I don't, he wraps his strong arms around me. I can smell his familiar scent —spicy cologne mixed with clean skin. I let out a huge

342

breath as I sag against his chest. He holds me tight, kissing my hair. His heart beats a strong, comforting pace against my cheek. I'm tempted to stay here forever and pretend that the last ten days never happened.

Pretend that the last twenty-four hours never happened.

"What's happened, Rach? Tell me, please?" His voice sounds heavy with emotion at seeing me in such distress. I know he's not used to it. No-one is. Rachel Jones doesn't cry. Rachel Jones is made of stone.

"Tanner?" Megan appears behind me.

I pull out of his arms and scrub at my cheeks with the sleeve of my sweatshirt, standing to one side so he can come in. He glances at me, seeking permission silently, and only when I nod does he pass over the threshold and into the house.

"What's happened, Meg?" His worried eyes dart back and forth between us.

Hearing him call her Meg is another blow to my heart. Realizing how close we all were just days ago, how much he had become a part of my life. But now isn't the time to think about that.

Today isn't about us.

Megan walks into the dining room as Tanner and I follow. She stops by the table and stares sadly at the towel-wrapped bundle lying motionless on top.

"Oh, God." Tanner's voice breaks as he reaches out a hand and lays it over the fabric. "Nigel."

"He'd been sleeping more recently, and we just...

we just thought it was old age," Megan mumbles as she cries.

I watch as Tanner pats the towel, hanging his head. "Goodbye, Nigel. You were a good little mate," he says softly before turning to look at me.

"We gave him his breakfast this morning, and he was laid between us on the sofa. We thought he was asleep. But then, he'd gone. It was peaceful," I say before my tears start again.

"We were just about to bury him in the garden," Megan says as I move to the table.

With great care, I lift Nigel's wrapped body into my arms and cradle him, my fingers stroking the soft cotton towel with tenderness. "We love you so much, Nigel." I sniff as tears drop onto the fabric.

"Can I help?" Tanner asks, his voice soft.

I look at him, and my feeling of brokenness is reflected in his eyes. I nod, and the three of us head out to the garden where I've got a shovel out ready.

"Where?" Tanner asks, not needing to say more. I know what he means.

"Over there, under the tree. He used to like that patch when the sun was shining," I say as we walk over the grass together.

Tanner picks up the shovel and digs. No one says anything as he creates a deep hole. He gets soil on his suit, but either doesn't notice or doesn't care. When he's finished, Megan and I whisper our goodbyes and kiss Nigel through the towels one last time before I kneel and gently lower him into the earth.

"Goodbye, Nigel," I whisper as we fill the hole with soil and pat it down.

I put my arm around Megan as she falls to her knees beside me. "I'm just going to sit here for a while," she says.

I nod in understanding and motion to Tanner to follow me inside. I lead him back towards the front door and open it. He hesitates, but then steps out before turning back to face me.

"Thank you for helping us do that," I say, not wanting to meet his eyes.

"I'm so sorry, Rach." His voice is heavy, as though there's so much more he wants to say.

"I believe you." I force myself to raise my eyes to meet his. He stares back. He looks hopeful, but I need to be honest with him. I take a deep breath. "Tanner. I know you had your reasons for not telling me. But you lied to me. How can I ever trust you again?"

He opens his mouth.

"Wait, let me finish." I watch his lips come back together; his beautiful mouth stills as he listens. The number of times I've kissed those lips, laughed with those lips, shared moments, and smiles. It's painful to look at them, so I shift my eyes back up to his. But that's just as bad, if not worse. I've looked into those eyes so many times and felt things I've never felt for anyone before. Things I never allowed myself to feel because I knew I never wanted to be vulnerable to the heartache that follows. Tanner opened a part of my heart I thought was sealed shut forever. Now it's closed again, but this time it's shattered inside.

I scratch at the sudden itch on my wrist as I begin again. "All the shit that's happened to me, this is the worst deceit. When I found out that our moms knew each other, I felt—" I tilt my head back and search for the right words. "I felt like I belonged again. Meeting your mom and hearing her stories and memories... it's made me feel my mom around me. It's helped me know who she was." My voice breaks as tears flow down my cheeks.

Tanner reaches out to me, but I step backward, and he drops his arms to his sides, his eyes shining as he looks at me. He looks distraught and as angry as I am at him; I hate seeing him like this.

"Now that you've lied to me, I can't trust you. I can't see you anymore, and that means I've not only lost you, but I've lost your mom. The only connection to my mom I've ever had. It's like losing her all over again. Only this time, I've got the memories that make it more painful."

"Rachel, I never knew about our moms, I swear." Tanner's voice is breaking as he pinches the bridge of his nose and draws in a shaky breath.

"I know you didn't. But it doesn't change the way I feel. I can't forget."

His haunted eyes look up to me, searching mine wildly. "Please, Rachel... I love you."

I gasp and take another step back. I suspected it; I even thought he was going to say it to me that night. I *hoped* he was going to say it. But now? Hearing the words, I don't know how I feel. Incredibly sad that we have both come to this point, I guess. If only I'd been the person I've always been. Kept him at a distance, not let feelings grow. We wouldn't be here now. I wouldn't have this gut-wrenching pain in my stomach, and Tanner wouldn't have his face screwed up with tears coursing down his cheeks.

I take another deep breath. I know once I say this, there'll be no going back. But I must. What else is there for us? I need to go back to being who I was before. I was stronger, then.

"I'm sorry, Tanner," I whisper, "but I don't—" I can't even get the words out as I see the pain in his eyes.

"Don't or won't let yourself admit it?" he chokes out, his voice thick with hurt. "What we have is special, Rach."

"No, Tanner. What we had… it was a mistake."

His eyes flash with anger as he looks at me. I hold my breath, not trusting myself. He's too close. It would be too easy to fall into his arms and say I forgive him, that we can work it out. But I won't do that. I can't do that. I can't trust him not to hurt me. He's proved he has the power to do it. I need to take that power back.

I can't ever feel like this again.

"If that's how you really feel?" He searches my face in a last-ditch attempt to break down the walls that are firmly back in place.

I suck in a deep breath, hoping to steady the

shaking which has started in my fingers. I clasp and unclasp my hands before answering.

"It is."

He holds my gaze long enough that I can tell he's hoping I will say something else. When I don't, his shoulders fall, along with any remaining light in his eyes.

"Then I guess this is goodbye, Rachel."

I nod. "Goodbye, Tanner."

I watch him walk down the path, get into his car, and drive away.

It's only after he's gone that I see the envelope on the table, my name written across the front in his handwriting. I stare at it. Today has been heartbreaking enough. Whatever's inside can wait.

Today's tears are for Nigel, not me.

TWENTY-EIGHT

TANNER

D{\small EAR} R{\small ACHEL},

The first time I heard your voice that day at the airport, I was drawn to you. You sounded so delicate. Your voice went hand in hand with your beauty. I was a nosy shit to listen in on your private conversation, but I would be lying if I said I was sorry. That day, almost two years ago now, is the day I met you. How can I ever regret a single second?

But that isn't what made me notice you. It was your strength. Your determination to push for something your heart desired. I didn't know your story then, not like I do now. But it was obvious to me that you were unlike anyone I had ever met before. You don't expect to be handed anything. You want to work for it, to earn it, and I respect that about you more than you'll ever know. You were NEVER a charity case, Rachel. I was just a stupid idiot who was so in awe of you that I had a crazy idea to invest in your business. It was a way of saying thank you for the impact you had that day. The deal with Griffin Parker only happened because of you, as I've told you already.

That whole year I lived in New York, and you sent the parcels to a PO Box in London—I never saw a single one until I returned. I used to look forward to your emails that accompanied them. You sounded so refreshing and upbeat. I never thought I would see you in person again. I never planned it. Please know it was never sinister. Maybe it was fate intervening when I saw you that day at the auction.

All the parcels are still sealed. Once I met you again, it didn't seem right to open them—despite my curiosity. It felt like a betrayal to you. Only, I know that my silence was the biggest betrayal, and for that, I will be forever sorry.

Meeting you is the best thing to have ever happened to me. Penny would agree that she and the rest of the team haven't missed 'Grumpy Grayson'. And it's all because a girl I call Snow came in and thawed out this wanker's frosty exterior.

I mentioned fate before, and although I'm not a big believer in these things, I feel as though something brought us together. When I heard you say those words, "difficult roads lead to beautiful destinations," I was selfish. I thought it was a message for me. That our paths were meant to cross for my own fortune. That fortune being you. Only now do I realize it was never about me and what I needed. This has always been for you, Rachel. Our meeting was the stepping-stone you needed to find the key to your past and what happened to your mom. Knowing that our meeting led to you learning about what happened to her and who she was makes me happy. Seeing the joy on your face when you talk to my mom about her is the most incredible sight I could wish for.

It makes me sick to think you might worry you've lost all that now because of my dishonesty and my absolute shit-headed stupidity. I couldn't live with myself if I thought I caused such unhappiness to you. I've only ever wanted you to be happy, Rachel. If that means me being out of the picture, then I will gladly do it. I will do anything for you, Rachel.

That's why I'm going to Las Vegas. I won't be here to cause you any further hurt. I had a long think after the kickboxing class. Seeing the look on your face when I mentioned your mom. I just knew, Rach. I know you better than you think. This way, you can spend time with my mom and not have to worry about seeing me. I'm beginning to think she likes you way better than me, anyway! That was a poor attempt at a joke, but you know what I mean. She would miss you just as much as you'd miss her, so please keep seeing her. I know how much she loves your visits—how much she loves you. It will never be as much as I do, though.

I love you, Rachel Jones.

With my heart and soul, I will always love you.

I hope you'll forgive me one day and we can at least be friends. I would do anything to keep you in my life.

Tan

TWENTY-NINE

RACHEL

Two and a half months pass by in a blur after losing both Nigel and Tanner. I'm in a hole of deep self-pity, thinking about how those I love leave. First my mom, Holly moving to LA, Nigel, and now Tanner. I don't know how I even function, but somehow, I do. I've re-read his letter so many times since he left. He knows me so much better than I gave him credit for. He knew I would be the most hurt over losing the connection to my mom I have when I'm with Nell. He'd written that letter long before coming over that day we lost Nigel. Long before I told him that's how I felt. He'd already planned to leave for Vegas. Maybe if I'd said something different, it would have changed his mind?

But I didn't.

I was too angry and hurt to do anything other than push him away.

Drew brought over Tanner's coffee machine, saying

he'd want me to have it. I didn't ask how Tanner is, despite wanting to. Drew, being Drew, though, left no detail out when he told me how miserable he is. How he's in Vegas, the "Adult Disney World", yet barely leaves his hotel apartment unless it's for work. I don't know whether this makes me feel better or worse. I hate the idea of him being unhappy, but I'm also relieved to know that he hasn't moved on with someone else already.

I volunteered to work Christmas. So many of my colleagues hate to be away at that time of year, so they bit my hand off when I offered days off in exchange for a flight. I can't say Christmas in Lagos, Nigeria was the most festive one I've ever had, but the other crew members were fun, and it kept my mind off Tanner and what he was doing.

The only problem with picking up extra flights is that now I have two weeks off as my flying hours were getting high, almost the top of the limit of how many we can do in a rolling year. It means I've spent some time with Nell, which has been lovely. She's careful not to mention Tanner too much, but he's her son, and he's also in a lot of her stories and photos from when she knew my mom. Besides, I don't want her to feel uncomfortable around me, so I ask after him sometimes. She always looks hopeful when I do. But it's a wasted hope. How can I ever go back on what I said to him, even if I wanted to? I let him think I don't love him—as though all our time together meant nothing. Yet here I am, acting like he was the cruel one for lying to me. Surely that makes me a hypocrite.

I sigh, leaning back into the sofa cushions as I cradle my mug. Even my favorite drink doesn't taste the same now. Everything is just so much... less without Tanner. I look around the living room. Megan's at work, and Matt is off in Hawaii with Stefan. Without Nigel here, the house is silent.

I'm alone.

I hate it.

My phone buzzes on the coffee table as a call comes through.

"Jay?" I answer quickly. "Is everything okay? Holly—"

"She's in labor," he pants down the phone. His voice is a mix of excitement and pure panic.

"She's what?" I cry.

"The doula is on her way. Holly's getting into the birthing pool. She said I had to call and tell you!" His deep voice is out of breath. It sounds like he's running around fetching things. I can hear Holly in the background telling him to relax, that they've got ages to go yet. That she sounds so calm and can still talk helps to slow my racing heart.

"I'm on my way!" I shout, prodding the end call on my phone sharply. I call Megan to tell her. She's caught up in meetings at work but insists I should go without her, and she will catch up in a couple of days if she can. I hang up from her call and dial staff travel to book a seat on this afternoon's LA flight. I grin as I rush around the house, throwing things into my case.

My best friend is having a baby!

"She's absolutely perfect," I say to Holly and Jay as I look down at the tiny bundle in my arms. "Your mommy did good," I coo, leaning down to her soft baby skin and inhaling her newborn scent. Her eyes are closed, and she's dreaming once again, her eyelids fluttering as her tiny breaths come out in puffs.

"She sure did," Jay says, wrapping his arm around Holly and beaming at her. "You were amazing," he says to Holly, kissing her as she tilts her head up toward him. His blue eyes sparkle as he gazes at her.

I swallow the lump in my throat at their complete and obvious love for one another.

Matt and Stefan gather around me and stare at the new member of our gang. They made it here before I did, cutting their trip to Hawaii short to get back.

"Can I hold her again?" Matt asks, dancing from foot to foot. "Me, me, Uncle Matt," he calls over my shoulder, pulling a funny face.

"She can't understand you yet," Stefan says, wrapping an arm around Matt, completely under Summer's spell, just like the rest of us.

"Little, Summer Robyn Anderson," I say in a sing-song voice. "You're going to have all the boys chasing you, maybe the girls too." I smile.

"She will not. No dating until she's thirty." Jay frowns, straightening up.

"Relax, Daddy." Holly giggles, stroking Jay's arm.

He softens at her words, and his eyes mist up. "I can't believe I'm a daddy."

"Better get used to it," I say as Summer's eyes peek open, and she looks at me, trying her best to focus.

"You are the most precious baby I have ever known," I whisper softly.

"I think she's hungry again, mama," I say to Holly, watching Summer's little fists come to her mouth as she roots around, looking for milk.

I hand her to Holly, and Matt lets out a disappointed-sounding sigh.

"You're going to be tall like daddy, aren't you?" Holly says as she nestles Summer in her arms and lifts her top, relaxing back into the sofa as she feeds her.

Matt stares at Holly breastfeeding. "That's incredible." His eyes are wide.

"Didn't they teach you about that at school?" I smirk, knocking his shoulder playfully.

He bats me off. "Ha ha, so funny, Rach. I just mean it's amazing how the human body can provide everything that Summer needs."

"It is, isn't it?" Stefan agrees as we all fall quiet again and listen to Summer's contented little snuffles as she works on getting baby drunk on milk.

Matt turns to me. "I'm glad you're getting back to yourself. I almost missed having you make fun of me."

"Only almost?" I fire back.

He gives me a wink before taking Stefan's hand. "Now, if you'll excuse us, we need to finish unpacking." They hug and kiss Jay and Holly, blowing extra kisses to Summer, who's still busy feeding in Holly's arms.

Once they've left, I sink down next to Holly as Jay heads off to get us all a drink. Holly's drinking more water than I've ever seen anyone consume. Breastfeeding makes her constantly thirsty.

"How are you really doing, Rach?" she asks.

The kindness in her voice draws a long sigh from my lips.

"Honestly? Shit." I mouth, "sorry," as I look down at Summer. "I was fine before I met him, Holly. I did what I wanted or *who* I wanted. I was happy."

"Were you, though?" Holly takes one hand and gently lays it over mine, effectively stopping my wrist from getting any redder. I didn't even realize I was scratching it.

"I didn't know I wasn't." I shrug, rubbing my hands across my eyes. I turn to look into her green eyes. "You're my best friend, Holly. You're literally one of the only people I trust in the world." She squeezes my hand in response. "Do you think I've made a mistake?" I whisper, searching her eyes as though they hold all the answers.

"I think you already know the answer to that yourself, Rach." Her voice is gentle.

"Fu... Fudge." I sigh, glancing down at Summer again. She's smiling in her sleep, her lips twitching up in one corner and exposing her gums as though being tugged by a tiny string. I smile at her little face. "Holly, she's just so perfect. I must get a picture of that face." I pull my phone out and take a photo before turning the screen to show Holly.

"Aw, that's a good one," Holly says, before smiling down at Summer.

I go to turn the screen off, but my camera roll flashes up instead. My breath catches in my throat as I see the photo of Tanner with Nigel asleep on his chest. Holly looks at it over my shoulder before speaking.

"You've spent your entire life being strong, Rach. Being in love doesn't make a person weak. Opening your heart up to someone and being vulnerable— that's one of the bravest things you can do."

I watch her closely as she smiles at me, her beautiful daughter in her arms—the ultimate creation of her and Jay's love. My stomach lurches.

I will never have this.

If I always keep people out of my heart, I will always end up alone. Where's the strength in that? My eyes sting. I've had it all wrong this whole time.

"You know, Vegas is only an hour's flight." Holly nudges me as if reading my thoughts.

The sun is shining as I step out of the taxi and onto the Las Vegas strip. It's not hot, but it's a world away from the frost back home. The giant hotel I'm standing next to reaches up to the sky. It looks a lot different from when Matt and I were last here, months ago. The fencing with the design posters on is gone. The hotel still hasn't re-opened yet, but it doesn't look far from being finished.

I walk up to the giant, black glass doors, which reflect my pale face back at me, and take a deep breath.

Here goes.

I wrap my hand around the large chrome handle that runs down the length of the door, and it opens effortlessly, allowing me entry. Inside is a hive of activity. Music blares from somewhere as people walk around carrying equipment. It looks like they're just doing the finishing touches. As with a lot of the hotels in Vegas, I've walked straight into the casino. The temptation to be pulled into the glamourous world of roulette and poker hits you the moment you enter. I look around at the re-model Tanner's company has done. It's incredible. Dark glass, mirrors, and velvet make it feel sensual. It's impossible to tell whether it's day or night outside. Exactly what hotels here aim for. They want you to be so immersed in your surroundings that you lose track of time spent here. That's why you hardly ever see clocks in the casinos. In here is a fantasy world, where time doesn't exist. At least, that's what they want you to think when you're spending money.

"Can I help you?" A young woman in a suit approaches, looking at me through her designer frames. She's immaculately presented with her blonde hair tied up into a chic bun that looks like it took hours and a million hairpins to achieve. Her manicured nails wrap around her clipboard as she waits for my answer.

"I'm looking for Tanner Grayson. My name's Rachel Jones... he will want to see me," I add as I feel her cool gaze assessing me. She stares at my tight, ripped jeans and slouchy blouse that's slid off one shoulder. I hold her gaze, and after a long pause, she smiles at me.

"Of course. Follow me." She turns and leads me down a side hallway past a sign saying *Conference Center*. "Mr. Grayson has his office set up here for the time being. I'll just let him know you're here."

"There's no need, Suzanne, thank you."

My eyes widen at the deep, gravelly voice, and every hair on my body feels like it's standing to attention. Suzanne's eyes narrow as she looks at me one more time before stalking off back down the hallway.

"Your assistant seems friendly," I say as I turn towards him.

His dark eyes are like lasers on mine the moment I turn. I swallow down the lump in my throat, my mouth suddenly dry.

His hair is a little longer, and he's got a new suit on, a deep blue with an emerald tie. He looks harder. The amber flecks in his eyes glow like they're on fire, but his lips are set in a grim line.

"She's not my assistant. She works for the hotel."

We stare at each other, neither wanting to

volunteer to break the silence. I straighten my back. He's not going to make this easy for me.

"Tan." I raise my eyes to his gaze, and I swear he flinches at the sound of me saying his name, his eyes pinching at the corners.

"I haven't heard from you in almost three months, Rachel. What are you doing here?" He crosses his arms over his chest as he looks at me. The motion disrupts the air around him enough that I smell his familiar, spicy scent. It pulls me back to a memory of him with his arms wrapped around me, comforting me when Nigel died.

I take a deep breath to steady my uncharacteristic nerves. "I came for you."

He raises one perfect, dark eyebrow, his face not giving anything away. "Really? You came here for me?" He leans against the doorframe to his office, making no attempt to move any closer to me or invite me in to sit down.

I thought his grey suit was my favorite, but this... *fuck,* he looks so dark, brooding, and sexy in this blue one, even if he is being so cold.

"I thought you'd be happy to see me."

"Did you?" he asks. His eyes drop down my body and back up again. "Well, now I've seen you." He stares at me, challenging me.

My throat burns and constricts.

Wanker.

"Fuck you," I whisper as my cheeks burn.

I know I deserve his coldness. I hardly expected a

welcoming party, but still. I didn't come here to have him throw it back in my face. I turn to leave; this was a stupid idea.

"Rach, wait." He sighs, uncrossing his arms and pushing his hands into his trouser pockets instead. "Tell me why you're here."

I look into his eyes and see the way they brighten under my gaze. I need to say what I came here to. He needs to hear this. After everything between us, I need to be honest now.

"I've missed you, Tan." My voice comes out shaky. "I never realized just how much meeting you changed me. You showed me a different life, possibilities I had never even considered." I stare into his eyes, searching for a giveaway to what he's thinking. He's looking at me with such intensity but says nothing. "I know I'm hard to love," I continue, "I don't make it easy." My voice sounds like it belongs to someone else. I feel like I'm on show standing here alone under a spotlight, as I wait for his reaction.

With what feels like excruciating slowness, the corner of his mouth lifts, and his eyes sparkle as though he agrees with my statement. The sight of it makes me want to jump into his arms and crush my lips against his. "I couldn't do it if I was the one standing where you are," I add.

He looks at me for a long time, his eyes caressing over my face in gentle sweeps. "You can do anything you set your mind to, Rach. It's one of the reasons I love you."

I stare at him.

"Do you?" My heart's beating so hard in my chest, I feel faint. I might pass out on this new, ridiculously extravagant carpet he's installed.

"Do I what? Love you?" He draws his hands from his pockets. My eyes fall to them, and I look at his long, talented fingers, recalling the way they felt against my skin the first time we really made love to one another in New York. The first time I ever made love with anyone. And if Tanner won't give me another chance, he will also be the last person I ever make love with. I know in my heart that he's it for me. No one else could stand a hope in hell of coming close.

He moves towards me, closing the distance between us, so he's just inches away. I swallow down the rising flutters from my stomach and nod, looking up to his face.

His eyes hold mine. "I will never stop," he says, his voice almost a whisper.

Although he may be trying, he can't hide all the hurt I've put him through by denying my feelings for him. It's in his eyes, behind the amber flecks I love so much. He wears it like a scar, hidden in their depths.

"I'm sorry I hurt you, Tan."

He sucks in a breath and frowns. "I'm sorry I lied, Rach. I will regret it forever."

I reach up and place a hand against his chest, elated that he doesn't move away. "I'm more trouble than I'm worth. I let you think I didn't feel the way I do about you."

"I don't agree," he says, leaning closer.

"I never asked you to fall in love with me," I say as my eyes blur.

"It was never up for discussion, Rach."

I stare back at him as my tears fall. This beautiful man, his big heart. How could I have been so stupid to throw away something so precious?

All because I'm afraid.

"I'm in love with you," I confess through my tears. "I was in love with you three months ago. I just wasn't brave enough to admit it. It was easier to be angry and pretend that was the real reason I was pushing you away."

Tanner places his hands on either side of my face, wiping the hot tears on my cheeks away with his thumbs. "These last three months have been hell, Rach. You do not know how much I've missed you... you and your snarkiness." He smiles. "I know you don't need to be taken care of. You don't need me, Rachel. But God, do I want to be there for you." His voice breaks as he rests his forehead against mine. "I want to support you, laugh with you, love you, grow old with you." He sighs. "If this is going to work, you have to let me in. Don't just open the door for me, Rach. Tear down the fucking walls altogether. I love you, Rachel. I want to marry you one day."

"Okay," I whisper.

Tanner's brow creases. "Okay?"

"Yes!" I nod my head as I wrap my arms around his

neck, my pulse racing. The rest of my life is waiting for me, and it's time I started living it.

Tanner looks confused. I gaze into his eyes, losing myself in them as I stand on my tiptoes and dust my lips over his. Their warmth against mine sends a tingle all the way to my toes. He smells sweet and fresh, like he's just eaten an apple.

"Yes, I'll marry you," I murmur as I press the lightest of kisses to his lips.

His eyes widen before he blinks, appearing to do a double take. Suddenly he barks out a laugh as he catches on. I know he didn't mean right now, but I'm done with being in denial. I don't do things by halves. He should know that by now.

He takes a deep breath, his eyes glowing. "Are you asking—?" I silence him with a finger to his lips.

"No, but you just did, and my answer is yes. I love you so much, Tanner Grayson." I smile at him.

The floor falls away from under me as I'm lifted off my feet and wrapped in warm, powerful arms. "You're the most complicated, infuriating woman." Tanner laughs, his eyes still wide in disbelief as his mouth turns into a huge grin.

"And you're still a smug wanker." I giggle as I run my hands through his hair, my tears turning to happy ones.

"Too fucking right, I am! I've got the sexiest fiancée in existence." He beams. "Are you sure about this—?"

I cut him off with a kiss.

He hasn't got the sexiest fiancé.

I have.

I melt into him as we pull each other closer, remembering what the other feels like, savoring being together again. Kissing away the hurt and pain. Kissing hello to new beginnings and to love. The salt from my tears mixes with our tongues. I've missed this. I've missed *him* so much.

He breaks our kiss, panting as he holds me up tight against him. His eyes glittering as his eyebrows shoot up. "You need a ring."

"I need you more," I groan, wrapping my arms around his neck, trying to pull him back to me. My body has gone into overdrive being back close to him. I want to feel his skin against mine more than anything.

"I can't believe I'm saying this—" he kisses me again. "But later. I'm making it official before you change your mind."

"I won't ever change my mind." I kiss him again, running my fingers through the hair at the back of his head.

"Well,"... kiss.... "I'm taking"... kiss "no"... kiss... "chances"... kiss. He grins, putting my feet back down on the floor and bending down on one knee.

"Rachel Jones, I'm on one knee, so it's definitely official." He looks up at me. "Will you marry me?"

I look down at this handsome man—his dark hair and deep brown eyes with their fiery amber flecks—gazing up at me with adoration and love.

"Yes, a million times yes, I've already told you!" I pull him to his feet so I can wrap my arms around him again. I look at him, at my future, staring back at me through his eyes.

The sight takes my breath away.

After all the years I've spent hiding from love, it's now blindingly obvious.

Tanner Grayson is my beautiful destination.

It really was him—all along.

THIRTY

TANNER

SIX MONTHS LATER

"Okay, Mrs. Grayson. Your turn to choose." I hold up the box as Rachel reaches her left hand inside. The light catches the giant pear-shaped diamond sitting next to the wedding band on her finger.

"Hmm, I wonder what we will get today." She lifts out a packet, tearing the top off and tipping its contents onto the bed. She carefully unwraps the red tissue paper. A tiny thong, resembling the size of one of my shoelaces, falls out. The string that goes at the back is made entirely out of pearls.

I cough back a laugh. "You did not work a flight in that." I point to the shred of material that Rachel's slowly stepping into and pulling up underneath her dress.

"I did too." She winks, turning around and lifting the back of her dress up so I can see the line of pearls running down between her ass cheeks.

"Fuck." I sigh, squeezing my cock through my

boxers as I lay back on the bed and watch her. "You look sexy as hell in that."

"Only the best for my favorite client," she teases, circling her hips slowly.

"Your only fucking client," I growl as I reach up and pull her down, so she's straddling me. I lift her dress up over her head, throwing it on the floor. Her tits are exposed at the perfect height for me to suck her rosy, pink nipples into my mouth. "You look so good." My eyes roam down her body and to the tiny piece of white lace fabric that's barely covering the front of her pussy.

She grinds her hips down onto me and bites her bottom lip as her eyes hold mine. A grin plasters itself on my face as I let my head drop back, enjoying the sensation of her against my throbbing erection.

I'm one lucky guy.

We got married a month after she came to find me in Vegas. Rachel didn't see the point in waiting, and seeing just how sure she was about us was the biggest turn-on. I don't know how I kept my hands off her long enough to even say the vows. We had a small ceremony, just our family and friends. Holly and Jay flew over with baby Summer, and that was everyone we needed, right there to witness Rachel become Mrs. Grayson. She looked so beautiful. The entire day is a memory I will treasure until my dying breath.

The day my Snow became mine forever.

A sharp tug on my balls causes me to suck in a

breath as my stomach tenses. "Earth to Tanner." Rachel smirks.

I love this game she likes to play. Ever since we came back from Vegas, Rachel seemed unhappy about the box of unopened lingerie in my cupboard. She said it was supposed to have been enjoyed and wasn't living out its purpose. She felt like it sitting there was a grim reminder of how badly things almost went wrong for us. The "cleansing ritual," as she likes to call it, involves one of us choosing a packet and then fucking each other senseless while she wears whichever pair of panties is inside. I can't complain about her quirkiness over it. Fuck, I'd be an idiot to do so. It makes my wife happy, and she looks incredible in every pair. I'm more than happy to oblige.

"Sorry, I was just thinking about the last time." My hands caress her ass cheeks, squeezing gently. I run my thumb underneath the pearl string and down between her legs, where she's slick with arousal.

"The last time?" She tilts her head, circling herself against my fingertips.

"Yeah, remember, against the window?" I grin, remembering the way her tits left marks that were visible on the glass the next day. I refused to wipe them off until she agreed to a morning re-run.

"I remember." She smiles, lifting herself off me so I can pull my boxers down and kick them off. "Why don't you focus on this time now?" She leans down towards me, her breath warm on my neck as she kisses me underneath my ear. "I'm so wet for you," she whispers, reaching two fingers down to swipe through her folds. She brings them, glistening with her juices, up to my lips as if to prove it.

I lurch forward, grabbing her wrist as I suck them into my mouth, hard. Her whole face lifts and her cheeks flush pink. "What a good husband I have."

"Want to see what else I can do?" I grin as I reach my arms under her legs and lift her, sliding down the bed underneath her at the same time. When I place her back down, it's onto my hot and hungry waiting mouth.

Rachel moans as I pull her panties to one side, and my tongue explores her.

"You're like fucking heaven." I swirl my tongue around, savoring her sitting on my face. My cock throbs and drips in response.

"I'm pretty sure you can't fuck heaven." Rachel's laugh is cut off by a sharp gasp as I pull her clit between my teeth.

"Don't be so snarky," I scold.

"Wanker," she fires back, but her smile is clear in her voice.

Maybe I'm wired wrong, but I fucking love it when she insults me. It means I'm hitting the right spot. I love giving her pleasure. Hell, I live for seeing it on her face, hearing it in her voice, and feeling it in the way her body reacts to me.

I go to town on her pussy, sucking, licking, and devouring it for as long as she will let me before she's clawing at my hair and panting my name.

"I need you, Tan," she groans, trying to pull her swollen clit away from my tongue.

"Busy," I murmur, clutching her hips and pulling her back down onto my tongue.

She struggles against me as her breath comes in short, sharp bursts. She's so close, I can tell. "Why don't you ever do as you're told?"

"Because I like it when my hot wife is angry at me."

"You're a wan—"

I don't let her finish; I suck on her clit, and she shudders and comes hard on my face, screaming out my name, along with a list of profanities, all aimed at me.

I drink her up as she rides her release down. When she stops shaking, she lifts her body away from me, her dark hair falling around her face as she looks down. Her red lips are parted, her cheeks flushed.

She looks beautiful.

"Bet you're pleased you married me, huh?" I grin up at her.

"You have certain redeeming qualities, I suppose." She looks at me, her eyes bright.

"Time to showcase another for you, Mrs. Grayson."

Rachel eyes me with amusement as I slide out from underneath her and spring up onto my knees on the bed behind her.

"I love it when you look back over your shoulder at me like that," I groan. She gives me a wicked grin in response as I grip her hips and pull her back roughly.

"Sit back on my cock like a good wife, Rachel," I instruct, my voice gruff.

Any other time these words would earn me a slap. But now, with her cheeks still glowing from her last orgasm, Rachel is more than happy to oblige.

She lets me be in charge... sometimes.

I line the head of my cock up at her entrance, electricity coursing through my body as she looks back and pushes herself onto me. The hot, wet caress of her body gripping me as I slide in deep is so fucking perfect. I could have this every day and never tire of it. I *do* have this every day, and all it does is make me crave her even more when we are apart. Thank God she agreed to move in with me straight away. With the understanding we would keep her house, and Megan could stay as long as she wanted.

Rachel clenches around me. "Fuck... what are you doing to me?" I groan, kneading her ass cheeks with my thumbs.

"Just enjoying what's mine," she says as she dips her back and grinds onto me.

"It's all yours, baby. It's yours forever."

I speed up, setting a steady pace to drive into her over and over. Rachel tips her head back and moans as I reach to her shoulder and pull her back roughly, keeping one hand there so I can deepen each thrust. My other hand clutches her hip with white knuckle force as I fuck her harder, spurred on by her rising volume.

"Tan, oh fuck, you feel so good. I'm going to come

all over that perfect cock of yours," Rachel cries out as her body convulses and her arms shake underneath her.

I feel every movement of her, every tremor, every tightening of her pussy as she orgasms again. That, combined with the sight of her perfect ass banging back against my body, is too much, and mine builds, reaching its peak.

The white pearls of her thong glisten against her skin where I've pulled them to one side. The first release of my orgasm is almost on me as I grab the pearls and yank them hard. Rachel lets out a gasp, and it's the final push that sends me free-falling over the edge.

"Oh fuuucccckkk!"

Hot, white heat from my cock fills her as she sucks me in and milks me dry. My vision blurs, and I see stars.

Literally.

I'm seeing tiny white stars flying around us both. There's a soft splattering as the tiny, pearlescent balls shower us like raindrops, landing on the mattress.

"I think this pair has definitely been cleansed," I pant, pulling out from Rachel's body and bringing her down to lie on the bed with her head resting on my chest. Both of us are covered in a sheen of sweat.

"I think so too. Let's open another."

My mouth falls open. "You wanna go again? Already?"

She smirks at me as she sits up to grab another

packet, pulling me up into a sitting position as she bounces back down onto the bed next to me and sits up straight.

"You open this one," she says, her eyes dancing.

"My balls are drier than the Sahara Desert, Rach."

She fixes me with a look that tells me if I want to continue being able to have sex at all, I should shut up and obey. I shake my head with a chuckle as I tear open the padded packet and turn it upside down.

"What's this?" I stare at the item that's fallen out onto the bed. The thing is small, but that's where the similarities between it and the panties I was expecting ends.

"Turn it over and see," Rachel says.

She watches me closely as I pick up the small object, studying it as I turn it over in my hand.

"Rachel..." Any tiredness my body felt a moment ago is eradicated. I feel like I'm on top of the world as I take in the immense meaning of what I'm holding in my hand.

The little blue and white stick only has one word on it. But it's a life-changing one.

Pregnant.

"You're pregnant?" My voice comes out high while my eyes feel like they may fly out of my head.

Rachel nods at me, her eyes wide as she bites her bottom lip. "Seems like your balls work fine."

I thrust my arms up and punch the air. "Did you hear that?" I call to the ceiling. "My balls work! I've knocked my wife up!"

"Never do that again," Rachel snaps, but when I look at her, she's grinning.

"This is fucking incredible, Rach." I pull her into my arms as I stare at the pregnancy test again. She tilts her face up to me, pulling me into a tender kiss, and traces her tongue along my lips as though this is the only place in the world she wants to be.

"We're going to be parents," she murmurs against my lips.

I place the pregnancy test down on the bed and reach up to hold either side of her face. Staring into the eyes of the woman I love, I know I must be the happiest guy in existence.

"No, Rach. We're going to be a family."

Her eyes widen as she whispers, "a family?"

I nod at her as I stroke her cheeks. Praying that she can feel my love and adoration for her and our baby seeping through my fingers.

"Yes. We're going to be each other's family." My words are soft as I watch Rachel process them.

She looks up at me, unshed tears in her big baby doll eyes. "I love you, Tan."

"I love you too, Rach. I love you too."

I wrap her in my arms, and she relaxes, trusting me completely to hold on to her forever.

And I will.

Because just as I am hers—Rachel is mine.

And what a fucking beautiful destination she is.

The End.

ACKNOWLEDGMENTS

My first thank you must go to the incredible TL Swan. As with book one—Meeting Mr. Anderson—you gave me the courage to chase a dream. You've had a huge impact on my life, and others too. No amount of thank yous will ever be enough for the support you give so selflessly. You are an inspiration.

Thank you to two wonderful author friends I have met on this journey: LM Fox and VH Nicolson. You two are stuck with me as a friend for life now! I've lost count of the number of times you've supported me, talked sense into me, celebrated with me... I am so blessed to be taking this journey with you both, and you are both beautiful, unique authors.

My beta readers; Hannah, Christi, Dana, Nicola, Kitty and Fred. It took all of you to help get Mr. X to how I wanted him to be, and I am so grateful, because now—what can I say? I absolutely love him!

To my editor, Ashley; thank you for all your hard

work and time! You are incredible! You really are! I can't tell you enough; your passion for getting the story right and making it shine is incredible. Thank you.

Thank you to Abi for your amazing talent getting Mr. X onto a cover. He looks exactly how I picture the character to be.

Stephen, thank you for the digital assistance! Writing is much easier when you have a laptop that works.

Thank you to my family. I know writing this book meant many late nights where I was sat typing, and you supported me. Girls, you give me a reason to be a better person and to chase my dreams, because I hope in my heart that you will always chase yours too, and never be afraid to take a leap of faith.

Thank you to all the Bloggers, Bookstagrammers, BookTokkers, and everyone else who helped read ARCs and spread the word about Books one and two. Without you, no-one would even find these stories. I will be forever grateful for all of your help and support.

Finally, my biggest thanks is to you, the reader. Thank you for reading Rachel and Tanner's story. I hope you enjoyed it. I loved writing it, so much. This one will stay with me forever. Please consider leaving a review on Amazon. It is one of the best ways to help other readers try out a new author. I never realised just how helpful they can be until I started on this journey.

Elle

ABOUT THE AUTHOR

Elle Nicoll is an ex long-haul flight attendant and mum of two from the UK.

After fourteen years of having her head in the clouds whilst working at 38,000ft, she is now usually found with her head between the pages of a book reading, or furiously typing and making notes on another new idea for a book boyfriend who is sweet-talking her. Elle finds it funny that she's frequently told she looks too sweet and innocent to write a steamy book; but she never wants to stop. Writing stories about people, passion, and love; what better thing is there?

ELLE'S BOOKS

Discovering Mr. X is book two in 'The Men Series', a collection of interconnected standalone stories. They can be read in any order, however for full enjoyment of the overlapping characters, the suggested reading order is:

Meeting Mr. Anderson

Discovering Mr. X

Drawn to Mr. King (Coming soon)

Captured by Mr. Wild (Coming soon)

To keep up to date with latest news and releases, find Elle in the following places:

https://www.ellenicollauthor.com

https://www.instagram.com/ellenicollauthor/

https://www.facebook.com/ellenicollauthor

https://www.bookbub.com/authors/elle-nicoll

https://www.goodreads.com/author/show/
21415735.Elle_Nicoll